The Breakfast Jury

Kenneth B Humphrey

Other books by the author

Elementary readers
The Hunts of Raimy Rylan
Book One: The World Serpent
Book Two: Chase of the Samurai
Book Three: Origins
Teen readers
Ghoul
Ghouls and Boys

Mystery thrillers
The Killing Arc
Book One: Killing the Man
Book Two: The Killing Face
Book Three: Arch Enemy

Title: The Breakfast Jury
Author: Kenneth B. Humphrey
Copyright © 2024

This is a work of fiction. The author acknowledges the use of real trial facts in crafting the plot of this novel. The portrayal of legal proceedings, courtroom events, and related details are inspired by real cases, but liberties have been taken for the sake of storytelling. Names have been changed in the interests of privacy.

For permissions requests, contact the publisher at the address below:
Wheatland House Publishing
500 Westover Drive, #6238
Sanford, NC 27330

ISBN: 978-0-9963659-9-4

Acknowledgment

My civic service started the same way as ten thousand others every year: With a summons in the mailbox. I'd never been on a jury before and really had no idea what to expect. It wasn't this, I can wholeheartedly confirm.

Maybe a quick dismissal because I didn't make the cut. Maybe a few days listening to testimony in a DUI or domestic altercation.

But this…

I didn't expect a month locked in a jury box with 15 strangers, consuming evidence for a trial that had been run once already and now came back around due to legal technicalities. I didn't expect getting to know anyone the way I did or the shared bond that emerged.

During our legal slog the germ of a plot developed in the back of my mind and so, on the last day we were together, I promised them a story for our one-year anniversary. Writing is slow work.

It couldn't be a standard legal tell-all. Those have been done to death and frankly, aren't interesting to me. I wanted something that left readers wondering what parts are real and what are utter fiction, grounded in the locale of Kenosha, WI. I also had a character from my *Killing Arc* series that deserved more airtime.

This book is a meld of both trials, playing liberally with facts and actors and settings, salted with healthy doses of fictional events.

And it's dedicated to my fellow jurors. We did our duty, folks.

1

MONDAY, JUNE 12, 2000, 8:14AM

I answer on the first ring. Might as well. My cellphone is already cradled in my palm like a useless appendage as I stare out the window of my tiny apartment.

"This is Aramis White," I use my professional voice. Just in case.

"Arch?" The response is less professional, gruff and abrupt, that of someone who can't wait to unload something.

"Only my friends call me that. I don't recognize the number. Who is this?" With a first name like Aramis and Archibald for a middle name, I'd learned long ago it was easier to use Arch.

Outside my window the morning sun blazes brilliant, Wisconsin sky so pure it makes my eyes water to look up. It's incongruent with my general mood these days; I have little room or time for beauty in the world. The wall clock ticks loudly in the background, some kind of metaphor, but for what I have no idea.

"It's Warren. George Warren."

Long silence, emphasizing the wall clock.

Of all the voices I expected to hear, his would be the last on my list. In fact, it's so far down, the list ends before he even appears. "Warren? The hell?"

Conversely, if I'm keeping a list of names I never want to hear again, his might crack the top ten.

"Yeah. Heyyyy, surprise!" His tone is forced mockery, falling on the ending note. He's nervous about something. "Your favorite cop."

Spoiler: Warren is not, in fact, my favorite cop. The one who did own that honor, my partner and mentor Tom Griffin, died a year ago, sinking my detective career. Despite being longtime friends with

Griff and knowing I desperately needed help, Warren disappeared into the ether.

"I've got about five seconds for guys like you."

He grunts, barely audible, as if agreeing with my assessment but unwilling to let me know. "You might want to give a little more. This is something right up your alley."

I don't know what he thinks my 'alley' is. I showed up in Chicago last year with a newly pressed detective's tin and a chip on my shoulder to prove I deserved it despite the way I earned it. All that followed was a series of highly public fuck-ups that, in the end, cast me out while costing me everything worth having.

"Five."

"Okay, okay. Listen. I got a good buddy, guy's like a brother, and he needs help. The kind of help cops can't offer."

Despite several decades living in the town of Grand Haven, snugged tight to the Wisconsin border, Warren still carried his southside Chicago accent and speech patterns. He had fled the hard work but you can never really flee the person you are. It's a lesson I've learned in the harshest of ways.

"Four."

"His wife, new wife, they got married not long ago, well she got herself in trouble. Maybe she caused it, maybe she's just a victim."

"Three."

"She's in the hospital and it looks like alcohol over-consumption but he thinks it was deliberate. I want to help him out because he's hurting and needs to know what happened. He needs that thing, whaddya call it, closure. Yeah, closure."

"Two."

"He's got bank and will pay someone top dollar to find out the truth."

I pause my countdown, hating myself for doing so, but resentment and indignation don't pay the bills. "And my name came to your mind. Why? We barely know each other, only through Griff." I'd formed my opinions of Warren in the few times we'd crossed paths. Apparently, he'd done the same of me and I want to know what they are.

"Well, you are a dog with a bone

when you get hold of something. Everything last year with the Noah Bell case, then all the stuff with that Covenant group and William Travian. You made national headlines and it was hard not to pay attention, especially when I knew the understory thanks to Griff. Someone else would have given up."

If his name was Warren, yeah.

"And tell me what I got out of that. Lost my partner, lost my dream job, friends…everything that mattered. What good is a bone when it's all you have left?" I fight to keep the bitterness from layering my words. This guy doesn't deserve that part of me.

Now it's Warren's pause. "Yeah. I heard about your daughter. Word traveled fast through people you don't even know. I'm sorry, I can't imagine what that's like."

"Right. Because you don't stay in the fight, you look for the first off-ramp. I'm no smarter than you and a whole lot less experienced. I just refused to let go. You tossed it up into the wind and didn't bother to see who would catch the pieces." At this point I'm just beating a dead horse.

"I know that and can't say you're wrong, but this is bigger than either of us. The truth matters and there's a truth here, buried deep. I don't have the chops to dig it up. You do."

He's buttering me up, giving ground so I'll think I won and take his offer.

"You don't know this," he continues. "But Griff talked you up, a lot. Several times a week we spoke, two weathered tins trading war stories. He was closer to retirement than me and I think the clock striking midnight on his career made him want to reflect on the years with someone he'd known since academy."

"And yet he never made it to midnight."

"No, no," Warren's voice drops a few decibels. I'd known they came up the ranks together and despite the different personalities had stayed close. It's believable he's sincere in missing his friend. I had months with Griff, those two had decades. "Did you know he questioned going through with retirement? He wondered if it really was the right time. Whether he had anything left. And that was because of you."

Now I'm the quiet one. "I did not know that."

"You showed up and he took you on, I think because no one else wanted to. You know, because of the lawsuit to get your shield and all."

Yeah, I know. I was there.

"He talked about you often, like you were one of his own kids. He only had daughters so maybe it was a father–son thing. I heard it in his voice, in the way he described you. I know more about you than you do me. More than you think. You need a mission, a purpose or goal. Something just out of reach to keep pulling you forward, that promise of reward. With that, you hit another gear and nothing stops you."

I hear my voice husky. "Griff said that?"

"You think I'm this eloquent?" Warren shoots back. "He said that and more. From what I hear right now, you have no mission, no glimmer on the horizon so you spend your time looking around for it. Well, here you go. There's someone who also needs that horizon and I think you're the only one who can deliver."

To the east open sky settles on the surface of Lake Michigan, straddling the border between two states. I can't see the lake from my window, but I know it's there and the metaphor is too obvious to ignore.

"Fine. Give me an address."

All the hysteria around Y2K and the turning of the millennium had turned out rather dull. There was no doomsday from computers failing to recognize double zeroes in the year column when the calendar ticked over. No collapse of civilization as our cars stopped driving, power grids locked up and planes fell from the sky. I'd read about extreme preppers digging bunkers and bagging up food before throwing it in the river to stay cold. I wonder if they sat by the river's edge even now, looking for the string to retrieve their food supply, feeling foolish. Probably not, those folks lack an amazing amount of self-awareness.

I wish I had the same failing. Ignorance truly can be bliss.

I'd spent 1999 rather busy, unintentionally destroying every single plan I'd made for the future. On the back of a contentious and highly public lawsuit, I claimed my tin as the youngest detective in Chicago history, moving my family across the country, intent on proving everyone wrong about me. I wasn't just a race hire and I intended to show them all.

Tom Griffin took me under his wing. I never knew why until Warren's words. Only months away from retirement, Griff spent his remaining time showing this over-eager cop the ropes, pulling back the cover on those little things that aren't taught in academy, only learned by working cases.

I thought I was ready.

Then Noah Bell was murdered. The crown prince of Chicago, a man who championed my right to be a detective, felled in a mugging that wasn't. My chain of command handed the highest of high-profile cases to a rookie detective, a passive Fuck You to my lawsuit.

'*Hey,*' they probably said in the depths of their fancy offices. '*Chicago's champion for racial equity was killed but we got ourselves a brand-new minority hire right downstairs. Let's assign it to him. That's only fair, right?'*

They expected me to fail, to publicly stumble until someone more seasoned could take over. But that's not how I roll. I'm more than the color of my skin. When the dust settled, an assassin lay dead with Bell's blood on his hands, giants of industry were implicated, and a conspiracy lay thwarted. I'd turned the tables on those guys sitting high in their towers and such pertinence could not stand. My tin was stripped, leaving me alone. The aftermath brought me to this point.

And I really need to stop dwelling on it.

Pulling my car over to the curb, I take a beat and surveil my surroundings. Not because I felt danger loomed, but rather at the picture-perfect image of wealth laid out in front of me. The June sun pulls High Street up and away from me in a gentle curve. Large houses follow the road, each one set back the same distance from a white sidewalk.

I'm in the village of Pleasant Prairie, tucked up against the south edge of Kenosha closer to the Illinois border. Looking at the idyllic scene through my windshield, I agree that 'pleasant' is the correct term for this area.

Checking house numbers against the smudged ink on my palm, I exit my car and stride up the nearest driveway. Granite river rock covers the façade of a two-story home, expensive shades of tans and grays and blues. Three wooden garage doors feature black wrought-iron buckles and the design theme is carried over to the arched front door. When I press the doorbell, a deep gong sounds from inside the house, solemn in its echoes. There's blurry movement on the other side of the frosted glass sidelights.

The man who opens the door is shorter than me, not an uncommon occurrence for my height. He's squat in build, guarded expression fixed to his face. He says nothing, simply looking up.

"Are you Teodor Wright?"

"Yes, is Ted."

In the response I catch an accent, maybe Polish or Czech. Straight brown hair and a bushy mustache complete the picture. I introduce myself and Teodor - Ted - steps aside to invite me in.

My shoes echo off the tiled entryway, soft clicks stretching up twenty-five feet to the second story ceiling. A glance shows Ted is in socks. Despite no longer carrying my badge, I still dress the part in hard-soled shoes, slacks and a sports jacket. The only concession to my current employment status is lack of a tie. Too damned hot for that.

Pictures clutter the walls to either side as a foyer takes us towards the rear kitchen area. Horses galloping against a mountain backdrop, forest stream trickling around intertwined tree roots, a somewhere distant beach at sunrise. All the images are beautiful, unveiling a keen eye for composition and color. Nowhere do I spy a picture of Ted and someone who could be his wife.

He motions for me to have a seat at the breakfast nook table, glass and chrome and metal chairs with padded seats. "You like coffee." It was either a statement or question, tough to tell with his flat accent.

"Black," I respond as I take in the adjacent family room. Leather couches are arranged in a U-shape and a flat-screen TV hangs over the brick fireplace. "What do you do for work, Mr. Wright?"

He sets a cup down before me. "Is Ted." The burr in his voice mashes together the words.

"Ted," I emphasize. "What do you do for work?"

A shrug. "Trucking, shipping, auto repair. Many things." Another shrug seems to indicate his vague answer was enough.

In my short time under Griff's wing, I'd learned about the Eastern European community prevalent in the Chicago outlying areas, which now apparently also included Pleasant Prairie. They created a closed-loop economy, specializing in businesses that weren't quite illegal but neither fully legal. These businesses catered mainly to others within their community, generating income from friends and neighbors, feeding that money back to friends and neighbors and their businesses. Once a dollar came in, it took a lot to bring it out.

The people also carried a common mannerism, not exactly evasive but blunt and clipped in their responses, forcing you to ask your questions in multiple ways to glimpse truth. Nothing was given, you had to work for an answer. I adjust my approach accordingly.

"Tell me why I'm here today."

Ted raises his eyebrows as he settles across from me. "You do not know why you came to me? Is this often happen to you?"

"No, I know why I'm here. I want you to tell me why from your perspective."

"Is odd question," he muttered and shook his head, then a sip of coffee. "It is this: My wife, some person tried to kill her, to poison her."

"And why do you think that? From what George told me she was at a bar and may simply have over-indulged."

He shakes his head, emphatic on this next point. "No, she did not. I have seen her many times drink and always she stops when it gets too many. Much tolerance and knowing when to stop. That is what she does. Was not alcohol."

I bite back on a sigh. This is the definition of flimsy but long as I'm here, might as well go through the steps so Warren knows I tried. Pulling a notepad from my jacket pocket I flip it to a blank page and click the mechanical pencil twice to extrude lead. "Can you walk me through the day? When did you last speak, what was she doing, that type of thing."

"She left house after lunch to run errands. I was in Chicago to work. Her party began at four. She calls me on way out of door."

I turn my notepad sideways and draw a straight line across the page, marking a notch for the noon hour. "She left around noon. When did you leave the house that morning?"

"Is busy traffic early in morning so I leave at 9. I call her at 10:30 to say I am arrived at work."

"And is that normal? That you call for things like that?"

"Yes. She likes to know I am okay."

Two more notches to denote Ted's

actions. "When was her party starting?"

"She say 4pm. At bar in Kenosha."

"That's three to four hours for errands. What kind?"

Ted shrugs and sips his coffee, wincing at the temperature. "I do not know. Just errands. Maybe dry cleaning, maybe shopping." He rolls his eyes and gives a half-smile. "She has new business, maybe stuff for that."

"What kind of business?"

"Hair. The cutting and styling," he motions around his head like someone with scissors in both hands. "She is to open soon and still trying to get chairs filled."

I put a big question mark above the timeline from noon to four. What did she do during that window? "So, she went to her party at four. What then?"

"She go, yes, at four. I am down in city to seven, home by 8:30, maybe 9. Eat dinner. I call her phone but no answer. But is okay. I know she does not answer in loud places. I talk with friends on phone for an hour, hour and one half. By now is after ten at night. I lay on couch to wait her return and fall asleep."

I dutifully note these items along the timeline. The answer to my next question is seemingly apparent but I ask anyway. "And you have no children?"

Ted shakes his head and I catch the glimpse of a smile peeking through his stoic expression as he looks down. "We are married only few months now. No children."

Not yet, his slipped smile reveals. *Someday.*

I turn to a new page and draw another timeline, this one starting at 10pm. "When did you receive a call from the hospital?"

He flips open his cell phone and puts on a pair of reading glasses. "It comes at 11:04. Is emergency room. She was brought by friend and they give nurse my number from her phone. Doctor says she is passed out. Too much alcohol. He does not listen when I say that it cannot be. I am there within half hour. She is not drunk. Is poison, I tell you."

I set down my notepad. "Ted, I have to be honest. There's not much here. People drink, sometimes too much. You saying it's poison doesn't point me in any direction for motive or opportunity. I need those two elements to identify a suspect. Otherwise, it's just me going around asking questions with no meaningful answers."

"Maybe I am wrong but I think I am not. Two hundred dollars per hour to ask your questions."

I blink at him for a few stunned moments. Then: "I'll start right away."

At the front door I turn back. "Oh, in all this I never asked your wife's name."

He looks up at me, face flat and unreadable. If there's hope that I'll be able to peel this tale apart for him, I can't see it. He may as well have been giving me the time of day.

"Is Nicole."

One Year Earlier

It was a trial built on the pillars of due process and hungry lawyers, aimed at a man accused of poisoning his wife. What started as an ordinary legal affair would metamorphose into the longest-running case in Wisconsin's storied history – a haunting testament to human vindication, leaving both legal minds and an unsuspecting public gripped by the chilling reality that justice sometimes begets its own grim consequences.

And the cause isn't always direct, clear, or logical.

MONDAY, MAY 10, 1999, 8:30AM – JURY SELECTION

Prospective jurors filed towards the courtroom, having dribbled into the building over the last hour, citizens mixed across age, occupation, status, and every other demographic present in the county of Kenosha, Wisconsin.

And like any other group of strangers thrown together, there existed this certain type of awkwardness normally found in high school dances and casting calls. People defaulted to their natural state. Some remained withdrawn, because they figured this was a one-day disruption to the rhythm of their lives, a momentary blip that would disappear once they were released from service.

Others took the opposite approach. They greeted those close in proximity, traded names, began the initial steps of forming a tribe. Within these pockets, the tempo was similar, a social pattern comprised of pregnant pauses, spurts of conversation and chattering laughter. Often one person took the lead in keeping the dialog alive when silence loomed, assertive in their words or mannerisms. In one corner, a lady named Nicole Redd finished her bawdy story, causing several people to nervously laugh and look around as if guilty by association.

"Anyone going to give us breakfast?" She shouted abruptly, to low chuckles and return comments. At the few looks sent her way, she merely shrugged. "What? I'm a hungry chick."

In another area a retired gentleman named Chuckie Fire leaned over to two females near his age and cracked some small joke. Both smiled politely and looked away, clearly humoring him. He shrugged and bit off a piece of licorice, sitting back in his chair with a mischievous expression.

Once all the courtroom benches were filled, bailiffs brought in folding chairs, extending the pews, packing people into a space never meant to hold this many. Though it was still early morning cool outside, the room felt stuffy, body heat and coffee breath warming the air.

The process of seating jurors lasted another thirty minutes, during which parts of the room began to reflect various attitudes. Many grumbled at the stuffiness and wondered how long this would all take. Why were there so many jurors? Was this normal? Law junkies and legal hobbyists understood why. They spoke in low tones, speculating on the docket, whispering and creating a buzz of expectation for those around them.

Others in the courtroom were oblivious, present simply because a summons showed up in their mailbox.

Kay Standin was one such juror. She fidgeted, folding the letter over and over into the smallest square possible. Her hair was chestnut dark and tied back into a ponytail. Lines at the corners of her eyes indicated early, maybe mid-forties. She was quiet and self-contained but stuffed with strong opinions which had brought trouble to her doorstep in the past. She'd never served on a jury before and a small part of her looked forward to the opportunity. Most of her, however, wanted to be done with all this and get back to looking for employment. She sat at the end of the second row next to a man named Travis Green. His dark hair and stubbled jaw, combined with steadfast eyes, gave the impression of someone secure in himself.

"How do you like that model?" Travis asked out of the blue, leaning over.

It took a moment to recognize the question was for her. "What?" She leaned an equal distance away.

"The Mercedes C-class," he replied. When she returned a blank stare, he clarified. "You were right in front of me when we parked. I noticed because my wife has the same one and loves it."

"Oh," she blurted. "Oh, yeah. It's my husband's. I don't drive it much."

Travis wrinkled his nose slightly. "Isn't that kind of a girly car for a dude?"

Kay gave a snort. "Well, he's got

issues." She followed with a laugh. "Mine is out for servicing."

"Yikes," he shook his head. "That's one part I can do without."

Unsure how to address the comment, Kay settled for: "Sure."

On the other side of Travis sat Margaret Art, elementary school teacher. She doodled in her ever-present notebook, head down but attention up, tracking stray conversations around her. "I know," she interjected. "My Chevy is the exact same way. American cars, right?" To soften the sarcasm, she gave him a smile, making her friendly face even more so.

He grunted and pointed to her doodles. "Nice flowers."

"Really? Thanks." Her appreciation was clearly genuine, a natural character trait.

A sudden bark of laughter broke out across the room from a juror named Justyna Lowder as she reacted to a joke. It startled several people into abrupt silence for a moment before conversation resumed.

"Holy cow," Margaret commented to no one in particular.

Up front, Larry the bailiff shook his head and smiled. He'd seen these behavioral patterns in his many years of court service. Short, squat and bald, with a neat white goatee, he looked forward to the general reaction of the room once they learned the scope of trial on the docket. He shifted his attention to a small grouping of people just entering the room and directed them to the empty folding chairs several rows back.

Kay shifted her posture towards Travis. "There's a lot of people here. Is this normal?"

He shrugged. "Beats me. I don't know what 'normal' looks like."

In front of those two sat Courtney Jotter. She fell into the category of trial junky and knew what was coming. She religiously tracked the crime section of the *Kenosha News*. Her dark hair and darker eyes, combined with a curious expression, lent an inquisitive air. Some would call her nosy. She turned in her seat. "It's a murder case," she whispered. "A man supposedly killed his wife with antifreeze."

Travis grunted in surprise. Margaret shook her head in disgust and kept doodling.

"Wait, what?" Kay stuttered. "You can die from antifreeze?"

"It's poisonous," Courtney remarked with a raised eyebrow. "That's what I heard anyway."

Before the conversation could evolve into the dangers of antifreeze, Larry straightened for effect and instructed, "All rise!"

With the cluttered sound of movement, everyone in the courtroom rose to their feet, looking towards the bench. Off to one side, a door opened and Judge Anthony Millick emerged. He was older, sporting a neat salt and pepper goatee below round spectacles with thick lenses. This was not the first murder trial he had overseen in his decades on the bench but knew it could be career-defining. The public scrutiny in this new age of internet communication meant millions of eyes could be following every motion and argument. Precedent and process would need to hew close in every aspect or he might find himself in the crosshairs of unkind attention.

He ascended to his bench and addressed the crowd. "You may be seated."

As the packed room rustled with motion, Millick dropped his eyes to the lawyers. District Attorney Robert Jambliss and his team would be prosecuting the case on behalf of the State. He was portly with white hair and a red face, prone to rambling statements in which he jammed in as many facts and asides as possible. Millick was long familiar with Jambliss's habits, he'd presided over many of the DA's cases.

To the right of Jambliss sat defense attorney Bridget Cruise and her lieutenants. Millick was not as familiar with her, a court-appointed attorney fulfilling pro bono requirements.

They were responsible for ensuring the defendant received a fair trial. The verdict of innocence was their goal. Whether through evidence or mistrial was irrelevant.

And at the far end of the defense table sat the accused: Mark Johannsen. Tall and lanky, long-jawed, draped in an oversized suit. He kept his head hung low, peering out at the prospective jurors from under his brow, giving the impression of a predator. Twelve people from this room would hold his fate in their hands and it seemed like he wanted to study them in advance, eager to glean an idea of their vote.

Millick could have told him to save his energy. There were simply too many people to weed through before final jury selection. He estimated the Voir Dire phase alone would last the full day, maybe into tomorrow.

Clearing his throat for attention, Millick re-engaged the room. "Good morning, ladies and gentlemen. Thank you for being prompt. I know it's crowded in here so I appreciate your patience as we got everyone settled." He paused and glanced down at the papers in front of him, even though he didn't need to. "We have a critical case before us today, potentially a historic one. I can tell you it's one I personally have never encountered. In speaking with both lawyer teams, we estimate this trial may last upwards of four, perhaps even six weeks, based on the evidence and quantity of witnesses. This will likely be a hardship for some, which is why there are so many of you packed in here like sardines. We must emerge with the best possible jury."

At the mention of the timeline, a buzz arose. Kenosha had a large blue-collar demographic. Trade and manufacturing laborers, service industry roles; these were hourly jobs that could not simply be skipped for weeks. Doing your civic duty was one thing, but losing a month's salary over it? That was the definition of hardship, one that a daily juror stipend of $16 would not cover.

Sixteen dollars. Per day. Four, perhaps even six weeks.

It meant this jury would be positioned towards a different type of worker: Retired folks, the white-collared salaried professionals, and those with gracious employers. Whether that was advantageous or not for Mark Johannsen remained to be seen.

"Before turning this over to the lawyers, let me brief you on the particulars," Millick continued, turning his eyes away from shaking heads and looks of astonishment throughout the room. "The defendant, Mark Johannsen, stands accused of murdering his wife Julie Johannsen, on December 3, 1998. The charges state he provided her with ethylene glycol found in antifreeze, in sufficient volume to cause death, also allegedly attempting to suffocate her. The prosecution contends these actions were premeditated on his part. The defense attests Mrs. Johannsen took her own life due to depression."

Millick set down his papers and looked over the mass of prospective jurors. Twelve people were soon to be weighted by the publicity of this case. They would be measured by their final verdict, rent asunder by opinions of people near and far.

"Please raise your hand if you feel there is a conflict or undue hardship to serving on his jury," he concluded.

The room echoed loudly with the rustle of hands shooting up. Millick gave a rueful smile and shook his head. He glanced over to the bailiff. "Well, Larry. Let's get this show on the road."

3

The first juror stood, a woman in her seventies, stiffly getting up. She objected to long periods of time sitting in the chair due to back issues.

"If we allow you to stand and stretch when needed," Millick countered. "Will that help?"

She paused and looked down, as if the answer lay on the faded carpet. "Well, I have knee issues too," she responded quietly, fooling no one in the room. It was obvious she simply did not want to serve jury duty.

Judge Millick moved through a few others who provided similarly weak reasons, some bordering on outright falsehoods. He came to a young female. Round spectacles mimicked her round face. A black t-shirt was emblazoned with the bright pink words *'Canine Mom'*. "I have to walk my dogs, twice a day," she said.

"I have a couple of dogs myself," he said. "Boxers. You have my word we'll never go past five. Does that help?"

"Twice. Per. Day." She emphasized with distinct syllables and shrugged her shoulders as if helpless to do any more. Like her daily routine revolved around pets and there was nothing she could – or would – do to alter it.

"Seriously?" Travis whispered.

Courtney looked over her shoulder. "I know, right?"

Millick visibly concealed a sigh and motioned for Canine Mom to sit. He pointed at the man next to her. Reading glasses were perched low on his nose and his dress shirt had no sleeves, crudely cut off at the shoulder. "And you sir, what is your conflict or concern with serving this trial?"

"Cuz I fucking think he did it," the man stated loudly. His voice carried across the crowd. Suppressed laughs and surprised gasps lifted up.

"Language!" Millick snapped back.

"We'll have decorum here."

"Sorry judge, but the guy is guilty as shit. Just look at him."

More laughter tittered through the room.

"I understand you think that, sir," Millick answered. "Are you able to maintain an impartial bias and arrive at a verdict solely on the merits of evidence?"

The guy shrugged and peered over the rim of his glasses. "Sure, whatever that means. As long as he's found guilty."

Silence settled over the room as Millick stared with a perplexed look. Finally: "You may be seated."

Attorney Bridget Cruise moved to the podium stationed near the front of the jury box. As Millick worked through the early stages of Voir Dire, many people had been excused and the seating order shuffled around after a morning break. The juror pool had shrunk, excised by the removal of those sent home. Final selections became more critical and her goal was to weed out anyone who seemed likely to find

Johannsen guilty, while the prosecution worked to retain them. This game of cat and mouse forced both sides to show their hand.

She looked down at her profile sheets, flipping through the stack. "Juror number 59," she said and looked up. Her eyes landed on a man named Terry Sharp. He sat in the rearmost row and raised his number card.

"Here," he replied.

"It says on your questionnaire that you are employed as a 'program developer'. What does that mean?"

Terry was tall, with his hair cut into a vaguely military style, shaved tight on sides and back. His rectangular glasses were steel-rimmed. "It means I sit in a chair all day and stare at the ceiling, thinking of stuff." This brought a ruffle of laughs and even Cruise smiled. "I develop software programs," he clarified.

"So, you know about computers and the programs they use," she added, not really a question.

"You could say that."

Cruise nodded and reshuffled her

papers. There was a significant technology aspect to this case, introduced as evidence by the prosecution. Having someone who understood the details could be helpful or hurtful and it was on her to determine which. She probed with a few more questions but with each answer he gave, she became less certain of her decision. He spoke above her head and clearly knew his business, to the point of overwhelming his audience with detail.

She drew a large 'X' across his name and moved on. Hopefully Jambliss had also crossed him off. "Juror 18."

In front of Terry, Shelli Dell raised her hand. "That's me."

"Your occupation is listed as a consultant. In what field do you consult?"

"Corporate taxes," Shelli replied. Like Terry she too wore glasses, but larger and rounder. Her hair was pulled back neatly into a bun, and she presented the image of someone composed with herself. "When companies conduct international relocations for their employees, I assist in making sure they are compliant to payroll and taxation requirements." The blank look in return from Cruise indicated the answer didn't reveal much but the lawyer notated her profile sheet and moved on.

And so it went. Numbers were called, a question or two asked and answered, perhaps a follow-up query. Juror 14, Lian Younger. Charles Wise, juror 21. Brian Snapon, Rick Crete, Danny Carpenter, Dennis Reader. All called out and made to reply. The inquiries were banal, seemingly innocuous, clarifying little, but it was all part of the game, a way for her to smoke out the prosecution's intended targets.

For his part, Jambliss remained quiet. He stared across the gallery, examining each juror as if they were mannequins behind a store window. Where he made eye contact, there was no human connection, no recognition of one person to another but rather that of someone surveying a collection of items to procure at market. Kay Standin found herself unnerved by the cattle call nature of this phase.

And it was not only Jambliss. The other defense lawyers also roved their eyes, flat and calculating, mentally picking up each juror to examine them before moving on to the next. However, it was the gaze of Johannsen that most unsettled everyone. He continued the dead stare from under his brow, long chin pulling his mouth down into the resemblance of a smirk, beady eyes almost reptilian.

All in all, the courtroom took on an atmosphere of uncertainty and awkward consideration. From all points of perspective, everyone wondered who would end up in the final jury. Who would have to eventually provide a verdict that determined the future course of one man?

As the clock ticked over at noon, Millick paused the Voir Dire and dismissed everyone to a large room in the basement. "The county is buying lunch for you today," he announced. "It's a working lunch for the lawyers and me. Please keep your juror numbers with you."

"Whoa. Free pizza," someone stated as the room's occupants began to shuffle out. "Your tax dollars at work."

In the makeshift lunchroom people

split up, some choosing to regroup with those they met in the morning, others retreating to their own isolation. Magazines and books appeared, a Nintendo Gameboy announced Mario's bouncing efforts to rescue Princess Peach. The rhythm of conversation ebbed and flowed, dwindling as slices of Italian pie were doled out and eating became the focus.

Nicole gathered with her morning companions, chatting as if they'd known each other for years. Her voice traveled the room, cracking jokes and commentary on the proceedings to which they were all subject. She had deeply dyed hair, a reddish-purplish tinge, and made friends easily. Her sense of humor was best described as coarse.

"I'm telling you," she spouted at one point. "It's hard out in the dating world. Might be worth the risk of poisoning for a good lay. Hell, it might even spice things up."

Across the room a guy in a biker t-shirt laughed, "I'll give you the spice."

Several tables away, Shelli Dell's eyes widened and she ducked her head. Kay, seated across from Shelli, frowned. She didn't care for mocking a serious matter where someone lost their life.

"Just saying," Nicole pressed. "I mean, I got a good guy but not everyone is so lucky."

No one else responded, killing that thread.

Jean Cook, sharing the table with Kay and Shelli, introduced herself as she wiped pizza sauce from her lips. A retired teacher, she was petite, talkative by nature. "This case is fascinating," she stated once they'd traded names. "I mean, antifreeze? Who knew? I barely know what it is."

"Right?" Shelli replied with an expression of dismay. "This stuff is just floating around in jugs. I know we have it in our garage and small kids running around. Now I have something else to worry about."

Behind her at the next table, Dennis Reader turned around. "It's also bright colors, like green, yellow or pink. That doesn't help keep little ones away." He was older, retired, with a full beard and deep smile lines at the corners of his eyes.

Tattoos on his right arm peeked out from the short sleeves of his black Harley-Davidson shirt. Kay thought he could pass for Santa, Biker Edition.

Shelli shook her head and gave a worried groan, looking back down to her food.

Jury selection resumed the next morning, albeit with a smaller crowd. Again they were provided pizza for lunch, pulling negative reactions from several in the room. "What, the county can't get us something different?" Nicole groused. "Like burgers from Spanky's or The Spot?"

At 1:07, Larry and two other bailiffs entered the room. Conversation abruptly died as their presence was noted, filling the air with anticipation. No one knew what to expect, but it was understood they soon would either be going home or going into trial.

Larry's voice boomed as he spoke, clear and unmistakable. "If we say your number, please gather out in the hall," he announced and then began calling out numbers.

Eventually, sixteen people milled around the hallway outside. Travis looked at Terry, Courtney, Kay, and Margaret. "I guess we're the Dream Team, eh?"

Dennis, Lian, Rick and Shelli nodded. Danny leaned forward. He was young and lean, black hair buzzed short. "Nice to meet you folks. Go team. Everyone on three. One, two, three…"

No one went on three and disappointment colored his expression.

Chuckie stood next to Jean. "We have the power," he intoned deeply then smiled. "It's you and me, huh?"

She smiled politely back but her look stated she had no idea what he was talking about.

Next to him, Justyna barked a laugh, sharp and loud.

The bailiffs led them upstairs to the courtroom, this time along a different route. They entered through a door behind the witness box. The courtroom population had changed considerably and now consisted primarily of reporters and photographers, along with a few docket junkies indulging in their hobby. Gone were the folding chairs, though the gallery was still packed.

Everyone stood as the jury entered, adding a layer of solemn silence.

"Feels like church in here," Courtney muttered to no one in particular.

The jury box had twelve fixed chairs in two rows. Larry directed them to enter but remain standing. As both rows filled, desk chairs were added to accommodate the four additional jurors. Terry and Kay took the back row, Travis and Justyna claimed the chairs in front of them.

A long pause filled the room as everyone settled into place then looked up at the judge.

"You may be seated," he stated, formality tinging his voice. The room rustled with movement. Cameras continuously clicked, even though no one was permitted to photograph a jury member. The shots were of the lawyers, Millick; other court personnel.

And Mark Johannsen. The man whose fate sixteen people now held.

"Okay everyone," Millick began. "I appreciate your patience yesterday and this morning. If it's any consolation, we progressed more quickly through Voir Dire than I'd predicted. I want to thank both legal teams for minimal haggling. Nobody gets every juror that they want so your cooperation in that regard is noted."

He turned to the jury box. "Now, onto you folks. There are sixteen jurors. Four of you will eventually be named alternates, but not until closing arguments have been delivered. That means you will not get to participate in deliberations. Despite this, it's important for everyone to assume they will be part of the final twelve. We can't predict what will happen during this trial and it's not that rare for someone to drop out. So please, stay engaged. Before we begin, let me emphasize that you are not to discuss this trial matter with anyone. Do not read the papers, watch the news or search out articles on the internet. I know it won't be easy but is highly critical to ensure a fair hearing. This case must be judged on the merits presented in this court, not opinion gained from external influences. In America everyone is presumed innocent until proven guilty and that burden of proof rests with attorney Jambliss."

Pausing to glance down at his papers, he continued. "As I stated in the beginning, this trial will be long. The witness list assembled from both legal teams is lengthy, producing considerable testimony as befits a crime of this nature. In addition, there is quite a bit of forensic evidence and testimony. To help you keep track, the bailiffs will provide everyone with notepads and pencils. These are not to leave the courthouse and your jury room will be secured at the end of each day."

It looked like he was about to ask if there were any questions. Instead: "Okay, it's time. Let the record reflect we have impaneled our jury."

"Amen, brother," Nicole added, just loud enough for the other jurors to hear. "Let's get this show on the road."

4

WEDNESDAY, MAY 12, 1999, 10:08AM - DAY 1

"That concludes our opening statements, both prosecution and defense," Judge Millick stated and looked over to the jury, seemingly arriving at a decision. "It's been a long morning. Time for our first break of the day. Ten-minute recess."

"Oh, thank god," Justyna said, loud enough for the bailiff to hear. Larry smiled and nodded. The courtroom stood for them.

They exited the box, single file like taught in elementary school, and down the back hallway to the jury room. A bathroom was located just outside the entrance and several jurors queued up along the wall.

After two hours sitting in the

uncomfortable jury chairs, no one had an urge to sit during break. In fact, Danny retreated to one corner of the room and began doing waist bends to loosen his back. "I feel like I've been roofing all day already," he groaned to no one in particular.

It was Chuckie who broke the ice for everyone's thoughts. "So, let me get this straight. Prosecution is going to show us toxicology reports, witnesses stating Julie Johannsen herself warned about what Mark would do, computer evidence and all sorts of other shit. But the defense is going to be like, '*Nah, she was depressed and committed suicide.*' Do I have it right? That's what they're going with?"

Several people laughed. Justyna walked into the room just as he finished and added, "Yeah. What kind of trial is this? Just find him guilty and let's all go home."

Travis, looking out one of the room's three windows, turned back. "You guys, we shouldn't be talking like this. Talking about the trial. You heard the judge. We need to decide on just the facts." His voice was steady and that of someone secure in his opinion. "Plus, it's only been two hours."

"I know, I know," Justyna laughed back. "Just kidding. Already feels like two weeks though."

Terry spoke up from his spot at one end of the table. "I think we can discuss the case without swaying opinions or developing a verdict in advance."

Next to him, Courtney nodded. "We just have to be careful."

Travis didn't reply but Kay could read on his face that he felt unconvinced.

"Well, I for one am excited to hear about everything," Jean said. "This is full of intrigue. I mean, a man kills his wife with poison. How much spicier can you get? It's like a murder mystery. What drove him to do that? How did it happen? Were there children involved? So many questions."

As other members of the jury would come to learn, Jean liked to voice her thoughts aloud, often leading into longer discussions. Perhaps it was the retired teacher in her.

"I'm with you, good stuff," Chuckie agreed, following with: "I'm your Huckleberry."

She displayed a bewildered look in response. On the other side of Chuckie, Dennis shook his head and laughed under his breath.

The table held fourteen, leaving two jurors to sit along the wall. Rick Crete, a man who made a living in the trades, picked a spot near the first window. At the second window, Lian Younger set up her position. She was the youngest juror, in her early twenties with dark hair, a quiet demeanor and wide eyes that watched everyone around her. She set her belongings on the ledge and sat silently, smiling occasionally at interactions from others, book unopened in her hands.

Larry the bailiff opened the door and leaned in. He held up his hand in a peace sign. "Two-minute warning, folks. Just like football. Go Pack go."

Several groans followed his statement.

"Well, I'd like to call a timeout," Charles Wise said from his seat next to Margaret. He was tall, the oldest appearing juror, with a calm look on his face contrasted by suppressed mischief in his eyes. His habit of inserting sly lines into conversation would be an appreciated element over the weeks to come.

As Margaret giggled and dipped her head, Larry wagged his fingers before closing the door.

"Everyone," Jean plugged into the silence that followed. "Let's do name tents so we all know who each other is. Are. Wait, what's the right word?"

"I got you," Chuckie replied, smoothing over her self-confusion. He began ripping pages out of his notepad and folding them in half. The remainder of their two-minute warning was quiet as everyone took a tent and wrote down their name. Once done, all eyes floated around the table, reading names, attaching faces to them and getting the most basic introductions in order.

"Seems like a long two minutes," Bryan remarked into the silence. He sat between Travis and Justyna, content to listen and laugh at other conversations. His hair was close-cut, peppered with gray that contrasted a young-looking face.

"I'm not complaining," Shelli

answered.

And, as if that triggered the magic bailiff genie, Larry opened the door once again, swirling a finger in the air. "Let's go."

In what would become a habit, the jurors filed out in the order of their seating positions. Courtney would check her notepad for the remaining pages to fill. Dennis would carefully mark the page in his book and fall in behind her. Travis brought up the rear, stopping at the automated sharpener and grinding his pencil whether he needed to or not. He followed this up with a flick of his eyebrows to Kay, or the bailiffs, or anyone else making eye contact.

Kay and Terry had a recessed window alcove behind them, allowing him to push back and stretch his long legs without crowding her. In front of them were Travis and Justyna in the two other office chairs. Initially Kay felt out of place, being outside the jury box proper, but as she watched others try and get comfortable in their fixed chairs, she realized the coin flip landed lucky side up for her.

She wondered if the non-ergonomic nature of the jury seats were intentional, keeping people uncomfortable enough to remain awake. If so, that was a diabolical approach.

On the other side of Terry sat Danny, erect, staring ahead with unmoving eyes. Of all the group, he did not bring a notepad into court. She'd overheard him talking with Margaret, stating he wanted only to go off his memory. Kay hoped his recall was better than hers.

"Mr. Jambliss," Millick ordered. "Please call your first witness."

"The State would like to call Dr. William Chambers," Jambliss responded, looking over his reading glasses at the jury.

A heavyset man entered the courtroom, dressed neatly in suit and tie. He made his way to the witness stand and provided his oath with the air of someone who had done this many times before. Although the way his eyes bulged from their sockets gave a misleading impression he was panicked by the procedure. Kay chalked it up to age, which appeared to be late sixties.

Nearly an hour was spent going through Chambers' resume to establish his expertise and his actions with regards to the autopsy. While a necessary step for the record, it was torture. Listening to dry recitation of educational requirements and medical examination processes wore down the jury. Margaret was seen either sketching in her notepad or struggling to keep her head up, it wasn't clear which. Charles stared forward with slitted eyes, perhaps asleep, perhaps not. Justyna dropped her pencil multiple times as she twirled it in an effort to stay focused.

As if Jambliss understood the numbing effect on jurors, he wrapped up the credentialing phase and directed the court's attention to the TV monitor hung on the far wall. "Members of the jury, please direct your attention there."

A picture of a woman's face filled the screen, up close in focus. Her head was lifted from a pillow, one eye pulled open to reveal a lifeless glare. Blue lips and a nose oddly canted to one side completed the final image of Julie Johannsen. The shock value was instant, perhaps intentional. Shelli stifled a gasp, clamping one hand over her mouth. Lian reacted in a similar manner. Courtney's eyes widened and she furiously began scribbling. Bryan hissed under his breath in disgust and Dennis sharply shook his head.

No one remained disengaged any more.

"Doctor," Jambliss continued as if unaware of the tactic. "What did your examination reveal as the manner of death?"

Chambers leaned forward into the mic. "The manner of death is homicide."

"And with a reasonable degree of medical certainty, what did you determine as the cause of death?"

"The cause of death is multiple and would need to be explained by indications of traumatic asphyxia to the lungs, along with the presence of ethylene glycol in her system."

Jambliss gave a dramatic pause, exaggerated look of surprise scrolling across his face. "Wait. Did you say asphyxia? As in suffocating?"

"That would be correct."

Kay didn't care for the grandstanding theatrics by Jambliss. If he thought that helped make his case, it didn't. She could see the picture and draw her own conclusion.

Terry leaned over and whispered. "Geez, act much?" He apparently felt the same way.

"So, let me see if I understand your testimony thus far." Jambliss turned to the jurors. "Julie Johannsen was poisoned and also suffocated? Why? Could it be that Mark thought the poison wasn't working and needed to make sure she died?"

"Objection, your Honor," Cruise interjected. "Speculation."

"Sustained," Millick answered. "Dr. Chambers, please confine your response to medical observation."

He nodded. "I cannot speak to any reasoning, just that evidence reveals traumatic asphyxia from being pressed into a bed pillow. This resulted in the facial distortion of her nose position."

"What kind of monster would do that?" The DA pondered as if hearing this for the first time. "Who could be so callous to murder the mother of his children in such a manner?"

Cruise threw up her hands in exasperation. "Your Honor…"

"And the Emmy for emotional over-acting goes to…Bob Jambliss!" Nicole hooted when the jury room door closed for lunch. She mimicked a bow.

"I know, right?" Jean responded. "He uses outrageous statements and demonstrative outbursts to emphasize his points. I don't know if he thinks it works but I can certainly tell you it doesn't do anything for me. You should be able to let the facts speak on their own. After all, that's how we're going to determine a verdict. All this grandstanding only makes it more difficult to focus on the testimony."

The room fell silent for a bit then Margaret turned to Charles. "Want to take a walk after lunch? I need to stretch my legs."

Charles nodded as he unwrapped his sandwich. "I would, yes."

"Who wants to hit Subway?" Courtney called out. Several others raised their hands.

Within minutes only a few jurors remained at the table. Chuckie had followed Jean out the door, saying he would go where she went. Charles and Margaret focused on their food. Dennis read his book while nibbling on vegetables. Lian sat silently along the wall also reading and eating. Shelli had a folder open, flipping through papers, trying to keep ahead of the work piling up while she served her duty.

Travis nodded his head towards Kay's notepad sitting open on the table. She had written '*Poison*' across the top of a blank page. "You getting ready for a lesson in serving antifreeze?" He asked, emphasizing the joke with an exaggerated smile.

"You bring the straws." She returned the smile.

Travis gave a laugh and leaned back in his chair. A fancy-looking lunch sat in open Tupperware before him, some type of Mexican dish layered with bright tomatoes across the top, and he stared at it for a moment. "You know," he stated to no one in particular. "We're going to be here for a long while. Weeks of doing the same routine at the same times, listening to good ole Bob over-act, watching Cruise object to his every word. It's going to drive us insane, we need something to keep it interesting."

"What are you thinking?" Shelli asked.

"Breakfast," he answered. "Start with that. Take turns bringing our favorites."

"Oh, I like that idea," Margaret chimed in.

"Well," Charles noted with a deeply serious mock tone. "It *is* the most important meal of the day. Might need to all eat our Wheaties for the way this trial is shaping up."

"Great idea. I'll go first," Shelli said. "But it won't be a box of cereal. Sorry, Charles."

His face fell into an expression that could only be described as 'droopy.'

"Dr. Chambers, you previously testified positional asphyxiation as a cause of Julie Johannsen's death but it wasn't the only cause, was it?" Jambliss stated, as proceedings resumed on the other side of the lunch hour. His voice retained that specific tone of disingenuity, a feigned ignorance.

Danny gave a tiny grunt and shook his head in irritation. Nicole echoed the gesture and added a subdued, "Bob, Bob, Bob," that only the jurors heard.

"That is correct," Chambers responded. "Asphyxia was the proximate cause but ethylene glycol poisoning was also evident. You can characterize it as an inputting factor to her death."

"Hmm, inputting factor. I like that." Jambliss made a show of noting the term down on his notepad. Attorney Cruise rolled her eyes and exchanged looks with her co-counsel.

"Tell us how you arrived at that determination, Dr. Chambers." With a flourish towards the screen, Jambliss brought up an image on the monitor. There were no discernable markings or reference points. Black and white shapes, clearly an x-ray but of what was anyone's guess.

Chambers glanced over at the jury. "You are looking at the decedent's kidney. The dark thick lines are tubular lumen, we can call them tubes inside the kidney for the sake of laymen's verbiage." He motioned to the largest tube. Several white blotches were visible along the length of the tube. "The octahedral shapes indicate the presence of calcium oxalate crystals, which can form during the renal stage of ethylene glycol ingestion, especially in sufficient quantities to cause luminal blockage as we see here. These crystals when found in urine support the diagnosis."

Several more images rotated across the screen, similar in quality, showing differing angles of the kidney. Each showed the same white crystals, shaped like tents seen in profile.

A drawn-out silence fell across the court. Jambliss seemed content to click from picture to the next, as if observing each one for the first time and finding it the most fascinating part of his day.

'Honey, I'm home. Guess what I saw

today? Calcium oxalate crystals! Incredible. Wish you could have been there.'

For his part, Dr. Chambers looked at the jury again and then to the gallery in the back. Cruise and her team wrote on their legal pads, ignoring the DA's grandstanding. Mark Johannsen stared at the jurors with a narrowed expression that appeared to be his default. If he sought to read anyone's mind, there wasn't much there. No one knew if they were supposed to be staring at the slow march of images showing the same thing, writing down notes or what. Kay looked down the row, catching Margaret's eye. The art teacher turned her notepad with a grin to show a sketch of Johannsen dressed in an old-time striped prison jumpsuit. Travis glanced around like he wanted to interrupt the silence with something, anything.

Finally, Jambliss pulled his attention away from the screen and closed the image view. The screen sunk to black. "I'm glad you mentioned the renal phase, doctor. Help me understand. Help the jury understand. What happens to someone if they drink antifreeze? In the last days of her life as she was being viciously poisoned by her husband, what did Julie experience?"

The doctor shifted in his chair as if physically settling into position for beginning a lecture. A sigh emerged from somewhere in the jury and it sounded like Chuckie.

"Yes, well. There are three recognized stages to the ethylene glycol poison cycle but it's important to understand many variables exist within those stages. Factors include the ingestion amount, metabolism, physical size, and stomach contents. These all play a role in the progression of impact and timing. Additionally, the stages are not distinct acts in a play, there can often be a blending. Some people can go directly from stage one to three if the conditions are favorable. I will describe it from a clinical position before addressing the matter of Mrs. Johannsen."

Jambliss interrupted him. "If someone were, say, only a hundred twenty pounds, is it more likely the antifreeze will have a greater effect than on someone who is two hundred and twenty pounds?"

"That is a reasonable assumption."

"And Julie weighed how much at the time of her death?"

"She was one hundred eighteen."

Jambliss nodded with a long look over to the jury, as if scoring a major point. He then motioned for Chambers to continue.

The doctor looked at Judge Millick and pointed to the flip chart mounted on an easel next to the witness box. "May I?"

Millick flapped a hand and Chambers stepped down from the stand, picking up a marker. He drew three vertical ovals, equally spaced across the sheet. "The first stage can occur within minutes. Our bodies are capable of metabolizing a certain amount of poisons before the volume exceeds processing capacity. Think of drinking alcohol, say a glass of wine. On an empty stomach you may feel light-headed after one glass. If you stop drinking the sensation eventually recedes, perhaps leaving you tired and sleepy. If you continue, the feeling progresses towards impairment of function. Balance, speech, emotions and so forth. These become affected."

He wrote the word '*One*' in the first oval. "This stage often mimics the effects of alcohol consumption. It is essentially what happens when you do drink liquor. The body is processing out chemicals found in the substance and when that limit is reached, the effects are felt." He scribbled '*Speech, Ataxia, Balance, Drowsiness*' inside the first oval.

"So, Julie could have thought she was drunk and not realized it was poison?" Jambliss asked.

"That is possible." Chambers wrote '*Two*' above the next oval. "From there we move into the cardiopulmonary stage, marked by symptoms such as throat irritation, hyperventilation and circulatory collapse. There are also secondary companion effects like acidosis which aren't necessarily felt by a victim. This stage generally occurs twelve to twenty-four hours after ingestion, again dependent on the factors initially cited. At this point the person feels as drunk. They may have a heavy chest, may encounter vocal issues and feel consumed by lethargy."

"What does that mean, doctor? They'll be lying in bed with chest pains, unable to move?"

Chambers compressed his lips, clearly not fond of the oversimplification Jambliss sought to place on his medical explanation. "Perhaps. There is nothing certain."

However, Jambliss wasn't done. His gamesmanship came into play. "And if Julie was in that state, she couldn't have possibly fought off Mark if he sat on her back and pushed her head into the pillow, suffocating her. He's a tall man, far heavier and stronger…"

Cruise shot up from her chair. "Objection, Your Honor. Counsel is constructing unsubstantiated scenarios."

"Overruled. You'll get your chance on cross." Millick turned his gaze to Jambliss. "Let your witness testify, Mr. Jambliss. Don't put words into his mouth."

"Sorry," the DA replied and waved for Chambers to proceed. His expression in no way conveyed regret.

Chambers wrote '*Three*' over the last oval. "Finally, we reach the renal stage. By this point the calcium oxalate crystals have formed and are detectable in urine. It's not necessarily the point of no return, but there is damage occurring to the kidneys." He drew a short line across the first oval then another, longer, line below it that crossed all three ovals.

"Again, I must stress that no two interactions will manifest in the same manner. Someone could ingest a large dose and merely wake up with a severe hangover. Someone else could pass away from a lesser amount and present as if they drank themselves to death. It is not a linear process by any means."

"Doctor, if it so closely resembles alcohol effects, how would someone know if they were being poisoned?"

"They probably wouldn't. Antifreeze is the most commonly available carrier for ethylene glycol. It has a flavor easily masked by juices or any sweet-tasting liquid."

Jambliss wrote a few notes then paused, staring at the jury as if in deep consideration. "Doctor, in your professional opinion, with a degree of medical certainty, could Mark Johannsen have fed his wife antifreeze in quantities enough to kill her and when that didn't happen fast enough, pushed her face into the pillow, suffocating her? Is that a plausible scenario?"

Dr. Chambers gave a considered pause before answering. "The evidence does support that finding."

5

MONDAY, JUNE 12, 2000, 10:18AM

Ted only had a single point of contact to provide. At $200 an hour he sent me on my way with one lonely name. Either he thinks I have superhuman powers of discovery or he doesn't care about money.

I call Warren from the car. He picks up just before it goes to voicemail. "Is this going to be one of those deals where you call me every time you need something?"

"You dumped this on my lap," I snap back. "You're not off the hook. You want your friend's problem solved? Pitch in with the things I can't get. Need an address. Justyna Lowder, from Kenosha." I spell out her name.

"Fine, fine," he mutters in response. "Two hundred bangers an hour and I'm stuck doing your legwork."

Interesting that he already knows my rate, meaning either he knew going in or Ted called him immediately after I left. It infers my moves will likely be under scrutiny and something worth keeping front of mind.

I'm parked in Kenosha, along Pershing Boulevard. Vehicles drift past at a sedate pace in the mid-morning traffic. Many trucks and SUVs are present. This is far different than what I'd known in Chicago. Gone is the constant chirping of horns from drivers communicating their displeasure, anger or various other emotions. I see no cars rudely jockeying for lane position, frantic to shave a micro-second from their drive time by cutting off someone else, which would then lead to yet another horn. There are no pedestrians clogging the nearest intersection, forcing drivers to wait, slipping between idling cars in a real-life version of *Frogger*.

This really is a world away, even though it's only a ninety-minute drive.

The strip mall I'm parked in hosts AutoZone and a UPS Store along with a couple local food shops. Chinese and Mexican, a Cousins Sub. It's an older area. I can tell from the houses showing mid-century elements on the other side of Roosevelt. There are common design features repeated across the homes.

"Okay," Warren mutters, interrupting my reverie. "Lowder, Lowder…here we go. Got it." He reels off an address I assume is towards the heart of town by hearing the street and house number. I write down the information and snap shut my phone, wheeling back into the flow of traffic.

Kenosha is an old town, established in the mid-1800s. It sits against the western shore of Lake Michigan, sandwiched between Milwaukee to the north and Chicago across the state line to the south. As such, it serves as a convenient stop between both cities, for travelers but also for commuters. The cost of living is lower, easier to find land and claim your stake perhaps. In return there's a thirty-minute drive to Milwaukee or a ninety-minute train to the Windy City.

AMC Chrysler is one major employer, with a plant manufacturing engines and employing over a thousand people. Snap-On tools is another, which makes sense. Got to build those engines with something. And then there's Jockey International, providing underwear to employees everywhere.

I squint up at road signs as my car follows an eastward path towards the lake, counting down the streets. Thankfully I'm not dealing with new millennium names like Sunnyvale Drive, Spring Lane or Lakeshore Boulevard. It's just straight up tenth, eleventh, twelfth avenues; sixth, seventh, eighth streets.

Clean and orderly, how I'd like my life but unfortunately not what I have.

Pulling over into an open spot on 14th Avenue, I scan the tree-lined road. Nearly every house is two stories with a front porch, driveway along one side and garage out back. Now this more resembles the residential Chicago I knew. There's a strange comfort looking at a block that I recognize in design, even if it reminds me of other times that went terribly sour.

Some porches feature two front doors, indicating the presence of upper/lower apartment units. It's to one of these I step up and rap my knuckles on the screen door. I feel a board literally flex under one foot and it creaks louder than my knock.

Heavy footsteps sound on the other side moments before the door cracks open. The eye peering out is mistrusting but young, near to my height. Tall kid. "Yeah?" His voice cracks with adolescence.

"This the Lowder residence?"

"Not if you're a cop. You sound like one."

I guess some things you never leave behind. "No. Just looking for Justyna. A friend of hers, Nicole, is in the hospital and I heard they were together last Friday when it happened."

"Don't know no Nicole." He moves to close the door.

"Look, wait. Is Justyna your mom? She anywhere around so I can ask her directly?"

He paused. "Yes. No." The door

opens fully to reveal a teenager with rumpled bedhead, gray sweats and a dirty white tank stretched over his belly. "You act like a cop."

His statement carries a weighty accusation, letting me know to choose my next words carefully. Otherwise, that door is slamming shut forever.

"Old habit. I used to be, down in Chicago, but those days are long gone." He has no idea how long and I'm not going to tell him. "Now I just take work the cops won't or can't do, like this. Nicole landed in the hospital Friday night and I'm trying to get some questions answered for her husband. Your mom might know something. You tell me where to find her and I'll be out of your face."

At that the kid's eyes waver and he looks down. "I got no idea. She ain't been around since Friday."

In the moment I get a glimpse of truth, of his uncertainty, caught between being a child who needed his mom and the man he'd eventually grow up to be. Tough to tell which one was more evident.

I sigh in the depths of my mind.

"What's your name?"

"Justice."

"Is that with an 'I' or 'Y'?" I ask with a smile, trying to break the surface. It doesn't work. He simply keeps looking down.

"Do you have anything that could help me find her?" I press on. "Phone number, address, names of other people she was meeting?"

He thinks a minute. Either that or he's comparing our shoe sizes. "Maybe. Her phone broke and she ain't got it fixed so there's a number to call if I needed. She don't like me alone."

And yet, here you are.

I sneak a look past him to the living room, at pictures hung on the wall. "Your dad around?"

"He's on a long haul this week. I told him everything is fine so he don't come running home."

"Brother and sister?" They appear older than him in the nearest picture I can see but it's also several years old.

"Both living on their own. So I ain't told no one nothing yet."

I bite back on a sigh. "Okay, I'll take that number."

He motions me inside and heads down the hallway. The living room is a cautionary tale of teenage boys left to their own devices. Empty bags of chips litter the coffee table, crumbs scattered across the surface. Soda bottles are lined up along the near edge, a mini monument to sugar intake. In the opposite corner a TV sits, *Madden NFL* on display, football frozen mid-pass. Justice is playing as the Minnesota Vikings, his faceless quarterback launching a deep ball to Randy Moss. I have a friend who would like this.

"Here." He pulls a sticky note from the fridge door. A single phone number is scribbled diagonally across it, nothing more.

"You call it? Where is this?"

His face turns sheepish. "Nah. Didn't know what to say."

Typical teenager. Awkward and unsure, covering with bluster when necessary, waiting for someone to give direction, unwilling to expose his own insecurity to others.

"You haven't heard from her in two days and didn't call?"

He flares up at my tone, instinctive. "Yo, fuck off. I can handle myself. What do you know about parenting anyway? You about five years older than me."

I'm not taking the bait. "I've been a parent." Typing the number into my phone, I hand the paper back to Justice. "If you don't hear from her by end of day, call your dad or siblings. Don't be pride foolish."

With that I spin, pressing the *Enter* key as I exit the Lowder house.

SUNNYSIDE BAR, KENOSHA –
10:41AM

The bar is less than ten blocks away. Justice could have simply walked here if he'd wanted.

On this late weekday morning the angled parking spots out front are empty. I take one directly before the entrance. The place looks more like an apartment building than restaurant or bar. Tan brick is prominent across the front facade, a row of second story windows arranged side-by-side like marching soldiers. The sign declares *'Sunnyside Club, Wine Shop, Super Bar'*.

I shake my head as I enter the dimly lit interior and down a long hallway to the *'Super Bar.'*

A petite chestnut-haired girl is behind the bar, wiping glasses dry. There's no one else around. I clear the threshold and walk towards her. "Are you Morgan? I called just a bit ago and think I talked with you."

She nods in response and sets down her towel. "Let me check our logs." Peering down at a piece of paper, her head shakes. "When did you say?"

"Like, five minutes ago. How many other calls came in?"

"None," she spouts and shows me the paper. It's a task list written in flowery cursive. "That's the joke. There's no one else. Some random dude calls and all he asks is who we are and where? I'm going to remember that." She laughs, clearly amusing herself. "Now, what can I get you?"

Already I'm off my bead here with this girl. Taking a stool, I say: "Need to ask you about an event here three nights ago."

A contemplative look crosses her face, arching one eyebrow high in thought. "Never heard of that drink. Long name. What's in it?"

"What?"

Morgan leans forward, closing our gap. "I am a bartender, not Yahoo search. I serve drinks. What would you like?"

"Oh, uh. Pepsi."

"We only have Coke." She draws a glass and watches as I take a sip.

"Now can I ask you some questions?" I hate the hint of pleading in my tone, but this girl is something else.

"Getting creepy, but sure."

I slowly pull out my notepad, keeping an eye on her like she's some mythical creature that will evaporate in a swirl if I look away. "Last Friday afternoon, around four, there was a group here. Do you remember?"

She wipes the counter in front of me despite the fact it's already clean. Her expression is deep thought. "Let me make sure I understand your question. You want to know if there was a group in a bar on a Friday, right near the start of Happy Hour? And of this far-fetched scenario, you would like to ask me questions about these specific people?" She made air quotes for 'people'. "Do I have that right?"

"Well, when you phrase it like that…" I look at my notepad, buying a heartbeat to center myself. "Let me start over. There was a woman, Caucasian, around five-ten, hair dyed a dark red color. She would have likely been with a group of others. Does that trigger anything?"

"Can you elaborate? What else about her?"

I shrug, thinking about Ted's offhanded comments, those things in-between the notes I captured. "Laughs a lot, loudly, happy lady, shakes her head often like she can't believe what she's hearing. Makes friends easily."

"Oh. Yeah. That helps."

"Really?"

"No, not at all. Anyway, I didn't work Friday. That would have been

Leonard."

I slap my notepad down with exasperation. "Then what have we been doing?"

"It's a Monday morning. I'm bored." Morgan gives a short laugh. "Let me go get him. He's got one of the apartments upstairs." With that she disappears towards the rear, light laughter tinkling in her wake.

I stare after her, disassembled by the encounter. What the hell was that all about?

Taking another sip of Coke to settle my jangled thoughts, I wait. The place is dark and old-fashioned. Square wooden tables line one wall. There are two separate bars, one straight, the other U-shaped.

Heavy footsteps pull me out of my interior design evaluation to see an overweight male in his 30s, flannel shirt untucked and rumpled over baggy jeans. Several days' worth of beard spatters across his jaw, uneven and patchy. Foggy eyes appraise me with suspicion. "Help you?"

Now this is more my lane. I can tell he's not interested in playing with me like his bartending partner. I glance around to make sure she's not hanging around. "I need to ask about a group of people from Friday afternoon. Specifically, one named Nicole, tall, dyed hair…"

"Yeah. Nicole Redd. I mean Wright. She got married."

I blink at the quick answer. "You know her?"

"Sure, for years now. We all do. She's a regular."

From the back area a giggle drifts out. Morgan, still amusing herself even when not around. I bite back my annoyance. "Can you walk me through Friday then? Who was she with? What did they do? When did they leave? Anything you can remember will help."

Leonard sips through his nose, holds it a second then exhales. Stale morning breath washes over me and I work to keep my expression neutral.

"It was a wild night. I mean, it usually is with her. She knows how to party. But Friday was new. Must have been something in the air. She was with a bunch of others I didn't know, maybe a dozen?

They seemed like they were celebrating something. There were rounds of shots and they toasted each time."

"No idea what?"

"No. Think I heard a guy's name but maybe not."

I fish out the picture plucked from the Lowder fridge, of Justyna and Justice. "Was this lady in the group?"

A squint. "Yeah, yeah. She was. Loud laugh, more like a bark."

His responses address my questions and can technically be considered information but nothing that moves my case forward. "Let's dig into more detail. When did they leave? What else did they do? Anything odd stand out to you?"

Leonard gives a shake of his head. "I've been interviewed plenty of times by cops. I know how it works. If I knew anything odd, I would have said it already."

I don't bother to correct his assumption of my role. "Humor me. When did they leave?"

"Starting around 10. For sure by 10:30. Those shots must have done the trick. Everyone looked wasted."

"Who bought the rounds?" Maybe now we were getting somewhere.

He shrugs. "Several of them. Taking turns I guess."

"And Nicole left with everyone else? You said she knew how to party. Is it like her to leave early?"

Now Leonard crinkles his brow. "No. You know what? She usually doesn't, she's a closer, but I also haven't seen her as much since she got married."

"See, that's what I mean by odd. Stay with me here. What else?"

He looks past me, out the front windows, eyes looking back three days. "They all got drunk faster than I'd expect. There were only, I think, four rounds of shots, plus whatever drinks each one had, but these people were sloshed like they'd been pre-gaming for hours."

I write: '*Did they drink before Sunnyside?*'

"How about payment?" I ask. "Credit cards or anything with a name?"

"Cash only."

"Did you know anyone else in the group?"

Leonard shakes his head. "Don't think so. No one looked familiar."

Holding up one finger to pause, I flip back through the pages, looking for something to trigger a new angle. I'm missing two windows. One, after Nicole called Ted in the afternoon before arriving here. Then two, the time between here and the hospital. Something occurs to me. I look up at Leonard. "You live upstairs, right?"

That makes him instantly defensive. I see it in shift of his posture, the subtle half-step back to create separation as if the incremental distance adds time for him to think. There's something to hide but it may not have any link to Nicole. The stale scent of weed on his morning breath tells me what the likely reason is. "Yeah, why?"

"Well, if they were all drunk, how did everyone get home? Taxi? Surely there were some who caught rides. You notice any cars still parked the next morning or over the weekend?"

Leonard hucks a choked laugh. "Dude, it's a Wisconsin bar. There are *always* cars left around. I don't keep track. Barely got off the couch except to work."

I can see in his eyes there's nothing more forthcoming. Setting down my business card and a five for the Coke on the sticky bar top, I give him the standard line about calling if he thinks of anything new. I know there won't be.

As I leave Morgan's voice calls out from the back. "Come again please!" Followed by more tinkling laughter.

The sun is blinding when I step onto the sidewalk, bright in the crystal sky. A sneeze overtakes me, then another. It's allergy season, stronger up here due to heavier pollen…

I snap my head around. A half dozen cars occupy spots on both sides of the road. I move among them, swiping my finger along windshields until one reveals a layer of greenish film. Heavy pollen alright. This car has been here a few days. Jotting down the make, model, and plate numbers I retreat to my own car with yet another sneeze.

6

THURSDAY, MAY 13, 1999, 7:48AM – DAY 2

Shelli waltzed into the jury room. True to her word, she arrived laden with a box labeled *Paielli's Bakery*, a Kenosha mainstay for pastries. Dennis was already in his seat, paperback propped up in both hands. He and Chuckie would end up becoming the first arrivals most days, two retired gents who rose early and liked good parking spots.

By 8:15 nearly everyone had arrived, letting loose commentary when they spotted the box.

"Yes, Paiellis!"

"Love their cream puffs."

"Cyclops pastry for the win."

"No way. Bear Claws or a Persian with coconut frosting."

This went on while the jurors picked through the offerings. A number of them – Bryan, Charles, Rick, Lian, Danny – hung back and allowed others to go first. They were still in the newly-introduced stage, conscious of being polite, not yet fully comfortable.

Not the case for Nicole, Justyna, Terry or Chuckie. They led the charge to pass out napkins, motioning others to step forward. Chuckie removed two bags of licorice from his bag and slapped them down on the table. "Lunch topic: Vines versus Twizzlers."

Courtney laughed as she bit into her Long John. In front of her sat two notepads. Travis nodded at them. "You take enough notes yesterday?" His sarcasm was pronounced.

"As much as I could," she replied. "I almost filled both. Did anyone else?"

Travis exchanged looks with Bryan. Neither had used more than three pages. "Were we supposed to?"

"You know," Terry interjected.

"There's a better way to do all this. Simple really. The stenographer is already transcribing everything. You take and run a conversion program on the machine, port it out into readable format, give us printouts. It's probably ASCII or some kind of Unicode which is easy." He elaborated with an example, speaking in technical terms, and finished with: "That's what they should do."

Silence reigned as the jurors nodded and avoided eye contact. No one understood a word he'd said.

All during this Kay sat in her corner of the oval table, between Travis and Charles, watching, observing. Her attention bounced from one conversation to another, dark eyes following. If they were truly all going to be together for a month she wanted to know who these people were, what they were like, habits and personalities, but not by engaging them directly. She preferred to absorb the information, a fly hovering overhead, attentive.

At 8:25 Larry knocked and opened the door. "Good morning, jury folks." He wore a gray suit with bright cheese wheels printed across the green tie. "We have everyone?" His eyes scanned the room, one finger dapping the air as he counted heads. When finished, he motioned for the jurors to follow him into court.

They did, a line of sixteen strangers continuing their journey to something more, though none knew it at the time. Travis brought up the rear after he sharpened his pencil and gave a flick of his eyebrows.

Robert Jambliss patted his tie as he stood up and faced the witness. "Mr. Clough, you were a close friend of Mark's at your place of employment, correct?"

Edward Clough, stuffed into his suit like sausage, nodded on the witness stand. "I'm not sure close friend is the right term, but we were friendly. We'd been working together for six months before this all happened."

"Would you say your relationship was close enough that he would confide in you?"

"This guy is smarmy," Terry whispered to Kay.

Indeed. Clough carried the air of someone who said whatever he thought necessary to look good; with the grease of a stereotypical car salesman. Maybe it was the slicked hair, the instant agreement he displayed to any question regardless of answer, or the way his eyes slid back and forth across the court.

"If he was drinking," Clough responded with a fake chuckle. "Then we were best buds."

"Tell the court what Mark said to you at a work conference one night."

"Well, we were down in St. Louis and it was late. Early morning, in fact, maybe 2am. He started talking about his marriage and the problems they were having. Although it didn't sound like anything more than problems everyone has. Money, roles in the house, how to raise kids, those sorts of things. He went on for a while bitching about her. Then, after a bit, started talking about how easy it is to kill someone with antifreeze. I guess there's a poison in it that's hard to detect. He spoke at length about how it could be mixed in with wine or juice without the other person suspecting anything."

"And how did this make you feel?"

"Uncomfortable, seriously. I mean, he was talking murder." Clough glanced over at the jury with a smile, as if to curry favor.

Danny merely stared back at him, unflinching and straight.

"It seems like an odd topic. Did he talk about why he'd want to do this?"

"Oh yeah. He told me how Julie had had an affair in the past. Maybe seven or eight years back. A fling with some coworker when he was out of town. She immediately told him and promised it would never happen again. They tried counseling but he couldn't get over the betrayal. His anger was obvious, even so many years later."

Jambliss smiled, greasy and smarmy in his own right. "And did Mark reveal any plans to poison Julie?"

"I wouldn't say plans. He mostly talked about how it could be done, like a mental exercise. I thought it was completely hypocritical of him though."

An exaggerated look of shock crossed Jambliss' face. "Oh? And why is that?"

"Because he was having an affair of his own."

"Now that's what I'm talking about!" Justyna busted out when they returned to the jury room for the morning break. "Damn, we finally got good sauce." She slammed herself down in a chair and reached for the Paeilli's box.

While other jurors may have phrased it a little differently, many shared the same thought. Thus far the testimony had been complex medical dissertations over most of their heads or bland attestations to Johannsen's character. Finding out Julie once had an affair brought the case into the stuff of soap operas, calling to the salacious interests of more than one jury member. Then, learning Mark never forgave her and embarked on one of his own juiced the trial up a notch.

Kay and Jean had opposite thoughts,

although neither said anything. Justyna's reaction was disrespectful. More importantly, infidelity in marriage was something Kay abhorred with passion. It added a new layer of consideration for her.

Danny scooped up a couple of licorice strips and waved them around as he walked around in his corner of the room, thinking aloud. "I don't know what's more fucked up," he commented. "That the guy killed his wife and got engaged to the other woman? Or that the other woman, who had to be suspicious, said yes. Did she really think Julie killed herself?"

Travis made a tamping motion with both hands. "Well, we don't have all the facts. This shouldn't slant our thoughts so early in the trial."

With a shrug, Danny refuted the statement. "I'm waiting for the defense to give some counter-facts. So far, nothing. Their cross game is weak."

"I agree with Travis," Nicole butted in. She'd been unusually quiet and thoughtful all morning. "There's still a lot more. Courtney, how many witnesses to go?"

Flipping open one of her notepads, Courtney, the default group archivist, dragged a finger down the page. "Seventy-one," she replied. In response, Bryan and Dennis shook their head the exact same way.

Chuckie pointed with his licorice stick at them both. "Jinx."

Charles raised his hand. "We're passengers on a judicial train. At every stop we get loaded down with more information and the end of our ride is the verdict. We've barely passed the first stop. Get comfortable."

"Well said," Margaret nodded next to him. She looked down at her doodles and murmured. "Riding the train, baby."

Perhaps feeling emboldened by the room sentiment, Bryan turned his head to Kay. Like her, he tended to sit back and observe people. "You have a look on your face." He didn't specify what type of look.

She shook her head. "This is all because of cheating. It's a rot in every relationship. I know she's the victim and murder is murder, but Julie's no angel here. She cheated first."

This sparked a reaction. Shelli's eyes went wide. "What? No!"

Dennis shook his head. "A one-night stand isn't worth death."

Terry, Courtney and Rick all spoke over each other. Margaret set her pencil down and stared. Even Lian, normally removed from the group, looked around with surprise in her dark eyes.

"Are you serious?" Nicole asked.

"Wow," Danny added.

Charles moved his chair away from her.

"I know, I know," Kay said, feeling heat trace up her cheeks. "But it's how I feel and I'm not apologizing. If I ever found out my husband cheated, I'd probably feel like killing him."

"That's a natural reaction," Jean stated. "But only a sociopath actually does it."

Chuckie made a show of writing in his notepad, reciting loudly for the benefit of everyone. "Reminder: Do *not* annoy Kay. Check."

Several jurors laughed, the tension broken, as Larry popped his bald head into the room. "Let's go, break's over."

The rest of the day brought more meat to Kay's infidelity bone. Jambliss was intent on grinding it down to the marrow.

"Your Honor," he began. "The State would like to display electronic email messages for the jury. Messages between Mark Johannsen and his lover Kelly Gorman."

Terry leaned over to Kay. "That's redundant. Email already means electronic mail." He snorted in derision and leaned back.

Kay didn't respond, intently staring at Mark. According to the testimony they'd heard so far, Julie's affair festered in his soul for years. He let it eat away at him until the only way to resolve the emotion was by murder. What does it take to arrive at that course of action? What ran through his everyday thoughts when sitting down to dinner? Or going on a family vacation?

Or making love to Julie knowing she'd tainted their marriage bed?

These considerations consumed

Kay's thoughts, swirling around her head like bats on a wing, charging again and again. For the first time when Mark looked at her with his beady stare, she did not look away. He was the one to break the lock.

"Members of the jury, while my partner queues up the emails for display, I want to lay out this particular exhibit. It is meaningful, it is impactful, and it is at the core of this case. On the night of Julie's murder, Detective Paul Richardson – who you will hear from soon – secured the Johannsen home computer. On that hard drive we found evidence confirming Mark willfully and thoughtfully planned Julie's death, that his anger over her minor transgression years before gnawed at him until he saw no other option than to do something. He plotted how to murder her, how to remove her from his life so a new one could be built with his mistress Kelly."

Attorney Cruise spouted: "Objection! Speculation."

Millick shrugged his shoulders. "It was in his opening argument. The State informed the court this is a core charge of their case."

"Your Honor –"

Jambliss jumped in. "It is absolutely relevant, speculation or not. Mark spent years seething over Julie's affair, over one little mistake. He tormented her with it, holding it over her head again and again and again. He launched a years-long campaign of terror and manipulation all because he could not bear to think of her with another man. And then, when he has his own affair, he immediately switches gears and makes plans to rid himself of her." His face turned red with indignation, as if he himself was the intended target.

Cruise threw up her hands. "Oh, come on."

But Jambliss wasn't done. He stood taller, on his toes, and began to repeat the same mantra, splitting his focus between the jury and Millick. The judge was forced to cut him off. "You've made your point. Don't overstay the welcome. Move on."

Cruise had a sour look on her face, contrasted by the smug smile from Jambliss as he motioned to the monitor now displaying an email. It looked like the message had been printed out onto a piece of paper then scanned back into an electronic file.

Everyone in the jury heard Terry's sigh of exasperation at this clumsy method. Even one of the photographers reacted, dipping his head and stifling a laugh.

The email was titled *'Speaking of…'*.

Jambliss wandered close to the monitor, pointing up at it with the bow of his reading glasses. "I want everyone to look at this email from Mark to Kelly, dated November 21, 1998. Take note of paragraph two. Mark references a future vacation cruise. From the context of this exchange, it's clear they're planning a trip together. This is not the first time it's been discussed. Now, let's scroll down to her reply."

The slide flips to another scan, Kelly's reply. "Look at what she says here," Jambliss again points to the monitor. "She asks Mark what he's going to do about his marriage."

Cruise stabbed her hand up in a halting gesture. "Objection, your Honor. Nowhere does it say 'marriage'."

"Sustained. Watch your

commentary, Mr. Jambliss."

The DA paused a moment, appearing to consider whether to argue the point. He continued with a nod. "Kelly asks Mark what he's going to do about 'his situation'. Now, I'm just a humble attorney and not very smart, but when I read that I think she means his marriage. You can make your own interpretation." He leaned his head towards the jury with a pandering smile.

At this Cruise tightly pursed her lips but didn't make another objection.

"More importantly, look at how Mark replied. And I quote: '*Details, just noise in the bigger picture*'. What could he mean by that? What are these details? If it was in reference to his marriage, is that how he views his wife? As nothing more than noise to be eliminated? Was he already plotting to murder her at that time?"

"Objection!"

"Overruled. This is foundational, Ms. Cruise."

Jambliss stepped away from the monitor, returning to his table and facing the jury. "As it so happens, this fact is completely foundational to the State's case. Mark Johannsen willfully engaged in a campaign of intimidation and harassment against his own wife, exacting revenge for her minor affair with one of his own. It's the old adage: 'Two wrongs don't make a right.' But that still wasn't enough. Unlike Julie, who immediately confessed and tried to make amends for her brief dalliance, Mark decided to take it one step further. The ultimate step. He researched numerous ways to murder her. We have testimony from multiple witnesses on that account. We have the detective who questioned Mark. We have a computer analyst who recovered these emails and more. Mark had many secrets he tried to hide. We have uncovered them and will show how these played into his mindset. We'll show the thoughts of someone warped enough to kill, even if it doesn't seem like there's any connection. Trust me, there is."

He paused, as if waiting for the defense to make an objection. When none came, he raised one finger, the motion of someone who just remembered something important. It was exaggerated for emphasis.

"Did you know, for instance, that Mark had a fascination with penises?"

An audible shift ruffled through the courtroom, gallery, and jury box alike. Shutters snapped to catch the defendant's reaction. Reporter's heads dipped as they furiously wrote in their notebooks.

Margaret slapped a hand over her mouth to stifle a gasp. Danny leaned back with compressed lips. Travis chuffed and shook his head. Chuckie choked back a laugh.

Nicole slowly murmured: "Oh, yeah."

Jambliss' theatrics had the desired effect. He stared at the jury while Cruise objected in the background and argued with Millick on the relevance. The DA's expression showed it didn't matter whether her objection was sustained or overruled. He had everyone's attention now.

"Shall we look at a few more of his emails?" He asked with a sly smile.

7

MONDAY, JUNE 19, 2000, 11:13AM

I call Warren with the plate number but he doesn't answer so I leave a voicemail. I'm at a standstill until he calls back, so this gives me space to think. The trail is thin, leading me down a path narrow and dark, forward as my only option. I followed the single name Ted remembered and it had paid off. That led me to Sunnyside, confirming the presence of Nicole with friends.

Now there are indications of splits in the path, other routes opening to me. Nothing concrete yet but hints like I've encountered in previous cases. A name, plate number, passing reference to another place. These are pieces of an eventual puzzle, collected to see if they fit. Some will be useful while others get pushed aside. I simply need to keep assembling them until an image starts to emerge. Once it does, I can then assess whether my ability to read the evidence is on track. A clinical and rational assessment supported by facts will be what's needed, not rushing to judgment, not thinking I know how everything will play out.

No need to have a repeat of my mistakes in Chicago.

It's near enough to lunch time that I should eat, if the rumble from my stomach is correctly interpreted. Kenosha is an unknown town to me, it's quirk and haunts still hidden just around the corner of a shaded street or behind a decrepit building on the other side of good days. I've got plenty of food options, the usual suspects like Applebee's, Perkins, and other chain restaurants, but I'm not interested in a generic offering on a laminated menu. I prefer restaurants that the locals know, those owned for generations by families who live in the area. It makes me feel connected to the town and its residents.

I have a feeling this case will spin around the people who personally knew Nicole and right now, they are walking just out of my sight, frequenting locations I have yet to find. Call it a hunch, my detective's intuition.

Winding in a roughly westward direction, alternating between side streets and main routes, I mentally map out the different neighborhoods and take note of business names that slide past. There is something unique about a store that's been in one family for years. Those are the places where owners make enough to live but gain the most by being involved. Things like providing schools with discounted sports team meals and sponsorships, consistently appearing at fundraisers, spending off hours showing their presence at the events hosted by other businesses.

They're not intent on buying fancy cars and houses, or dreaming of a luxurious lifestyle, or sinking money into the latest building signage trend. No, the money that would go towards these things instead gets invested back into the customer base.

Eventually I wind up at a place called Big Star. It's a throwback to an older era, where you remain in your car and roll down the window for service. A waitress notes my arrival and walks over. I'm disappointed she's not on roller skates.

The menu is displayed on a large board outside and I scan it while she stands silently beside my door. The menu is mostly variations on the hamburger, fries, and soda theme. Looks like I'm having a cheeseburger, fries, and root beer.

After she leaves, I notice the car next to mine is a family with two little girls in the backseat, twins, maybe eight or nine, laughing at their own private game. I avoid eye contact with them or the parents. Reminders are everywhere it seems.

My phone rings and I snap it open without looking. "Warren. What do you have?"

Reminders come in many forms.

"Arch, it's me."

The voice is soft and undeniably female, so…not Warren. Not even close. I shift mental gears, quickly and without care for the damage caused by doing so. These types of calls are not my strong suit.

"Sheila."

In that name are many things, wound tight and packed into a storage corner with no declared expiration date. Memories and emotions make up most of the bundle, frozen snapshots I can't ever un-see, a life I can't outrun.

Sheila rushes in, threatening the sanctity of my bundle. She has an ability to speak clearly and quickly, denying me the chance to interrupt. "Look, I know you've been avoiding me, and I understand why, but we can't keep on like this. So much has happened in the last year. I get it's not always fair but what's going on now isn't fair either, to both of us. The memories of our daughter are all we have left and if we don't remember together, they will fade. Is that what you want? To forget Anna and everything she meant? Because I can't bear to think of that happening, nor can I stand watching you let your pain eat you from the inside out. Will you talk to me?" She pauses, expecting an answer, but I'm not strong enough to bridge the silence. I need a beat.

"Arch, please."

I dip my head, as if the response is to be found on the floorboard of my car, nestled neatly between my feet. It's shadowed down there, details hard to see, a metaphor for my thoughts and words. When you don't know what to think, how can you know what to say? Worse, when you don't *want* to think, what words are used to fill that void? Nothing changes the past and the future is black, devoid of anything glimmering bright on the horizon. What's the purpose of it all?

What's my purpose?

I try to lid my emotions, but the response still comes out bitterly tinged. "You're damn right it's not fair, Sheila. There's nothing fucking fair about any of this. Anna survived every odd all those doctors gave her. She survived us dragging her across the country, from one group home to another. She survived being kidnapped by those supremacist ghouls. Things that would make a normal six-year-old kid crumble, she survived. And then…" My voice cracks, louder than necessary from restraining the rawness scraping my throat. "And then after all that to lose her to something as stupid as pneumonia? How am I supposed to be okay?"

The twins stopped their laughter, looking over at me through the open window. So does the mother. I put a hand on my forehead, shielding my eyes. No one gets to see me this way. Their window slowly rolls up.

None of this phases the mother of my child – our child – because the words are not new, the emotions well-worn. All our conversations over the last several months have sounded this way. "You said it yourself. She beat the odds but they kept coming and she couldn't keep up. She outlived her medical projections, Arch. She's gone but can't you be grateful we had six years of her blessing our lives?"

Sheila's not wrong. Born into a body that refused to function on its own, Anna never learned to speak, never smiled with joy or cried from pain. Machines supplanted her organs, keeping her alive in a state doctors explained with fancy words but never the words we needed to hear most.

'She does not have the cognition to

recognize the external world. Her impairments are too severe.'

'Our facilities can assist with daily needs but not much else. It's likely she doesn't understand your presence.'

'You may want to think about end-of-life care.'

But I know what I know. When I spoke her name, whispered it into her ear because the machines made too much noise, she moved. A gurgle, a slight squirm, some minute shift of her head. Anna knew dad was there, she always did. Doctors can go fuck themselves.

I feel the anger surging once again, railing on a universe that cares little for one man and his personal loss. There's nowhere I can go to fight back against what happened, no one to blame.

No justice to be had.

As if Sheila senses my dark thoughts – and she probably does, the woman knows me well – she pushes on, desperate to keep me clinging. Like, if she stops I'll simply slip away to endless night, never to be seen or heard again.

"It's not dishonoring her memory if

we grieve and also look to the future. The two things are not the same. It's all we can control. Don't let your wound fester until it infects everything. That would be a true dishonor to Anna. Can we meet and talk? Just be together like we once were?"

My phone beeps and I see Warren's name displayed on the screen. "I'm sorry Sheila, I have to go."

I hang up before her protest is fully formed. Sometimes running away is an explosive sprint, a sudden leap from emotional danger. It can be easier to let the reaction dictate the response.

He's got a hit on the plate.

Travis Green opens the door to his residence. Bags are under his eyes, stubble graces his jaw and a golf glove is tight to his left hand. He shows a guarded expression. "Hello."

I give my spiel, adding Justyna's name to Nicole's. Two women now, unknown in what truly happened to each, and the car left outside Sunnyside belonged to him.

"Oh," he responds with an emphasized nod of his head. "Yeah. I was there Friday. Christ, I'm still hungover. Come on in."

I step in and point towards his glove. "On your way to a round?"

"No," he returns a puzzled look, as if it's natural to wear a glove for no reason. "Why do you ask?"

I skip any follow up and motion to the couch, taking a seat when he nods. I pull out my notepad as he settles across from me in a leather recliner. The side table has a golf ball and two tees scattered on it, along with a TV remote and *People* magazine.

"I don't know if you heard, but Nicole is in the hospital and Justyna hasn't returned home yet."

"Really? No, hadn't heard. I mean, those two are pretty wild from what I know. Is Nicole alright?"

"Well, she's in a coma so take that for what it's worth. Can you walk me through the night? Assume I know nothing, because I don't. Who were the others there? Why were you together? What happened?"

"Coma, wow." Travis fiddles with his glove, leaning back in the chair. "Let's see, square one. All the way back. It starts last year when we all served jury duty on a pretty big case. After it was over, we promised to regroup around the one-year anniversary and celebrate the verdict. That was Friday."

That's a new one to me. "Celebrate? Is that normal? I mean, I get the civic duty aspect and all…"

"No, dude. You don't understand. This wasn't a piddly DWI case lasting two days. We were together almost two months to decide the fate of a man who murdered his wife. Longest trial in state history. You never heard of the Johannsen case?"

I think back to this time last year. I'd been handed my first case as a rookie under Griff's tutelage, which precipitated meeting Warren. That case led to an assassination plot, which led me to break nearly every Chicago police department policy, leading to my dismissal. And then all the fallout that followed through end of year…

"I'm not from around here and

things were a little hectic for me then."

Another shake of his head, another snap of his glove fastener. "Okay, from the top then." A sip of breath. "May 1999. A bunch of us were on a jury for Mark Johannsen, accused of killing his wife Julie. Sixteen jurors – four alternates – stuck in uncomfortable seats eight hours a day, five days a week, listening to a hundred witnesses and several annoying lawyers. We were stared down by a creepy defendant and every reporter in the gallery, like zoo specimens or something. It's hard to explain unless you've done it."

"And that warranted an anniversary celebration?"

"Well, yeah. Like I said, it was a big deal around here. You end up becoming close after that long stuck together. We all stayed in touch."

I write that down, buying a little thinking space. "Yet you just said you don't know Nicole well. It seems inconsistent."

Travis' skin is deep tan, presumably from the hours spent on a course under the sun. Combined with his dark hair and salt-peter scruff, it gives him shades of leading man looks. His dark eyes wander the room searching for words. "You know *The Breakfast Club* movie?

"Is that the one with high school kids in detention?"

"Yeah, yeah. They're all stereotypes. The jock, princess, criminal, brain and weirdo, thrown together in a room for an entire day. At the end of it, everyone discovers they aren't so different after all. Well, we were like that. You come to know each other, their habits and personalities. Like, I know Chuckie collects old tractors, Lian works in a factory, Dennis reads every chance he can and Margaret can't not doodle when bored. But I don't know their history, spouses, kids, what makes up their lives. I don't know their last names even. They are in my contact list as Shelli Jury, Dan Jury, Rick Jury."

In a way it does make sense. I remember liking *The Breakfast Club* and relating to it as a kid. "Okay, so you were a bunch of strangers brought together for one reason and ended up getting to know each other well. I can accept that premise. Let's work the party. You showed up when?"

"Around 4:30. Rick, Lian, Dennis and Chuck couldn't make it. Danny and Courtney came not longer after."

"Then what?"

His eyes squint in confusion. "What do you mean, *then what*? What always happens when people get together in a bar, especially one year later. Drinks, catching up on lives, shots and cheers, making the rounds, rinse and repeat." The expression shifts, letting out his suspicions. "What exactly are you looking for?"

"Nicole's husband wants to know what happened."

"She got over-served, that's what. We all did. I'm sure mine wasn't the only car left there that night."

"Did she interact with anyone outside the group? How many rounds of shots? What did she drink?"

Travis raises both hands. "Hey, hey, ease off the question cannon. I'm telling you what I know. She talked with everyone. Nicole is the life of the party, our jury foreman. Or forewoman. What do you call them? Foreperson? I remember her and

Kay in heavy conversation at some point, but I don't know about what. They both looked wasted. She got into an argument with Terry and neither one made any sense. I never saw her talking with anyone else outside of our group, though the bartender knew her by name."

None of this is helpful, barely worth writing down but I do anyway. "When did everyone leave?

He shrugs. "Dan, Shelli and Courtney went first, kids at home and all. Maybe 9pm. I left not long after, my wife had to come get me. Man, I was loaded. The bar made money that night." A short laugh, followed by a groan. "Can't believe I still feel it."

"And Nicole was there then?"

"Yeah, that's when I saw her and Kay talking, leaning against each other. She may have been holding Kay upright." He laughs again. "Or maybe the other way around."

"You don't know when she left or with who?"

"Nope, I was comatose the minute I got home. Wife yelling at me and everything. Woke up on the floor." He points to a spot at my feet. "Guess I fell off the couch."

I do some math. Leonard stated everyone was gone by 10:30, Ted receives a call at eleven. It seems plausible she got completely shit-faced and someone who knew her – maybe Kay – brought her into the emergency room. The scenario starts to form. Ted may not want to believe his new wife drank herself comatose and is looking for a scapegoat. It's not unknown. I've had numerous other cases where someone doesn't want to hear the facts. I'll need to track down the other jurors and find who last was with her.

Travis is helpful and recites everyone's number from his phone contact list. I diligently record them. Afterwards he stands and cracks a knee joint. The bags under his eyes appear deeper now. Guy looks like he wants to faceplant on the couch and say night-night.

I take the hint and stand also, turning for the door. "That trial must have been quite an experience. Certainly seems to have made an impact on you guys. What made it so special?"

"Just all the evidence and testimony. Witnesses, forensics, porn, infidelity. You name it. All the things that cause divorce. But it didn't end with a beating or shooting or whatever passes for violent in domestic crimes. Not for this guy. He was a special kind of psycho. He fed his wife antifreeze so it would look like she drank too much and then…"

His voice falls off a cliff, instantly silent.

Our eyes lock as the same thought lands on us both. My hand is frozen on the doorknob.

"Holy shit," we say.

8

WEDNESDAY, MAY 19, 1999, 8:02AM – DAY 6

"Do you think they'll show them today?" Nicole asked.

This morning's treat came courtesy of O&H Bakery, in the form of a local pastry known as Kringle. One raspberry, one cream cheesecake, baked in oval shapes. She picked up a wedge and placed it on her napkin.

Travis grunted through his bite and let loose a muffled, "So good."

"Show what?" Jean asked as she cut her slice into smaller pieces.

"The penis pictures. He talked about

them last week and then nothing. I want to check out the goods." A guttural laugh followed. "You can't tease a girl like that."

"For what purpose?" Margaret countered. "I don't know why it matters."

"Well," Jean said slowly as she finished her bite. "The guy clearly has issues. I mean, tormenting your wife for years over a one-night stand instead of sticking with counseling? Letting it eat at you until there's only one option out? It goes to his mindset, I guess."

"I don't want to see those pictures," Dennis abruptly announced. The other males in the room grunted in agreement. Bryan tapped his chest and pointed upward, "Hear, hear. No dick pics."

"I don't want to get self-conscious," Travis declared, and the grunts turned to laughter. Even Lian joined in, giving a shy smile.

"We'll tell you when to close your eyes," Courtney stated. "We care like that."

Nicole was set to be disappointed. Once everyone had convened for the morning, Jambliss called his first witness of the day. Jason Ruffalo, forensic analyst for the Wisconsin Department of Justice. Young and heavyset, Ruffalo portrayed the image of a smart but sedentary guy recently out of college. His technical forensic group was new, still feeling their way through the explosion of internet usage and what kind of evidence such use provided. It fell to simple luck that he'd drawn the Johannsen case.

"Mr. Ruffalo," Jambliss began once preliminary witness credibility was complete. "Can you tell us a little bit about what happens behind the scenes of internet searches? I'm not an internet user at all and some of the jurors might be in the same boat." He looked over to the jury box with a pandering smile. "Although they all look smarter than me."

Ruffalo nudged up his glasses and angled towards the jury. Travis, the closest juror, sat less than ten feet away from the witness stand, but Ruffalo did not maintain eye contact with anyone as he spoke. "When you conduct an internet search, those results are captured and recorded in three spots on your computer hard drive. The first spot is associated with an application like Internet Explorer or Netscape Navigator. Let's call it the browser space. When someone types out a search request, the entry is saved to a file for that 24-hour period. So, when you go into your browser menu and look at history, you'll see a series of hyperlinks that have been returned from a search. If you clear history, those are the files being deleted. However, they are not completely gone. They will no longer appear in your browser history, but there is a second place, an area of system folders that contains essentially the same information. This is your temp space. Computers will create these temporary files to help speed up search results and graphics rendering. To the average user these system files may look like nonsense but if deleted they also help to erase the search history."

"Duh," Terry the software designer whispered, as if Ruffalo spoke on the most basic things everyone should know. Kay ignored him. She didn't know this. Her husband was the computer user in their house.

Nodding like someone participating in a master class, Jambliss prompter further. "And what about the third place a user's search history is stored?"

"This is generically called your unallocated space. Information like date and time stamps, automated processes and so forth are saved here. These are not intended for human reader comprehension. There's a lot of other purposes but for the sake of this trial, think of them as a backup of a backup, only harder to find. A casual user would not be likely to stumble across these files and deleting the wrong ones could negatively impact their computer's functionality."

"Thank you, Mr. Ruffalo." Jambliss turned to the jury. "This might seem confusing and overly technical, but trust me, it's critical to your understanding of the case." He turned back to Ruffalo. "Can you tell us why this is important?"

"When I analyzed the hard drive of the Johannsen computer, it was obvious someone had purposely deleted search history in both the browser and temporary folders but not from the unallocated space.

Perhaps they were unaware it existed."

"And why would Mark Johannsen have reason to do that?"

"Objection," Cruise stated. "Witness cannot speak to intent."

"Sustained," Millick agreed.

Undeterred Jambliss took a different angle. "When you see evidence of someone deleting their search history, what does that tell you? In your expert opinion."

With a glance towards Cruise to see if another objection was coming, Ruffalo paused a beat before replying. "It tells me the user wanted to cover their tracks. These aren't folders you normally would access, you have to look for them, intentionally look for them. The user of this computer was tech savvy enough to know of two memory storage locations but not the third. Deleting the data in both locations is the action of someone seeking to remove evidence of their browser activity."

Kay looked at Johannsen, gauging his reaction to this revelation. The defendant sat perfectly still, staring back at her from a lowered look, the expression of someone caught in a lie. She looked along the row at her fellow jurors, seeking someone else who witnessed it. Nicole met Kay's look and held up her notepad.

It read: *'Dick pics. Dicksdicksdicks!'*

Chuckie saw the page as well and snorted aloud, just partially successful in stifling a laugh.

Jambliss glanced over, distracted by the noise. His eyes scanned along the jury box, but no one met his eyes. On the far wall the monitor flared to life, and this pulled him back to the task at hand. "Oh, yes. Let's look at Mark's search history. Mr. Ruffalo, what's displayed are internet pages you reconstructed from those files in the unallocated space, correct?"

"Correct."

"And so, we're really looking at the path Mark took during his searches, seeing the pages one by one as he would have seen them?"

"Correct."

The next ninety minutes were devoted to dry explanations of each internet page, from the title to the topics to the images. After the first few, fascination over being a virtual voyeur to Mark's searches faded, leaving the jury slack-eyed and bored. One slide after another of reconstructed website pages, Jambliss' line of questions following the same script: *'Tell us what this page is, tell us when the user viewed it, tell us about the page content. Let's view the next.'*

As they reached the end of the slides, Jambliss summarized the testimony. "So, on the same day that Mark answered Kelly's question about his 'situation', he began searching for ways to address it?"

"I don't know about any question. All I can say is on that day, a user of this computer began searching out how to kill someone with antifreeze."

Jambliss raised his finger in emphasis. "Not only searched but then tried to cover his tracks."

"The deletion activities suggest that."

Satisfied, the DA looked at the clock then Millick. "Your Honor, we have a lot more to go. I'd suggest a break before we continue."

Millick nodded and thumbed over his shoulder to the door leading towards the jury room. "Ten minutes, folks."

Back in the jury room, Charles nodded with his head towards Kay's notepad, open to the page replicating the ethylene glycol poisoning stages. She was in the process of over-writing words, an unconscious habit when deep in thought. "That's very thorough," he said through a bite of Kringle.

She flipped to her diagrams of internet search history and displayed them. Every inch of the page was packed with writing. "It's important to be accurate."

"No kidding," Margaret chimed in. "I tried, but…" She trailed off and opened her notepad to show where some kind of diagram morphed into bulbous flowers with looping lines.

Charles laughed and shared his attempt. Written at the top in shaky letters were '*browser, temp, unallo…*'. The rest of the page was blank. "They were talking too fast for me."

"I wrote everything down," Courtney chirped in from the other end of the table. How she'd picked up on the conversation was anyone's guess. She patted the stack of five notepads before her. "Killing trees and taking notes."

Danny shook his head. "I don't think I've written that much in my entire life."

Several others could be seen looking at their half-empty notebooks then over to Courtney's collection.

"Hey," Jean said, teacher instinct taking back over. "We should all trade phone numbers, just in case someone's going to be late one day or needs a ride or something like that."

"Sure," Chuckie immediately agreed. "Why not? Beats feeling inadequate next to Courtney."

A sheet of paper circled the table, everyone listing their name and phone number. Kay came last and stared so long at the list Charles eventually leaned over. "You don't have to memorize it. We can have copies made."

She grunted a short laugh and wrote her number down. "Sorry, got distracted."

Travis sat back in his seat looking pensive. No one else in the room had much to say, as if they all recognized this moment signified something. It had only been a week but in that short time they'd gone from complete strangers to the next stage of familiarity. Trading phone numbers marked the point when connections could move outside of the courthouse walls. It remained to be seen where this would all lead.

"You guys ever seen that movie *The Breakfast Club?*" He asked.

After the jurors were seated back in court, Jambliss stayed upright, watching them with a practiced eye. The tech analyst Ruffalo once again sat in the witness box, hunched and placid.

The DA began without preamble. "The State has established frequent communication between Mark Johannsen and his mistress Kelly. We've heard testimony from law enforcement, not the last time mind you, and gotten a glimpse into the mind of the defendant. I want to continue the journey so that you, our jury, get a full picture of the man on trial today."

In her seat, Nicole began to bounce

with a growing smile, little movements revealing anticipation.

"Mr. Ruffalo, during your forensic analysis, you uncovered more than just emails, correct?"

"Correct. In the user section of the hard drive were many folders created by someone with access to the computer."

"What were in these folders?"

Nicole's bouncing increased. Next to her Shelli dipped her head, covering her eyes as if that would keep anyone in the gallery from seeing her. More than one reporter glanced over at the jury box, noting the motion.

"Image files. Photos downloaded from sites on the internet."

Jambliss snuck a glance over to the jury. Kay sensed he relished this dramatic build-up and fought to keep a distasteful expression off her face. The application of law should be above this kind of theater.

"What were the subjects of these files? What kind of images?"

Ruffalo shifted in his seat, clearly unsure how to frame his reply. The pause unintentionally added to the drama and he finally said: "Penises."

Nicole hissed in approval and gave a small fist pump.

Though all reporters had heard the revelation last week, this was the first time it came back around and once again the gallery buzzed with palpable anticipation. Sex sells.

"How many of these images would you estimate there were? How many did Mark save to his computer?"

Leaning forward, Ruffalo replied, "Three thousand, one-hundred sixty-two."

"That's an estimate?" Danny whispered. "Christ."

Cruise stood. "Objection. What does the number have to do with anything?"

"I believe the State intended for this to go towards mindset," Millick responded. "Overruled."

"But this is nothing more than a blatant attempt to sensationalize the case and paint our defendant in a defamatory light."

"I said overruled."

Cruise sat back down, clearly unhappy. For his part, Mark Johannsen gave no expression of shame or concern. Kay found herself studying his face, looking for something that exposed his thoughts, and came up empty. She supposed if he was sociopathic enough to murder his wife, letting the public know about his warped obsession was no big deal.

However, Jambliss wasn't done twisting the knife. He had a point to make and make it he would. "You stated there were many folders. Can you explain how these images were organized within those folders? After all, three thousand and change is a significant number. If someone is demented enough to search them out, I would assume there is also some type of organization."

Cruise didn't even bother objecting to this statement. She rolled her eyes and shook her head. Johannsen looked over as if expecting a different reaction.

"Well," Ruffalo adjusted his position and pushed his glasses up. During the time of his testimony, the jurors had come to recognize it as a tell that he wasn't comfortable with the answer. "They had names like *Big, Small, Huge. Soft. Hard.*"

"And, in your forensic expertise, what did these folder names mean?"

Now Ruffalo looked like he wanted to be anywhere else but here. The thrill of testifying for a high-profile case had given way to feeling like he was involved in this warped hobby. Nonetheless, he was under oath.

"I would say they related to the type of penis images in each folder."

"Oh," Jambliss replied. "So, would the picture of a large penis be in the *Big* or *Huge* folder? In your expert analysis?"

"Come on," Cruise blurted. "Objection."

"Sustained. Move it along, Mr. Jambliss."

He moved it along, hounding the topic of tawdry habits, painting Johannsen as someone obsessively typing search terms for a male penis on his keyboard and saving those images that fit some criteria only he knew. Cruise made numerous objections but Jambliss was in his element, re-working his question to satisfy her objection while still making his point. A portrait emerged: Mark Johannsen, hunched tightly over his desk, face to the screen as he repeatedly typed search terms, studying an array of male appendages and either nodding in approval or dismissing with a headshake.

Sadly, this would be the limits probed by Jambliss through end of day. No actual penis pictures were ever shown on the monitor. He merely referenced them with oblique terms and descriptions, keeping Ruffalo squirming in his seat.

Nicole left the courthouse grumpy.

THURSDAY, MAY 20, 1999, 8:34AM – DAY 7

The courtroom gallery was packed shoulder to shoulder. Yesterday's topic of Johannsen's penis fetish had made its way through the courthouse halls, drawing those who wanted the dirt. In addition to more reporters and photographers, there were other attorneys, administrative employees in the building and even a couple of sheriff's deputies who wandered in before their own cases. Everyone came to verify the rumors.

And hopefully be treated to more twisted facts.

Jambliss stood behind his table as the jury filed in. His stance was the same, his suit like others he'd worn but the look on his face was new. Satisfaction, confidence; he'd scored major points yesterday probing the penis photos. Even though not core to his case, in the court of public awareness they were a hit. He knew this case would be historic and left nothing to chance. The smile he gave the jurors as they entered was made of triumph.

After the morning roll call formality was completed, Millick asked for the first witness.

"Your Honor, the State calls Gus Hoover."

The rear doors opened to allow a tall man. All eyes turned towards him. He moved with studied care, distinguished in appearance with a full head of gray hair and professor's specs perched low on his nose, all the while darting looks everywhere except at Johannsen.

In the jury box, Danny leaned towards Terry and Kay. "He looks nervous, really nervous."

Terry nodded. "Maybe all the spectators?"

"I think more than that," Kay countered. "Something's going on, guys."

Sure enough, as Hoover made his way past the prosecution table Jambliss also sensed the emotion. His confident expression faltered.

"Mr. Hoover," he began once the witness had been sworn in. "Tell us your relationship to the defendant."

"We worked together."

"But not just coworkers, right? Your relationship extended beyond the office."

Hoover nodded, still avoiding eye contact with Johannsen. "Yes, that's true. My wife and I spent time with them outside of work. Dinners, mostly."

"You knew Mark as a friend?"

"That is correct."

Jambliss looked down at his notepad, seemingly pondering the next question. "And as part of this friendship, were you aware of Mark's fascination with penises?"

New members in the gallery found themselves rewarded for their attendance. The rumors they'd heard yesterday had just been founded. A shifting occurred across several rows as they straightened, eager for more. Even the sheriff's deputies glanced at each other and smiled.

"Not until later in our friendship."

"Describe for me how you discovered his fetish."

Hoover was clearly uncomfortable but Kay felt it was more than just talking about this topic. Travis reacted, too. He looked over his shoulder at her and Terry then shook his head with a frown.

"I went into his office one day looking for a client's phone number. Mark wasn't around and I thought to look for myself before calling him. A writing pad was on his desk, just a standard one like hundreds of others around the office. So, I flipped through it hoping to find the phone number."

"What did you see instead?"

"Drawings. Pages and pages of them

starting from the back. The first half of the pad was just work notes."

"And the subject matter?"

"All penises."

"Did you ever find that phone number?" Jambliss asked with a sly smile.

"I stopped looking."

Someone in the far back of the gallery let out a cough of laughter, quickly choked off. Millick looked up from his bench.

Jambliss spent time grilling Hoover on the drawings, asking similar questions in different ways. Types, shapes, quantity. Cruise objected several times, winning a couple, losing a couple. None of this, however, eased Hoover's nerves. If anything, he became more tense, more fidgety. The jurors, who had a side view of the witness box and could see him more clearly than the gallery, traded looks. Even Margaret looked up from her own drawings and paid attention.

"Mr. Hoover, let's move on to another aspect of your relationship with Mark Johannsen." Jambliss' demeanor had settled down, back into a semblance of the earlier confidence. Maybe his witness's answers set him at ease. "Did he share with you a desire to rid himself of Julie?"

Hoover shifted and looked over to Millick before answering. "No, he did not."

At this Cruise shot up her head, zeroing in. Her pen hovered in mid-air above her legal pad, poised for use.

Jambliss rocked back like some invisible hand had shoved him. His mouth clapped open and closed, and color started to creep into his cheeks. "Mr. Hoover, during our discovery sessions you answered differently. I'll remind you that you are under oath."

"I know. I think I misspoke."

"You think?" Now Jambliss' forehead was a shade of crimson. "We deposed you multiple times so I don't know how you can suddenly say your words were wrong."

"It is what it is," Hoover stated flatly. His eyes shot all around the court, the look of a man cornered and seeking the nearest exit. Larry the bailiff leaned forward in his chair behind the witness stand, alert.

Jambliss wasn't done. "You stated that on the night of June 17, 1998, the defendant confessed to you a desire to kill Julie. That he'd had enough of her infidelity despite it being seven years earlier. That he'd…"

"Objection," Cruise blurted. "Leading."

"Sustained." Millick looked at Hoover. "Sir, it is your duty to tell the truth as you know it."

Hoover nodded sharply, rapidly. Sweat beaded along his forehead, visible only to those close enough, like the jurors and bailiffs. And attorneys. "There was a lot of conversation and alcohol that night. The more I think about it the less sure I am."

"You are changing your testimony," Jambliss said, and it was not a question.

"I'm saying it's hard to be sure. I don't know any more. A lot of time has passed."

The tonal shift in the courtroom was a palpable thing. Jambliss looked at a loss for further words.

Cruise smiled and stood when her turn at cross-examination arrived. The case which seemed a lock had suddenly developed a crack and she intended to widen it.

9

THURSDAY, MAY 20, 1999, 12:22PM – DAY 7

"I've had enough of this Hoover guy," Chuckie announced over lunch. "The defense has been tearing him a new asshole all day. He doesn't know his right from his left anymore. Glad we're done with him."

"Shady as hell," Danny agreed. "He and Johannsen are stockbrokers? I'd be safer just sticking money under my mattress."

Bryan laughed, mouth full of sandwich, and choked. He slapped the table once then shook his head.

"I don't know," Shelli chipped in. "The fact that his story changed makes me wonder why. Maybe he did really think more about it and began doubting. I mean, it's his friend's life here. That's a lot of weight."

"Bullshit," Terry spouted. "Someone got to him. Made him change his testimony."

This prompted several stares from around the table. Even Dennis took note. He pulled his attention up from the tattered novel before him. "Where did you come up with that?"

Terry shrugged. "It's the only explanation. A guy under oath doesn't change his deposition statement unless he's forced to. Maybe their company is putting pressure on him from a PR standpoint. Maybe there's a book angle he's working. Who knows."

"Oh, come on," Travis laughed. "This isn't a movie. I think he got scared and started doubting himself. Happens to us all. Happens to me every time I line up for a putt. Like Shelli said: It's a dude's life at stake, a friend of his."

"You're really comparing testimony to golf?" Nicole asked, shaking her head as she did.

"It's an analogy," he shot back. "Or metaphor. Whatever."

Justyna snorted in disbelief. Rick shook his head, although it wasn't clear exactly what he disagreed with. The room erupted in discussion pockets, rife with noise and loud opinions. Jean tried to talk but Terry overrode her, so she turned to Chuckie. He in turn looked at Danny. Courtney repeated herself several times, but no one listened. Lian watched with wide eyes, focusing from one conversation to the next.

What had seemed a unanimous opinion on the case was clearly divided now, all over the doubts of a single witness. If she was able to see the arguing, defense attorney Cruise would have nodded in approval. All she needed was one juror to hold out and her client walked.

Under the growing chatter and opinions, Margaret turned to Charles. "Ready for a walk?"

He nodded and stood to his full height. "Good idea. Things are getting a little tense in here."

As they left, no one paid attention,

wrapped up in their own conversations. Several lines of argument had emerged, splitting the jurors along opposing lines. Voices rose, making point and counterpoint, creating two opposing tribes of thought.

By the time Margaret and Charles returned, the room had grown thick with tension, remaining jurors silent in resentment or plotting their next argument. Even Jean, normally the peacemaker, sat and scribbled idly in her notepad.

Detective Paul Richardson was large, barrel-chested with hands that looked like they could encircle someone's neck twice. Yet his voice was soft and carefully modulated, expression serene, patient. Watery blue eyes peered out from behind glasses that were small for his face.

Jambliss seemed to have recovered from the disaster that was Hoover's testimony. At least his forehead no longer showed a vein pulsing in anger. "Detective, did you have contact with Mrs. Johannsen prior to her death in December 1998?"

"I did, yes." He shifted in the chair, which creaked alarmingly under his weight. "A number of times since 1992 in fact."

"What was the nature of these conversations?"

"She reported finding pictures of a pornographic nature left around the house, in the backyard or shed. Mr. Johannsen also stated he'd received similar pictures in his office or left on his vehicle."

"And how long did this go on?"

"Up until the time of her death. Approximately six years."

A buzz rolled through the gallery. Reporters sensed this was a sub-plot to the story and recorded the details so they could figure out how to wind it in. Was there someone stalking the Johannsens? What was behind the harassment?

"Please describe the nature of these pictures, detective." The jury recognized Jambliss' tone. He was leading towards a shock statement.

Richardson took a breath and leaned into the microphone. "The majority were penises. Some pictures showed couples engaged in sexual acts."

Now the buzz took on life as connections were made. Mark Johannsen tried to keep a neutral expression but the way he shot looks from under his brow revealed anger at this revelation.

Nicole merely rolled her eyes, resigned to the fact that none of these would be shown either.

"Detective, did you find any of these pictures on the computer hard drive?"

"We did not."

"And yet, you expressed to me the opinion they came from Mark. Is that correct?"

"That is correct. There was similarity in the type of image, background, framing and such. It appeared they all came from the same collection."

Justyna snapped up her head. "There's a collection?" She whispered, drawing a laugh from Bryan.

"So," Jambliss continued. "Mark could simply have printed the image from a web page instead of saving it first?"

"Objection," Cruise stated flatly without even looking up from her notes. "Speculation. The detective is not a computer expert."

"I withdraw the question, your Honor." He pondered his next angle of questioning. "On the day of Julie's murder, you personally responded to the call."

"The on-scene officer called me."

"And is that normal procedure for all murder investigations?"

Richardson shook his head, never wavering his gaze from Jambliss. "There is no normal, each is different. Because we'd had numerous interactions with the family, he thought it important I come by."

"Did you speak with the defendant?"

"Yes, I received the call around 4:30 and arrived within 30 minutes. I conducted a site interview with Mr. Johannsen before doing an evidence sweep of the house."

Jambliss interrupted. "Your Honor, the State will present a video recording of this sweep as evidence later today or tomorrow morning."

Returning his attention to Richardson, he asked, "Even at that time you sensed Mark had murdered his wife?"

This caused Richardson to shake his head. "I didn't have any inclination either way at this point. My focus was on understanding the situation and collecting evidence to determine how I would proceed."

Jambliss didn't like the answer, obvious from his pursed lips. Perhaps he thought law enforcement officers should help prosecute his cases instead of simply presenting their facts.

"And yet, you felt it necessary to call and request my presence."

"Yes. Due to our department's history with the Johannsens. You arrived at 5:20, at which time I walked you through the scene."

"In the course of this you made some observations."

"I did. I noted how Mr. Johannsen seemed unaffected and calm."

"Which is not normal."

"As I said, there is no normal in homicide investigations."

FRIDAY, MAY 21, 1999, 10:12AM – DAY 8

Margaret nibbled at a carrot from her Tupperware container during the morning break. Charles had vacated his seat between her and Kay, leaving an opportunity to chat. "So," she said, breaching the gap. "What do you do? For a living, I mean?"

"Right now, nothing." Kay opened her baggie of crackers, meat and cheese, sorting them into stacks. "I'm between jobs but a stylist by profession."

"Any luck finding a spot? New salons are popping up everywhere. Someone has to work them."

Kay nodded her head, focused on the task of assembling a cracker sandwich. "You would think, right? Not a lot of places are taking applications. I've tried a bunch."

"How about Joan's Designs out in Twin Lakes? I heard about a chair that's been vacant for months now. I guess one of their employees went nuts on a customer. Ended up in a stalking case or something like that. Crazy."

Kay bit into her ad-hoc sandwich. "Never heard of it. Thanks for the tip."

Charles caught the exchange as he returned to his seat. "Let me know when you get settled. I could use a good barber to control this tangle." He ran one hand over a balding scalp.

"I bet," Margaret laughed and patted his head. "Look at all that. How do you get by?"

"Not a barber," Kay replied in a clipped tone. "Stylist."

"Just a joke." Charles held up both hands in surrender. "Don't fire."

"Then learn the difference," she shot back and bit from her sandwich.

After the break, attorney Cruise had her chance to cross-examine detective Richardson. She moved dangerously close to the Well, that space just ahead of the judge's bench where the clerk and court reporter sat. It was a breach of protocol for lawyers to enter that space without permission. Millick could be seen watching her position.

"Detective, you stated Mr. Johannsen did not show any normal reaction to his wife's death."

He politely leaned forward into the mic. "I believe I said there is no normal but that I found his demeanor odd."

Cruise nodded, dismissive of his answer. It was not clear she even heard it, plotting her next question. "Can you tell the court whether you are a trained psychologist?"

"I am not."

"Then what training qualifies you to assess a person's reaction to such extreme events?"

Richardson looked around the court, blinking several times before answering. "Well, I'm human."

Laughter rolled through the gallery. Justyna let out a barked laugh, startling Travis, Kay and Danny. All three shifted in their chairs. Even Millick broke a smile.

Unfazed, Cruise moved on. "So, your investigation was launched with an assessment that had no professional basis, just your reaction as a 'human'. How do you expect the jury to believe this reaction didn't taint your actions?"

"Because we simply follow the evidence. What I thought of his behavior had nothing to do with medical examinations or witness statements or computer forensics. It had no bearing on any of the facets of our investigation. Our role is simply to collect the evidence and present it to the State for prosecution or dismissal. We don't decide guilty or innocent." He pointed to the jury box. "They do."

Millick shifted in his chair. "Let the record reflect the witness indicated the jury pool."

Cruise did not give the impression she'd expected such an eloquent answer. Perhaps she misread the detective's ability to counter cheap courtroom tactics like implied questions. She stared a moment at him before continuing. "Let's assume your statements are truthful and delve into other aspects of the case."

If the passive-aggressive tone bothered Richardson, it failed to show. He nodded and smiled. "Yes. Let's."

"Dayum," Danny whispered. "Dude

is stone cold."

After the lunch intermission, Jambliss moved onto his next witness. "The State wishes to call Aaron Daball to the stand."

The rear doors were opened and held by a sheriff's deputy. Behind him came Daball in an orange jumpsuit, hands cuffed, closely followed by a second deputy. Those in the gallery turned with expressions of surprise. A jail prisoner testifying against Mark Johannsen? Plot twist.

Once formalities were completed and Daball sat in the witness box under oath, Jambliss came right out with it. "Your testimony today, Mr. Daball, is that while in jail awaiting this trial, Mark confessed to Julie's murder. Do I have that correct?"

Daball was broad in build, salt-peter hair and two-day scruff across his jaw. His voice was smooth and modulated. The voice of a con man. "You are correct, yes."

As Jambliss led him through his testimony, Travis could be seen tilting his head left and right, like a dog trying to make sense of a strange sound. He sat closest to the witness box, with a clear view of Daball's profile. In the second row, Danny and Margaret exchanged glances, catching the attention of Chuckie and Terry.

Suddenly Travis leaned forward and tapped Larry on the shoulder, whispering to him. The bailiff's eyes darted around then he stepped up behind the witness box, motioning for Millick. He spoke into the judge's ear. "Folks," Millick immediately said, directing his attention to the jury. "Take a break."

Confusion scrolled across the faces of Jambliss and Cruise, along with the other jurors. They'd been seated less than ten minutes. What was happening? As the court stood and the jurors filed out, Larry led Travis to a different room ahead of the rest. Their normal migration from the courtroom had Justyna right behind Travis and then the rest of row one before those in row two. As Travis walked towards a different room, she blindly followed only to have Larry hold up a hand and stop her. She sent a puzzled look back to Bryan. He simply shrugged and motioned for her to continue onto their jury room.

"What the hell is all that about?" Courtney blurted when the door closed and no bailiffs were present. Her sense for detail has been triggered, alerted by the abrupt nature of Millick's dismissal. She couldn't recall other trials where something like this had happened.

"Yeah," Chuckie chimed in. "Something's going down."

There were no answers forthcoming so they stopped looking around at each other and fell into silence. Shelli broke the ice. "So, what's everyone doing this weekend?"

"Drinks," Nicole declared.

"Cheers," Justyna agreed. They clinked imaginary glasses together.

"Girls have soccer," Margaret added.

"Roofing a buddy's house," Danny said, causing several groans. He patted his stomach in response. "I'm getting fat just sitting in that chair every day. Need some exercise."

He was already whip-lean, the last person in the room who should be worried about gaining weight.

"I'm taking care of my honey," Terry offered.

"How sweet," Shelli replied. "Lucky lady."

Terry gave her a confused look. "No. Bees. I got bees." Dennis choked on a drink of water, laughing.

A few minutes later Travis entered the room. All eyes went immediately to him and he stopped in place, reluctant expression on his face.

"Bathroom emergency?" Chuckie asked with a smile. "Mexican lunch come calling?"

"No." Travis considered his next words. "I know that guy, Aaron Daball."

Exclamations filled the room, overriding each other, blotting out clarity. He raised his hands and when the noise subsided, "It took me a while to recognize him. Been a couple of years. He dated my sister for a while and stole money from her. I wanted to notify the judge in case there's any conflict but he's letting me stay on."

"Kenosha is a small town," Jean said. "I'm kind of surprised no one else has run into this yet."

Travis nodded. "I need to call my wife, have her set the home alarm and make sure the guns are in our nightstand."

Silence followed, pregnant with the weight of consequence.

"Wait. Are you that worried?" Bryan asked, glancing around to see if anyone else felt the same. From the concerned expressions, others did.

"The guy's a career criminal and I helped my sister get him arrested," Travis said. "Who knows if he recognized me or not. He's probably got friends on the outside. One call and I'm getting an unfriendly visit."

Serious looks raced around the room. Gone was the jovial banter of weekend plans. Stakes had been raised.

That evening, hours after court let out, Travis sat in his living room, nerves jangling, running through mental scenarios. He tried to quell the thoughts, to keep things in perspective. Daball never looked over at him during testimony, never gave any sign of recognition. Still what if that was all just cover? What if he'd seen Travis right away and simply ignored him but deep down planned out a delayed revenge? Travis looked at the handgun lying on the coffee table, oiled and ready. He'd only ever fired it at the range for sport. What if he had to hold it with different intentions?

Suddenly noises drifted from out front of his house. Multiple voices lowly murmuring, the scrape of metal on concrete. Blood pulsed in his temples, beating with increasing rhythm. His wife was upstairs and he contemplated having her get ready to call 911. But that would result in panic and signal to her he thought there was potential for something bad to happen.

That would make it real and Travis was not prepared yet to make that leap. Better to check it out on his own first.

He padded over to the window blinds and paused for a few deep breaths, dreading what he might see. The gun, now gripped tightly in his hand, felt ice cold, heavy with consequence. He pushed the curtain open a fraction, just enough to peek out.

People were camped out in his driveway. A loose circle of chairs, coolers on the concrete next to them. Chatter and laughter, mixed conversation, relaxed body language.

Bryan held a portable grill, in the midst of setting it up. Courtney, Rick and Shelli were unpacking burgers and buns. Chuckie was halfway up the driveway towing a massive cooler on wheels.

They all turned as Travis opened the door and stepped outside, stunned expression on his face. "What the absolute fu…?"

Nicole raised her drink. "Sir, Breakfast Jury reporting for guard duty."

10

MONDAY, JUNE 12, 2000, 2:48PM

I'm driving with a fog of conspiratorial thoughts swirling around my head.

A jury finds a man guilty of using antifreeze to poison his wife. Antifreeze has an ingredient that mimics the effects of alcohol, but if there's enough of it, the victim dies. One year after this jury rendered their verdict, the foreman – forewoman – is admitted to the hospital looking like someone who drank way too much. Her husband thinks otherwise. He thinks she was poisoned.

Justyna is still missing, three days now. Travis is hungover, three days now. I have all the other juror numbers. When I call will I find others missing or suffering, three days now? Or will it be worse?

This can't be right.

The coincidences are too many.

Leonard is my obvious next step, visiting him again with targeted questions since he's the only person thus far with opportunity, if not motive. But I'm not ready yet. I need to sort out a plan, something that will serve as my blueprint. Because if this leads where I'm afraid it will, it moves from an unofficial look-see at $200 per hour to a criminal investigation handled by the local police department. And if so, I want – *need* – my ducks to be precisely in a row.

I back my car into a parking spot at a place called Simmons Island Park. It's a small spit of land sticking out into Lake Michigan. At mid-afternoon on a hot June day the beach is crowded with families. Towels and umbrellas are strewn everywhere, children laugh and splash and run through the shallows.

With effort to slow my racing thoughts, I open a new page in my notepad.

Creating lists always helps me define order, even if the tasks are obvious. Maybe it's the act of writing that settles me down. I even number them.

1. *Pull the trial transcripts.* Ground myself in the facts with an assumption Nicole's condition is related to her service.

2. *Study up on antifreeze and its poisoning agent.* How much can kill? How long does it take? What does that look like forensically?

3. *Call Ted.* Let him know what I've found. He may be right about this after all. Have him request someone to test for the presence of antifreeze.

I stare at my short list, knowing it's only a draft and will flesh out. I flip another page and re-write, moving Ted to the top. Knowing whether there's a poison in Nicole's system will drive all other actions but lab processes are slow. It can take time to convince authorities there's a need to test in the first place. Bureaucracy is maddening and I can't sit around waiting. My list grows branches and now looks like:

1.   *Call Ted*
2.   *Trial transcripts*
3.   *Antifreeze research*
4.   *Contact the remaining jurors.* Get a current accounting of their situation. Is anyone missing? Did anyone else have similar reactions?
5.   *Build a list of suspects.* Several question marks follow this item. How I will build that list is still unknown.
6.   *Get Warren's assistance with next steps.* If it moves into criminal investigation territory, it's out of both our hands, but he has friends in the Kenosha department. Maybe he can help push it along.

The beating wings of conspiracy settle somewhat as I scan up and down my list, thinking and notating. I add a few sub-points:

2.5 *Find out who testified on behalf of the defendant.* It will be part of the trial transcript but worth jotting down as a reminder. Maybe a close family member or friend who thinks the verdict unjust?

4.5 *Find out who the judge and prosecutor were.* They could be viewed as targets.

5.5 *Dig into Leonard.* Are there connections that would give him motive?

6.5 *What do I need to convince Warren this is a criminal case?*

Now, for open questions.

Flipping to a fresh page, I ruminate through everything I know so far, the needed answers that aren't covered by my punch list. These are free flowing notes, sometimes closer to ideas than questions.

I'm most worried about this becoming an official investigation and the effort to convince Warren of such. I'll need evidence he cannot poke holes through, evidence that bypasses my reputation. As far as the public is concerned, I'm that rookie detective who made a mess of Noah

Bell's high-profile murder. The man who reigned as Chicago's prince of peace, who stood as my champion in the lawsuit to earn my tin…well, he deserved better than Aramis Archibald White fumbling around and uncovering a plot to stir up a race war.

He deserved someone who resolved his fate in a manner befitting his legacy.

Those are the chains I drag with me, always present, and my argument will have to be compelling enough to remove them. Warren will be putting his neck on the line to get an investigation opened. If there's one thing I know about him, he does not like risking any portion of his career on the unknown.

Then again, what are the odds I've stumbled across another secretive plot. No one can be that unlucky, twice in a row.

Can they?

A glance at my watch shows I've been idling in my car nearly forty minutes now. The day is slipping and I've got stops yet. Pulling out of the lot, I dial Ted's number and leave a message to call me back immediately. Nothing about my suspicions or theories, simply: *'Call me.'*

My first stop at the courthouse yields an interaction with a records clerk who looks like she'd rather be scraping gum off her shoe than take my request for trial transcripts. Her gray hair is shaved short on one side and she peers at me over the top of red-rimmed bifocals. She makes no promise when I'll receive the records before telling me her day is ending. Her stare indicates our business is completed.

Nearby to the courthouse I find Yee's Oriental Inn and enjoy some good Chinese food while adding thoughts to my punch list and open questions. I'm at five full pages now.

Afterwards, bogged down by a stomach stretched with General Tao Chicken, I head towards the Kenosha Public Library and grab a table. By the time overhead lights start darkening and librarians push to close, I've learned more than I ever needed to know about ethylene glycol.

And I'm fully convinced Nicole was a victim of intentional poisoning, along with her fellow jurors. The Why seems easy to answer, the Who…not so much.

TUESDAY, JUNE 13, 2000, 7:21AM

My cell vibrates loudly across the TV tray serving as my nightstand. The imitation oak laminate peels from one corner, exposing a particle board core.

Blurry eyes watch the phone migrate towards the edge, my mind trying to engage from a sleepless night spent tossing every conceivable scenario over and over. I answer just before it goes to voicemail.

It's Ted. "Nicole, she is gone."

His Eastern European accent compresses the message flat, unemotional. I misunderstand at first, at the use of the word *'gone'*, thinking he meant she was discharged. Then it rolls over me.

The blurriness snaps away as I shoot upright in my bed. "Mr. Wright, I'm so sorry…"

He cuts me off, clearly in no mood for platitudes from someone he barely knows. "You left message. No details. Tell me of what."

Roosting myself from bed, I pad across the tiny apartment to another TV tray. This one is my coffee table but there's no couch. Just a ratty armchair donated by the previous occupant. My notepad is there, left open to the last page, little more than rehashed scribbles of previous notes.

"I have good reason to think you were right about Nicole's condition. It may not have been alcohol overindulgence. There's a working theory she was targeted for her role as foreman of the jury that sentenced Mark Johannsen to prison last year. The Friday party was the one-year anniversary for the verdict."

"The others are dead too?" Disbelief is rampant, injecting emotion into his words.

"I haven't spoken to everyone else yet but no others so far. Did you ever meet any of them?"

"No, I never meet. Nicole," he pauses, and I suspect he's taking a beat to compose himself. "She spoke little of the trial. We were new then as couple, still strange to each other."

Taking a deep breath, I plunge ahead. "I know you have a million things going on and my condolences, but I need Nicole's phone logs, home and cell. What are the regular calls? Who did she call in the days leading up to Friday? These are pieces important to solving this puzzle. Can you get those for me? The last six months is fine."

He grunts. "I pay you money, good money, but you assign me tasks. Is this always how the police work in America?"

"Well, I have no authority to requisition your records…"

"Relax, is not serious question. I will do."

It seemed like an odd moment to bust my balls. I gloss over it; we all grieve in different ways.

"Next thing is the autopsy. The medical examiner will conduct one as a matter of procedure. Please contact their office and request a full toxicology panel. That's not always done and we need to make sure they don't overlook anything. Specifically signs of ethylene glycol in the kidneys." I rattle off the ME's phone number. "This is critical."

He mutters in echo, apparently writing down my requests. "I will do."

"You have my word, Ted. I will unbury the story in this. If your wife was poisoned, I'll find out who did it and bring you justice."

He was silent a moment. "Is true then, what George says. You will not stop chewing bone even if it means you bite yourself, yes? Good, good. Find me the answers."

Without another word the line clicks dead, leaving me staring down at a page of scribbles.

By 10am I've either spoken to or left messages with the remaining jurors. Courtney, Shelli, Chuckie and Jean all reported feeling the same as Travis. Rick, Lian, Dennis and Charles confirmed they had not attended the party and felt just fine, if a little baffled by my call.

That left Terry, Bryan, Margaret, Danny and Kay to reply. I'll give them a few hours before trying again.

Warren hasn't yet responded to my messages, so I make the snap decision to pay a visit. Sometimes the in-person approach is more effective. Plus, I think better on the move and the thirty-minute trek to his station gives me time to process my thoughts.

Once across the border, I navigate through the swank town of Grand Haven along Jordan Way. It's a four-lane road, bordered by markers of the new millennium. Chain restaurants and big box stores occupy prominent spots at major intersections. For a Tuesday morning there's quite a bit of traffic and I note the volume of high-end cars. Audi, Mercedes, BMW, Range Rover; all of them shiny and filled with signposts of upscale suburbia. Blond housewives running their equally blond children around, dark-haired businessmen with severe expressions barking at their cell phones, carefree teenagers in a black convertible, laughing.

Grand Haven is the epitome of wealth, expanding at a rapid pace, spawning small villages like seedlings.

The last time I visited here Griffin

piloted our unmarked slick-back, regaling me with tales of him and George Warren as rookies in a different era of Chicago. When the city's southside grew dark and dangerous, Griffin dug in to help become part of the solution. It was his home, his beat. Warren bailed to posh Grand Haven where his days were spent taking reports on graffiti and packages stolen from unlocked Cadillacs.

I can't stave off the memory of Griff bleeding out on the floor, eyes glassy as he stares up at me, and it derails my thoughts. I'm forced to acknowledge my role in his death before I can revert to the present. This may forever be my penance.

Grand Haven's police precinct mirrors the facade of the town. Fancy and new, long entrance bordered by decorative trees in full June bloom. The glass and stucco exterior makes it resemble a corporate office more than a place where criminals are processed and detained.

I park and enter the wide lobby, asking the desk sergeant to page Warren.

He gives a look as if wanting to verify my request but instead shrugs and picks up the phone.

Behind me a janitor buckets his mop and sets out a *'Caution Wet Floor'* sign. I step aside to give him room just as my phone rings.

It's Warren, finally. "You don't think I check my messages?"

"You may, you may not. However, you don't answer your messages and that's what I care about."

"Despite your low opinion of me, I do have other cases I'm working, just as important. Since you're here, let's get it done. Careful, wet floor."

I look down by reflex then around. Warren is standing behind me, separated by the glass wall of a conference room. His phone is pressed to his ear, and he gives me a smile with no humor. The dark sport jacket strains to hold his ample belly, revealing weight he's gained in the year since we last met. We snap our phones closed at the same time and he opens the conference room door with a sarcastic flourish.

Twelve seats ring the long table, a speaker phone the only item atop it.

"Your office has gotten bigger. Promotion?"

"Haha, wiseass. Like I'm bringing you into my space. You've got enough entitlement already."

I ignore his jab and sit down. "I assume you've heard my messages. What do you have?"

He holds up a quick hand. "No, before that, let's talk about the dog you're hunting. Poisoning? Conspiracy? Christ, Arch."

"So, you talked to Ted."

"Yeah, of course. We're close. His wife dies, he's going to call me."

I mentally reorient myself. This discussion was farther down my list. Maybe it was a bit naïve of me to think Ted wouldn't call his detective friend with an update. "I didn't plan on talking this soon. That's why I've been making requests, to get the right read on the situation."

"And your first read is homicide?"

There's no point holding back now. Despite the lousy timing, I must get

Warren on board. He's my key to pushing it all forward for resolution. If he thinks I've asked a lot of him so far, he ain't seen nothing yet. "What do you know about the Mark Johannsen trial last year?"

His expression is surprised, caught off-guard by the change in topic. "Lots. Everyone around here does. Biggest thing to happen across the border in years. Decades maybe."

"Right, so a husband having marital problems decides to kill his wife using ethylene glycol. One year after a rendered verdict, the jury foreman dies, and her symptoms are suspiciously similar. Others with her that night also look to be targets. I've spoken to half of them so far and each one confirmed the same effects."

Warren is unfazed. "It was a party. People drink, some better than others. Your logic is thin, paper thin."

"Don't look at the logic. Look at the parallels." I modulate my next words carefully, knowing this comes out of the blue. "How well do you know your friend's marriage situation?"

His eyes narrow and harden.

"Watch it, rook."

"From what I know it was a short and sudden deal. One month they're dating, the next married. There can be a lot of second-guessing when the trigger gets pulled that quickly. And with him as a successful businessman, Wisconsin being a marital property state…" I trail off, letting it hang on purpose.

"He'd never."

"Detective 101. Rule out no one until the evidence forces you to."

Warren slams back in his chair, staring at me but now also inside himself. Doubt flickers across his face. He may be lazy and self-interested, but even he recognizes a thread worth tugging. The silence stretches until he finally slaps a hand on the table. "Goddammit, White."

We suddenly went from a first name basis to last name. Interesting shift.

"It wasn't supposed to be like this. I did a favor just to get him off my back. Nicole was a lush so I figured that would be the end of it. I mean, it sucks for him. He's been wanting a wife for so long and to lose her this way. But what are you gonna do?

Now this? Fuck."

I could be petty and pile on, emphasizing why my calls are important, but I've got bigger fish. This is my bone to chew. "Exactly why I need your help. I'll follow the path of someone getting back at the jury but if it leads back to Ted, you've been warned."

Warren nods, resigned. "I know, I know. What's critical?"

"Trial transcripts and autopsy panel. Start there." I state it with finality, ready to move.

He's not done, however. "You know, if something comes of it, I'm out of jurisdiction. This would go to the Kenosha police, someone else."

Typical Warren, weaseling his way out before there's any indication of anything worth investigating. I keep the distaste out of my reply. "You'll make a credible character witness. You suspected something and took the proper, if a little unorthodox, steps to reveal it all."

"Yeah, okay." He stands and turns for the door. "Anything else you have to ruin my day?"

I also stand and return his stare, unwilling to play further into his martyr complex.

"Do you realize what this means?" He's still processing, unfolding the pieces one at a time, slowly, like a person dreading what lies at the center. "I have to consider my friend is capable of murder. Or raise the flag on a potential serial killer running loose in the area. What a choice. Goddammit."

I stop in the doorway, looking down from my height advantage. "You asked me. And with that ask comes everything else. Never forget it."

11

TUESDAY, MAY 25, 1999, 8:41AM – DAY 10

"Please state your name for the court," Millick said after swearing in that morning's witness.

"Perry. Perry Tarrell."

He was soft-looking, bald and pink-skinned in his gray suit. Sweat beaded heavily across his bare scalp as he twitched in the chair and glanced around at the jury, the lawyers, the stack of reporters staring back.

"Dude looks like he's going to freak," Justyna whispered.

Jambliss took his time, writing carefully. Finally, he seemed satisfied with his notes and stood. "Mr. Tarrell, can you tell the jury what relationship you had to Julie Johannsen?"

"We were co-workers," came the reply in a reedy voice.

"How long?"

"Approximately a year I'd say."

"But it wasn't always professional, was it? What else were you to each other?" There was gentleness in the DA's voice, as if consoling a lost soul.

This caught Tarrell off-guard. He blinked several times before answering. "Lovers."

The gallery reacted as expected. Murmurs rolled through the reporters, cameras clicked and clicked again.

"Lovers, yet both of you were already married. So, an affair really. Am I correct?"

Tarrell nodded quickly, then cleared his throat and whispered an affirmative. The red flush crept down from his forehead, coloring both cheeks. He licked his lips multiple times.

"Describe this affair. Who initiated it? How long did it last? When did you meet? What made each of you betray your sacred marital oaths?" Now Jambliss' tone flipped, becoming hard and accusatory.

"Whose witness is this?" Danny muttered, confusion on his face. Kay felt the same way. Jambliss had called Tarrell for the State, meaning he was expected to help support the prosecution's charge but with a couple simple questions the DA treated him more like a defensive witness.

"It wasn't like that," Tarrell refuted, his voice rising an octave. "We were close friends, first and foremost. There was no intent."

Jambliss waved away the answer. "Regardless of any labels you wish to apply, it was an affair. There was attraction, a deepening of emotional bonds, maybe some dirty talk. Sex."

"That makes it sound crude, tawdry. We only made love one weekend."

"Yes, one weekend in 1991 when Julie's husband was out of town. A weekend when you two could consummate the affair in the Johannsen bed. Did you spend all weekend with her? Or have sex and then leave?"

For the first time in this trial Mark

Johannsen showed a reaction. His normal glowering look turned dark, eyebrows crunching down in anger. His eyes pinned to the witness, sending daggers.

"I said it was not like that." Tarrell's voice grew ragged, face now completely flushed as he leaned forward.

Jambliss cut him off. "The State has no more questions."

Even Millick showed surprise. "That's it?" When Jambliss nodded in response, he looked over to Cruise. "You wish to cross?"

She shot up from her chair. "Absolutely, your Honor." Pausing to adjust her jacket, the look on her face could best be described as predatory.

Tarrell also sensed this. He straightened his chair and set his jaw, though it was far from convincing. A tremble lurked along his jowl.

The jurors, though not trained legal pros, had been immersed in testimony for weeks now. Many of them suspected Jambliss misplayed his witness. After Hoover's appearance, had he become desperate and pushed too hard?

Cruise smiled at Tarrell with little warmth. "Please, if you could, describe the deceased as you knew her."

Wariness colored his reply. "Wonderful. Great friend, great mother. Very good at her job. Just the greatest person."

"Mm-hmm," Cruise pondered. "And were those the qualities that made you pursue an affair with her, despite knowing she was married?"

"No, no. You don't understand. There was never a conscious decision…We were just friends and talked a lot."

"Always in the workplace? Or maybe sometimes outside of business hours?"

"Sometimes. Every now and then we'd talk on the phone when Mark was not around."

Cruise nodded again, not listening to his answer but rather planning her next question. "And what were these phone calls about? Work situations? Meetings with the boss? Favorite TV shows?"

Her tone was purposely bland, as if talking about curtains or carpet. That made it seem more insidious. For his part Jambliss leaned forward intently. He didn't have the look of a man who thought he mishandled a witness. It was the only sign there might be something else going on.

"She just needed someone to talk to. Mark wasn't giving her any emotional support. I did, and she needed that."

"And so, because she relied on you for emotional comfort, you were able to parlay that into a visit to her house?"

"What?" Tarrell slammed back in his chair. "No! You make it sound like I had an agenda. There was none of that. Things just…just happened."

"You mean it just so happened that you came over one weekend when Mark was gone and spontaneously erupted in sex?"

He hunched, tight and quivering. "I know what you're trying to do. This wasn't some casual one-night stand. Neither of us meant for it to happen."

"Yet, it did happen. Imagine, if you will, how such a betrayal would affect a loving husband like Mark. He left on a work trip, providing for his family, sacrificing time away from them, only to come home and find out that another man had defiled his bed. It's enough to drive someone insane. Enough to eat away at their soul for years."

"You're trying to cheapen it," he shot back, lips compressed in anger. By now his jowls quivered so deeply creases were developing. In the gallery, camera shutters snapped constantly, adding a low soundtrack.

"Did she not perform sexual acts on you? Did she simply lie there and let you have your way?"

"No!" He shouted. "That's wrong! We made love. Passionate lovemaking between two people. Nothing disgusting. I don't even like oral."

Terry grunted. "Weird redirect."

In the front row, Bryan wrote *'oral'* in his notepad, followed by a circle around the word and then a slash through both. Charles glanced over, saw the note and dipped his head to hide laughter. Behind him, Chuckie held up his notepad so only the back row could see it. Down one page it read:

'What.

The.

Fuck.'

As if Tarrell never spoke, Cruise gave him a confused look. "You two did commit intercourse, correct? How many times while Mark was gone? In the kitchen, the den? When did you take it to the Johannsen marital bed?"

"Objection," Jambliss offered, in a subdued voice, almost like he felt duty-bound rather than affronted. "Badgering the witness."

"Sustained," Millick agreed. "This isn't a soap opera, Ms. Cruise. Get on with it."

Tarrell was coming apart in the witness box, apparent to anyone in the courtroom. He trembled with emotion from the embarrassment of his sordid acts brought to life. His emotion was matched by a murderous expression from Johannsen. The defendant looked capable of leaping the table at any moment and choking out the witness. Jambliss looked over at him, then to the jury.

"Thank you, your Honor," Cruise

said, looking anything but thankful. "Mr. Tarrell let's move on from the events of that fateful weekend. I can see it upsets you and have no wish to bring back what I'm sure are powerful emotions."

The oily nature of her tone completely negated the words and no one in attendance believed she wanted to move on. At all.

"After the affair ended, the Johannsens began receiving harassing pictures left around their house. You knew the layout, based on the amount of time you spent on Julie. I mean, with Julie. Was this harassment your doing?"

"No, never," he said. "I would never do that." If the shift in topic was intended to bring down his boiling point, it failed miserably. Tarrell's face remained crimson tight.

"Sure, but if someone had asked whether you'd have an affair with a married woman, wouldn't you also say, 'No, never'? If you can't hold yourself to a moral standard for that, why should the jury believe your statement about harassment. Am I making sense, Mr. Tarrell?"

He failed to answer, shaking his head back and forth. His eyes were reddened, a man on the verge of cracking.

Cruise pushed. "It's clear you had feelings. How deep were they? Did you want…?"

He erupted, jerking forward in his chair, hands gripping the arms like they were the only thing keeping him tethered. *"I LOVED HER!"*

She paused, stunned look on her face, letting his disjointed words hang in the air. When she resumed, her tone was softer. "Loving someone means doing anything for them, would you agree?"

"Of course," he spat. Hatred for the attorney rose off him like vapor.

Travis leaned back towards Terry and Kay. "If this guy wore glasses, they'd be steamed up right now. Kettle going to blow."

Both jurors could only nod in agreement.

"And love can have a dark side, too. I'm sure you'd agree." Without waiting to see if indeed Tarrell did agree with that assessment, she plunged on. "Like encouraging her to leave her marriage by any means possible?"

"I did not send her those pictures."

"That's not my question. Did you remain in contact with Julie? Phone calls, perhaps letters or email?"

"No, I respected her wishes."

"Does respecting her wishes include sending a Christmas card? One which you mailed to her sister and asked to have passed on in secret so Mark wouldn't find out?"

At this Tarrell's face blanched. The crimson shade grew mottled with white pressure points building at the bridge of his nose, his compressed lips. "That was wrong. I wanted only to express my regret at our mistake."

"And tell her you missed her too? How much you cherished your time together? That you still loved her?"

He hung his head and whispered, "Yes."

"I'm sorry, Mr. Tarrell. Can you speak up for our court reporter? I don't think she caught that."

"I said: Yes."

Jambliss still had a sly smugness about him, like only he knew the outcome of this testimony. Several jurors caught themselves torn between watching Tarrell melt down and Jambliss appearing to enjoy every moment of it. None of them could figure out why.

"Did you know Julie sought treatment for depression afterwards?"

"I heard," he said through gritted teeth.

"So, if you're a woman who betrayed the sanctity of her vows, regretted it and now the cause of that betrayal is sending cards to keep you engaged, wouldn't that make you depressed?"

"Objection. Witness is not a mental health professional."

"Never mind," Cruise said and waved away her question. "If you made a mistake you deeply regretted and pictures keep showing up to remind you of that mistake, would that make you depressed?"

"I didn't leave any pictures."

"Again, not what I asked. How would you feel if you betrayed the trust of your loved one? Would you feel happy?

Satisfied?"

"What? No. Of course not!"

"Is depression then a reasonable reaction?"

Tarrell looked around, at the jurors, the reporters, then Johannsen. By this point his entire body trembled, a man cornered and letting loose his animal instincts. "I don't even live in the Midwest anymore. I couldn't have left the pictures."

"Just answer the question. Would it make you depressed?"

He shot to his feet and jabbed a finger out. "If I was married to a monster like that you bet I'd be depressed!" He roared.

The courtroom burst into noise. Reporters buzzing, cameras clicking, Millick banging his gavel for order. Shelli gasped out loud, Danny exclaimed, "Whoa."

The deputies moved forward in case Tarrell left the box but he simply sank back down, now emotionally deflated.

Cruise rested her questions, going unheard against the crowd noise.

Jambliss sat in his chair, wearing the face of someone who'd overplayed his hand.

"I think he wanted Tarrell to accuse Mark of something," Terry stated back in the jury room later.

"I think he wanted him to confirm she was not depressed," Kay added.

Danny shook his head. "Makes no sense."

"Well, it kind of does," Jean countered. "Papers love to report that stuff, not the boring scientific things. Get pictures of the guy pointing, repeat what he said. The public remembers drama."

He grunted in reluctant agreement.

"You know what I remember?" Bryan stated. "I remember opening arguments when the defense stated she took her own life from depression. Now this guy is giving justification for it. Just saying the word keeps the possibility front and center for us."

Courtney shook her head. "Jambliss underestimated how much Cruise would get under that guy's skin. He really screwed the pooch."

12

TUESDAY, JUNE 13, 2000, 10:35AM

Warren wasn't completely useless. He'd provided information for most of the jurors. Critically, I now had addresses for those who hadn't returned my calls. Time for some visits. The lure of an answer to all this tantalized me, a glimmer just over the horizon, always drawing me forward. It was an effort not to let my imagination run wild in search of ideas supporting that answer, which in turn would direct my path.

Let it come from the evidence, Arch.

Terry Sharp lives in the town of Salem, not far off my route back to Kenosha. I'm heading north on highway 83, just crossing into Wisconsin when my phone rings and it's him. What timing.

"Returning your call," he abruptly states after giving his name. "What's this about?"

I provide my standard cover story, editing out the part of Nicole's death, and pull into a gas station on the corner of highways 83 and C, ready to take notes.

He cuts me off. "What's really going on? Cops don't look into someone over-drinking without good reason."

For once, letting someone think I was a detective worked against me. So, I come clean. "I'm not law enforcement, not anymore. I'm just looking into this as a favor to Nicole's husband. He's concerned about what went down on Friday."

"She's married?" Terry's voice reveals true surprise. "I didn't know that. She seems too wild. I couldn't keep up with her, none of us could."

I straighten and unbuckle, as if that allows me to hear better. "Why do you say that? Was she drinking more than everyone? Separately?"

"No, I don't think so. I bought a round, Chuck did, Kay, maybe Danny. Honestly, I'm not sure, things got hazy."

He pauses. "Fun, but wow was Saturday painful. I haven't puked like that since I got alcohol poisoning in college."

Ethylene glycol will do that.

Another pause and I can practically hear gears spinning. Then: "Hey, wait a minute…"

"Appreciate the call, Terry. Thanks." I cut the line and snap my phone closed before he can get through his suspicions. Hopefully he doesn't dwell on it and start calling the other jurors. I don't need side conspiracies popping up.

Crossing Terry off my list leaves two remaining jurors. Hopefully Justyna turns up. There's little more I can do to track her, other than checking local hospitals. Warren can do that more efficiently than me if needed.

So, Kay Standin is the last.

I head back towards Lake Michigan, threading along major roads until turning south on Lake Shore drive. The Great Lake surges under the summer sun, waves winking from a steady breeze outside my open window. As I roll along the two-lane road, neighborhoods begin to thin, transforming from clustered blocks into smaller pockets of six, ten, twelve houses separated by stretches of vacant land. A drive-in movie theater slides past my passenger window. Don't see many of those anymore.

This region is strange to me. It feels like a place where time lags, with people and ideas slow to change, clinging to years past. The discussions I've overheard in public, the way houses and buildings are designed, even the appearance of average citizens. Everyone knows everyone. Table talk centers around cousin Ed and his kid Joey who just started building a new garage, or the Thomas family and their recent vacation; the new farm stand off highway 50.

There's little conversation on the larger topics of the world, those social hallmarks that drive culture in the year 2000. Forgotten is the Y2K panic – misplaced as it was – dismissed is any DotCom enthusiasm and stock market heights. These people would rather talk about the weather.

Eventually I reach Kay's address in the community of Carol Beach, tucked between Pleasant Prairie and the Illinois border. Her house is directly off Lake Shore Drive. There are no curbs, no sidewalks, just blacktop butted up against grass. I pull over next to the driveway and exit. A lone car sits in the open garage, nice white Mercedes sedan, providing hope that there's someone home right now.

I step onto the stoop and press the doorbell, then move back down to the front walk, using a standard method of minimizing the appearance of threat from strangers at your door.

It takes a few seconds before I hear footsteps inside. A pause in which I envision someone looking through the peephole before the door cracks open to reveal middle-aged female features. Only part of her face is visible, like she's hiding.

"Mrs. Standin? I'm Aramis White. I called and left you a message yesterday."

"Yes," comes the flat reply. "You said your name was Arch."

I'm not sure how to interpret her

reply. There's neither welcome nor rejection in it. "Sorry, it's a nickname."

She says nothing more, so I plunge forward. "Do you have time to talk?"

"You drove all the way out here to ask me questions you could get answered over the phone?"

"But," I work to keep my reply neutral. "You didn't answer them."

"Correct. I did not." Her eyes flick around and behind me. "You a cop?"

"Once. Now I'm private. Can we chat?"

She opens the door and steps away. Now that I can see her full face, both eyes are reddened and tired, the eyes of someone crying. I'm inwardly alarmed by the emotion and curious whether the reasoning will come out. It's not a can of worms I plan on opening unless it seems related.

We sit at a small dinette table. A late morning cup of coffee sits before her, but she doesn't offer me any, which is fine. I've already had my daily fill. Papers and envelopes are strewn across the surface, some opened, others still sealed. A notepad with female handwriting, looks like a shopping list. Car keys with a metal Mercedes emblem. I'm reminded of the apartment Sheila and I shared. Our table looked similar, more bills, less German autos. Maybe every household has a spot like this.

She collects the notepad and envelopes, pushing them aside. "This is about the party, isn't it? What did Nicole do?"

I'm surprised and know it shows on my face. Then again, should I be? The group has clearly stayed in touch with each other. It's reasonable that the rumor line fired up and calls have been going around. "You heard already then."

"No, I just figured. You consider the amount of liquor she pounded on Friday and it's easy to do the math. I left before her. She set fire to the place or something?"

"Sounds like you're not her biggest fan." This is a new facet. All the other jurors I'd spoken with gave the impression of closeness that transcended their duty. Like Travis said, they were all strangers that became friends through circumstance. Charles and Margaret still convened for an occasional walk along the lakefront. Chuckie had taken Jean out to dinner a couple of times. Some jurors visited Shelli at the county fair when her daughter showed her prize cows. Terry sold his honey to the group.

Kay shrugs. "We didn't see eye to eye on a lot of things. Oil and water, that type of situation. I didn't hate her; we'd just never be friends."

I flip back a few pages and review my notes. "You and Nicole appeared to be in heavy conversation Friday night. Do you recall the conversation?"

"Oh God, who knows. We were all drinking and fuzzy. I think it was some stupid evidence detail from the trial. Ridiculous. It's been a year, who cares. The night was a blur."

"Did you guys do that often? Rehash moments from the trial?"

She gets up and dumps the remaining coffee, rinsing her cup. "We didn't do anything often. It's not like we have regular meetups. We were a bunch of strangers thrown together for six, seven weeks, forced to endure the same regimen and weigh the life of a man. Some chose to stay in contact, others not so much. I'm in that latter group."

It makes sense that if she didn't stay in contact, she'd be unaware that others did. I take a moment to assess her words, her body language. Kay Standin is completely average on the surface. Average height and weight for her seeming age, non-descript hair, no makeup. Only her reddened eyes mark a distinguishing factor. Yet I get hints of an edge buried shallow beneath her tone, sharp intellect married with some other undefinable trait. There's a sense she knows more than most, that her relationship with Nicole might put her in the best place to dig for information. We tend to focus more on the things we like or dislike, skimming the rest.

"The other jurors conveyed alternate opinions of your time together. They said a kind of family developed, a realization that no one was so different from each other."

She laughs coarsely. "Let me guess. Travis and his *Breakfast Club* analogy?" She flaps one hand to emphasize the emotion.

"It was rather funny at the time. He kept saying this person was Bender, that person was Claire, another was Andrew. We didn't have anyone playing the principal, apparently that defaulted to Johannsen. Travis watches too many movies."

I smile at her characterization. "Yes, but not just him. Shelli, Courtney, Bryan, Charles, to name a few. Maybe they didn't use the movie but all relayed similar stories about friendships emerging from a unique experience most people never have."

"Yeah, well. Long enough to know each other, not long enough to learn their secrets."

There it is again, a glimmer of keen insight. "Let's circle back to Nicole and Friday night. Did she hang with the group the entire time? Or did she wander off? I understand she was a regular there."

"Was?"

"Is." I give a disarming smile to cover my gaffe. "Sorry, not good with my prepositions."

"Not a preposition. Singular present indicative," Kay replies with straight eyes. "Anyway, yeah. She hung with us. I mean she flitted from person to person, but so did Terry, Jean and Danny. Nothing unusual in her behavior."

"And she drank equally with everyone? Did the same number of shots?"

Now Kay gives a hard laugh. "I think she did ALL the shots. Never seen someone who can pack it away like that. I would have been laid out in half the time. I'm not a drinker, not at all."

"You don't seem too worse for wear. Shelli and Jean were bed bound all weekend. Charles needed his wife to drive him into urgent care for fluids. Terry hasn't puked like that since college. Travis' car was still at Sunnyside yesterday."

"Some of us know when to say when."

I pause and look around. Much of the living room is visible from my angle. Nicknacks are everywhere, little kitschy things like small porcelain animals. Cows, horses, frogs and cats line the edge of a bookshelf. Glossy ceramic dogs sit in a circle atop the TV. Kay apparently really likes her animals.

The room's walls are adorned with

family pictures. A thick dark-haired man who I assume is Mr. Standin, two daughters who carry Kay's features. Images in a park, on bikes, at the entrance to Disney World when the daughters were young, another of them in graduation caps. It's all the artifacts of an archetypal family life, something I was denied when Anna passed.

Focus, Arch.

"How was your Saturday? Any aftereffects? I see pictures of your husband. Were things the same as usual over the weekend?" I'm trying to peel something off her, a little fact she doesn't think matters but that leads me onto my next step.

Instead, we take a hard left.

Kay looks down, breaking eye contact for the first time. A stifled sob follows.

When she looks up again, her eyes are deepened red, tears glistening. "No, nothing like that at all. I'd have loved usual and boring. Instead, my husband left. While I was hanging out with people I wouldn't exactly call my friends, he disappeared. I think he was having an affair and went to the other woman. Took all his stuff. My girls are grown and living in southern Illinois, so I've been abandoned." She tilts her head to the ceiling and releases another sob. "Twenty-six years. Poof. Oh, God. What am I going to do?"

This utterly derails me and my purpose here. We went from a homicide interview to domestic strife in the blink of an eye and if I'm not careful our conversation is going right off the cliff. I open my mouth to offer sympathy, but she cuts me off.

Her sob twists to scorn. "So, if you ask what I care about from Friday, if I seem a little jaded, well there you have it. I don't give a flip about the Breakfast Jury or Nicole's drinking problems or a weekend hangover. I'll answer your questions if you think I can help, but I really don't give a shit. I've got bigger problems."

I hear a weak condolence come from my mouth in response, something trite and overused. She either doesn't hear it or, more likely, doesn't care. She gets up from the table and moves to the front window overlooking the lake across the street. "I suspected something was going on. He would take calls and walk outside, or I'd catch him deleting numbers from his phone log. Every time it was '*Oh, nothing big, boring work stuff.*' You don't want to believe your spouse can betray you, so you nod and rationalize it away. You think it's something innocent that you've misinterpreted. After all, this is the person you're supposed to grow old with. Why would he lie? Then he's just gone. No note, no explanation, just evaporated. I've called everywhere. His friends and family. His work. I checked out our boat in the marina. Nowhere. He doesn't want to be found. What am I supposed to tell our daughters?" Her words are soft now, cycling back from angry wife to lost woman. Her emotions are a roller coaster and there's a sense she's speaking more to herself than me.

I try to get us back on common ground with a fluff reply. "Marina, huh? What kind?"

"The boat? Beats the hell out of me. Big, white, fast. It was his. I know nothing about them, except that falling overboard and drowning puts a damper on the day." She chuffs a half-laugh as if trying to lighten her own mood.

Well, there goes my lame attempt. Now what? I look around, like the answers I need are randomly floating in the air. My eyes land on the stack of envelopes she'd moved aside.

A few bills, plenty of junk mailers, one handwritten card. They are mostly addressed to Jonathan and Kay Roberts but I spy one addressed to Kay Standin and realize she never took his last name, maybe wishing to retain a level of individuality. *Twenty-six years.* Now, listening to her, I wonder how much the Standin last name means, whether she thinks they'd still be together if there was only Kay Roberts.

As if remembering she was not alone, Kay turns back and pins me with her dark stare. "I'm sorry. I don't have much else to say. You can let yourself out." She points, like I'm unable to see the door.

I cross the room and place my hand on the knob. "Well, good luck." I mentally cringe even as the words leave my mouth, lifting off on their own. It was a reflexive response and probably the worst one I could have chosen.

There's no reply as I leave, shutting the door on my best chance to understand what happened to Nicole Wright.

Good luck? Christ, Arch. Get it together.

I'm stuck idling while I wait for Warren to come through with trial transcripts and autopsy findings. This leads me to drive aimlessly through the city of Kenosha, heading north, then west, then again north until I eventually wind up at a place called the Mars Cheese Castle. Parking along the outer edge of the lot, I conclude that it doesn't look very much like a castle. Not a single parapet or cannon to be seen.

Flipping through my notepad, I review everything for the thousandth time, adding a word or two here, circling something there, generally killing time while I think of what to do next.

The juror notes I'd recorded during calls are insightful. Margaret and Shelli were worried for the others, showing elevated levels of compassion. Courtney was curious, picking for details. Both she and Terry had sensed more to the story. Danny laughed off the night, giving the impression he was close in age to me and unsuspecting of anything unusual. Jean talked for a long while, regaling me with tales from the trial.

When my phone buzzes I jump from my stupor and realize I'd been nodding off.

"This is Justyna," she says after I answer. "My boy said you came looking for me. What do you want?"

I give her an abbreviated version of my purpose, leaving out anything related to the death of Nicole. It's become a rehearsed speech. I end with asking where she's been.

"Not that it's anyone's business but I had a hell of a hangover and spent the weekend with a girlfriend. I called Justice and left a message but he never listens to the machine. Kids."

"It's Tuesday." I try and fail to keep the recrimination from my voice.

"And believe it or not, returning calls to a stranger is not my highest priority. Some of us have jobs. I was home last night. My kid is fine, thanks for your concern."

"Right, understood. Mind if I pick your brain?" Without waiting for a response, I start down my gamut of questions, asking her the same ones I'd asked of others. Despite her initial clap-back attitude, she's helpful, considering each answer, clarifying when I probed. Eventually I work us to the core questions, taking a roundabout path to avoid raising her suspicions.

"I didn't know Nicole before the trial but it turned out we know a lot of the same people, our paths just never crossed. She wasn't overserved, I can tell you that. I'm not sure you *can* overserve her."

"Who brought you guys drinks?"

This returns a laugh, punched and loud. "Dude, it's Sunnyside. Whoever bought the round fetched the round. That's the way it works. This isn't some fancy big city place. You want a drink? You walk up to the bar and order, not raise your hand and twiggle two fingers for attention."

Another laugh and I realize the culture of Wisconsin is far different than what I've ever known, even during my time in Chicago. It's evident in the sheer number of bars I spot on every corner, in the casual way people have referred to drinking. It's in their blood, literally, to have liquor present for any situation. These people are hard-drinkers, hard workers and the two things are not separate.

"What was Nicole's drink?"

"Some rum and Coke combo, I think."

Antifreeze is brightly colored, easy to hide in dark soda mixes.

"And her husband? You never saw him?"

"She's married? I had no idea. So, no." There's a pause. "What a great night though. Travis fell off his stool. We found Chuckie hugging a coat stand that he named Miss Molly for some reason. At one point I remember Danny drawing on a napkin, some diagram about figuring out the proper angle for roof trusses, and people were listening to him like it was a secret to the universe. Hell of a hangover but worth it. Fun group of people."

It's clear Justyna suspects nothing untoward happened on Friday, just another wild gathering amongst friends. She doesn't even wonder why I'm looking into the night. Her statements align with others and don't add much to the picture. I feel like I've tapped out the witness line of inquiry. Now it moves onto science, specifically the autopsy results.

"Okay, well thanks for your help. Glad to hear you're back on your feet. Liquor is a hell of a kicker." Not that I speak from experience, I don't drink.

This brings one last punctured laugh, a wizened pro humoring the novice. "Mister, you don't know." The line clicks dead.

Thirty minutes later I'm still in my car, ruminating on swirling thoughts while chomping on the Cheese Castle's finest.

A dead woman and no leads, except her husband who wanted this investigated in the first place. So, while it's possible he's suspect, it's not probable.

A trial of the century and one man sentenced to life in prison. There's your motive but who's taking on the task of vengeance for him? Who cares enough about his fate to risk a similar one? It sounds both logical and batshit crazy at the same time.

The fact that jurors reported effects identical to ethylene glycol poisoning cannot be a coincidence. The universe isn't big enough for these two things to be unconnected.

Warren calls during this interlude of disparate pondering. I won't say he came through as promised, simply because guys like him never promise anything that can be held against them. But at least he gives me what I need.

"Stop at the records window and ask for Rebecca," he orders. "She'll have your trial transcripts."

"Great, thanks."

"I pulled a chit that's been hanging out there for a long time. You better be on track because if I wasted it for nothing, I'll be pissed." He sounds bitter.

I ignore his mood. "You ever been to this Mars cheese place? Someone told me if the curds squeak when you bite into them, it means they're good."

There's no response. Whether he's confused by my statement or doesn't care is anyone's guess.

"Okay, great talk." I snap my phone shut and put the car into gear.

It feels like my last two days have been spent mostly driving back and forth through Kenosha, to the point where I no longer need to reference the paper map sitting on my passenger seat.

In the courthouse basement I'm helped by a short squat woman, with carefully coiffed hair and heavy makeup. She doesn't verbally respond to my request for Rebecca, merely pointing to a row of chairs along the opposite side of the hallway. It's not apparent whether she's annoyed by or resigned to my presence.

I take a seat, the only person waiting. It's a long quiet hallway, black and white tiles reflecting the sound of hard-soled shoes as a man in an ill-fitting suit walks by without a look. He's got an aura of self-inflated importance. Maybe my history as a cop makes me biased, but I peg the guy for a defense attorney, haughty and weasel-like.

Across from me the records room door opens. A tall female exits, light blond hair, neutral expression, heels clicking. She doesn't bother introducing herself as she stops before me. "Aren't you a special one, Mr. White?"

I stand, still taller. "Excuse me?"

"I've got detectives loading my voicemail with requests to expedite retrieval of a closed case. These transcripts have been public a year now and no one's asked for them. Suddenly it's urgent and I need to assign staff to make copies? Why? Who are you? Which department?"

"I'm no longer active, formerly Chicago until a few months ago."

There is long silence as she assembles the connections. When it comes, her face blanches. "Oh, shit. You're *that* guy, White…White…"

"Aramis White. Call me Arch."

Recognition floods her expression, this person I've never met, and it's unsettling. "You brought down the Covenant group last year. That was you! Dozens of arrests rolled through here because of it."

"Thanks, but you're giving me too much credit. I didn't do anything in Wisconsin."

"You cut off the snake's head. That's what you did. Suddenly, our police had access to information needed to make arrests." Her expression darkens. "You also made a shit-ton of work for us."

I want to snap back: *You mean like doing your job?* But I still need this woman's help and instead bite my tongue, ending with a shrug.

Her eyes search mine, looking into her own mind for what I can guess are wide-ranging questions. The Covenant case was big enough to make national news, starting from a mugging gone wrong, to the homicide of Chicago's prince son and my mentor, to the takedown of a domestic terrorist group intent on bringing race wars to middle America. When the dust settled, I'd been publicly hoisted as a reckless wild card, offered up as the sacrificial lamb. The brass in my chain privately cleared me of any wrong-doing but bent weakly to political pressure. They could not be held accountable for allowing such a serpent to grow under their noses, the backlash would have burned too many shiny shields and that's what mattered most to them. In the end they stripped me of my detective's tin while patting my back behind closed doors. It's all I ever wanted to wear and in doing so, lost the right forever.

Rebecca blinks her eyes and we're both returned to the present. "Anyway, never mind. I pulled the files. There are a lot. It was the longest trial in state history if you didn't know."

"I did. Do."

"Something like eighty witnesses and tons of medical reports." She motions back to the records window ledge onto which the squat clerk placed a file box.

"That's it?"

"No, that's the first. Of many. Now you have a shit-ton. Enjoy."

It takes me nearly a half-hour to carry all the boxes to my car and I'm dripping sweat by the end.

13

FRIDAY, MAY 28, 1999, 8:12AM – DAY 13

"Watch out," Margaret stated as she entered the jury room, last to arrive. "Friday before a holiday weekend. Today is going to be some kind of day."

All around the room heads nodded and no one thought otherwise. Three solid weeks now, locked together listening to witnesses, trying to retain information that may or may not be important, striving to fulfill a juror's commitment to impartiality. The bleary eyes and sagging looks revealed a toll being extracted in a variety of ways. The holiday weekend came at an opportune time.

Travis tried to break the mood. "Three days free of this place. What's everyone doing? I'm…"

Every juror interrupted him. "Golfing!" A second of silence followed, then laughter erupted at the look on his face.

Chuckie pointed at Nicole. "Drinking."

She nodded and rolled her eyes. "I need it."

Courtney: "Organizing her notebooks." Several barks of humor as Justyna reached over and patted the stack which now stood a dozen high.

Shelli: "Helping her daughter with a cow."

Dennis: "Heading out of town on the back of his Harley."

Lian: "I have no idea. What do you do?"

Danny: "Probably re-building a house or something."

And finally, Terry: "Taking care of his honey."

The mood lightened as the Breakfast Jury fell into the rhythm and grooves that had developed. Margaret and Charles chatted and planned the lunchtime walk. Chuckie nibbled on licorice and elbowed Jean as he told her a story. Bryan laughed at something Rick said which caused Lian to laugh as well.

Kay sat back and took in the atmosphere. She didn't engage in the banter, simply letting her attention roam the room, thinking about these people who were strangers just a few weeks ago. Now they interacted like friends who'd known each other for years. It was interesting how Fate had a way of knotting random threads together, unveiling connections that would never have been discovered otherwise.

Larry knocked on the door, giving his two-minute signal.

Jambliss rested the State's witnesses on Wednesday and the defense had spent the last two days calling their own witnesses. The docket was significantly slimmer for people willing to testify on behalf of Mark Johannsen, but it could be argued these witnesses carried greater impact because of that.

Cruise stood at her table. "The defense would like to call Kelly Gorman."

Instantly the courtroom came alert. Kelly's name was already well-established from prior testimony. The mistress, the homewrecker, asking Mark what he was going to do about his marital situation so they could be together. She was portrayed by Jambliss as a catalyst, the spark that ignited Mark's plan to murder Julie. Now they were going to hear from her first-hand.

"Juicy," whispered Justyna. Bryan rubbed his hands together to emphasize her words and gave a Dr. Evil laugh from Austin Powers. Then he laughed at his own impersonation.

Gorman walked to the witness stand, brown hair cut short in a bob, glasses perched on a pointed nose. If she sensed the scrutiny from reporters, cameras, and others in the room it didn't show. Her eyes remained fixed forward. After swearing in, she sat and focused her attention solely on Cruise.

During this, she never once made

eye contact with Johannsen.

The initial questions by Cruise quickly revealed her agenda in bringing Gorman to the stand. "How often did Mark discuss Julie's depression with you?"

"Um, quite often. He'd say she was still lying in bed. Or that she never wanted to do anything with him. Or she was losing weight. Things like that."

Jambliss peered at her with intent. To the jurors it was clear he sought anything he could use on cross-examination. He wanted to crack open the shell of their relationship and cast his questions against the backdrop of infidelity.

In Kay's eyes this was the proper way to attack. It galled her that Gorman sat up there like she was a distant observer, as detached as the medical examiner or computer forensic analyst who never met the victim. No one was innocent in this case and acting as if you had no role in what happened was wrong.

She agreed with Jambliss that this woman was the catalyst for Mark's descent into evil. Julie may have set the kindling for this fire with her affair, but Gorman was the critical fuel.

Cruise picked at the thread of depression, asking the same question in different ways to produce an answer that portrayed Julie as someone capable of taking her own life. Her examination lasted until morning break.

The argument arose from a casual comment, spanning an emotional barrier previously erected between several of the jurors.

"No," Kay replied to Jean. "I don't like Gorman either, but Julie *should* have been depressed. She's the one who cheated first." It was Kay's same position from two weeks earlier, nothing had changed. Except now she knew the room better, knew the other personalities and how they would react.

This stirred a similar reaction as last time. "You can't be serious. No one commits suicide by drinking antifreeze and stuffing their own face into a pillow." Jean's tone was affronted.

"You don't know that," Kay replied,

unmoving.

"And you make it sound like she had it coming."

Kay didn't respond, simply shrugging her shoulders and looking down.

"Wait," Courtney interjected, paying attention from the far end of the table. "Do you?"

Others fell silent as invisible tension stretched across the table like a band ready to snap. "I'm just saying things are never as cut and dried as they seem," Kay said. "Everyone shares some level of responsibility."

"Except the wife who's dead because her psycho husband killed her," Nicole muttered.

That triggered Kay. "What do you know? You're not married. Half you people in here aren't. You don't know what it means when two people build a life together and one of them decides to throw it all away because the rainbow's faded. That kind of betrayal that can never be forgotten. People willing to do such things are selfish and crazy."

"Pot, meet kettle," Nicole shot back.

"You've said more crazy things in the last three weeks than anyone else here."

To which Kay returned: "Fuck you."

Margaret played peacemaker. "Okay, let's take it down a notch."

"I'm not listening to someone that clueless," Kay spat.

"Takes one to know one," Nicole said and turned away.

Margaret shook her head as everyone purposely kept their own tongues leashed. No one wanted to fan the flames of drama. They understood Kay was prickly, with strong opinions that would not be swayed. At the same time, personal attacks coming from Nicole weren't helpful.

Thick silence reigned for the remaining break.

Jambliss struggled to keep the smug look from his face as he buttoned his jacket and prepared to cross Kelly Gorman. His goal was to thoroughly negate her credibility and, based on her answers to Cruise, he had all the ammunition needed.

"Ms. Gorman, when did you begin

with your affair with the defendant?"

"Sometime over the summer. I don't remember exactly when."

"Do you have a better memory when you consummated that affair? In other words, when did you first engage in sexual acts? Was it at his house? His office? A hotel room?"

Gorman showed the first hints of being uncomfortable. Clearly the DA was angling to force testimony personally embarrassing to her. "It would have been around the same time. Never at his house. I think the first time was in a hotel when he visited our corporate offices in St. Louis."

"At the time you lived in St. Louis." It was not a question.

"Yes."

"And since then, you've relocated to Kenosha to be closer to Mark so you can continue your relationship despite his pending conviction." The jury noted how he assumed there would be a prison sentence following this trial.

"Nice touch," Terry murmured to Kay, referencing the subtle play. She didn't respond.

"I did move to Kenosha, yes," came the non-answer.

Jambliss didn't belabor the verbal sleight of hand. "We've seen emails between you and Mark. In many of them you sign off with the word 'idly.' Both of you did. Can you tell the jury what that means?"

She nudged her glasses up but remained otherwise perfectly still. "It's an acronym for 'I do love you'." Her mouth was small, and her lips barely moved when she spoke.

"So, you both confessed love for each other and spoke it often. We also saw email references to a cruise planned for the following year, which would have been several months from now if the plan went through. What was that about?"

"We wanted to go on a vacation."

"Yet he still had a wife. How would that work? Was she invited? Was she even aware of it?"

Now Gorman's stillness began to crack. She showed signs of nervousness. When she again nudged up her glasses, jurors saw her trembling fingers. "No, she was not invited."

"And in fact, you two discussed that, correct? We saw an email where you asked him how he planned to handle his 'situation' in the context of taking a cruise. Remind us again of his reply."

Gorman looked at Cruise, who had her head down, scribbling notes. There was no help to be found. Still, she did not make eye contact with Johannsen. "He said he was handling it."

"You paraphrased your answer. I believe the correct wording was 'Details, just noise in the bigger picture'. How did you interpret that?"

"I…I didn't really know what he meant."

"But you did want him free of marital encumbrances so the vacation could happen, correct?"

Gorman dipped her head before answering and when it came, it came as a whisper. "Yes."

"Even if that included murdering Julie his wife?"

This shot her attention back up. "No, never. That's not what I wanted."

"And am I correct in the recent

development that you two are engaged?"

Another soft "Yes."

"You are engaged to a man charged with the murder of his wife," Jambliss said in a ruminating voice, as if he was alone and pondering aloud, reminiscent of a Shakespearian aside. Theatrical but effective. Charles shook his head as if he too thought the same thing. Jambliss re-directed his attention to Gorman. "Did you think then he was capable of it?"

"Of course not."

"Given what's transpired since, seeing and hearing the evidence presented, do you still think that?"

Then it happened. For the first time all morning, Kelly Gorman looked over to Mark Johannsen, a man accused of heinous crimes. Her lover. She'd shared her life and her emotions and her body. Did she know he had murder within him? Had she suffered guilt over her role in ending another woman's life? If he was capable of this, what else lurked beneath his surface?

She leaned towards the microphone. "Not really."

"His side chick even thinks he did it!" Courtney exploded once they returned to the jury room for lunch. "That was the weakest 'No' I've ever heard."

Jambliss had continued grilling Gorman throughout the morning, but he'd shot his wad with her response and everything else that followed was a pony show to hammer home her lack of credibility. By the time Kelly was excused her face burned red and she looked on the verge of tears.

The DA gave her a smug nod as she passed his table on the way out, like he'd never been the author of her testimonial demise.

"Tell you what," Rick said. "Jambliss is an asshole but if I need someone prosecuted, he's my guy."

"No shit," Danny agreed. "And if I need a defender, that lady lawyer *is not*. Johannsen's going to prison because she's losing this case."

The earlier tension in the room faded away, everyone moving on from the confrontation between Nicole and Kay, superseded by Gorman's words. The opinion of her weak defense for Johannsen was universal across the jurors, even Kay. No one bought it. She may as well have said: *'Now that all this is happening, probably yeah.'*

14

WEDNESDAY, JUNE 14, 2000, 8:56AM

"I'm not looking through all that shit," Warren huffs as I meet him outside the rear precinct entrance. He nods to the brown expandable file folder in my hands and takes a sip from his Starbucks cup.

"You don't even know why I'm here." I follow him through the door without waiting on an invitation. His office is around the first hallway corner. Stacks of paper on the desk are arranged like a bulwark against the inevitable surge of additional cases. I set the five-inch-thick folder down in the lone open spot and loudly tapped it to keep his attention. "I've gone through the entire trial witness list and narrowed them down to people who have motive and opportunity. These are the starting suspects. There are only three. What I need is a second opinion on my logic and workups. Is that something you can handle?"

He hangs his sport jacket off the back of his desk chair and rolls one hand in circles. "Okay, fine. Whatever it takes to get you out of my hair for another day. Let's hear it."

I suppress a smile and sit, then talk him through my process and rationale in creating a suspect profile. It's nothing ground-breaking and I'm not seeking his admiration. Despite reluctance to do any dirty work, Warren has a sharp mind for investigations. More importantly, he's got decades of experience. I'd seen it on display last year when we crossed paths.

His role is to poke holes in my work, to unveil some angle I'd overlooked. It's a risk in detective work, getting too wound up or focused on one theory early in a case and then seeking evidence to support it. I'd once heard it termed Confirmation Bias during a training seminar.

When I finish, he leans back in his chair. It creaks loudly from his weight. "Sounds good."

I mimic the move in my own chair, minus any creak. "That's all? Just '*sounds good*'?"

"I don't know what you think I'm supposed to add. It's the same approach I'd take. You don't always need to peel back an onion very far, Arch. Sometimes the obvious motive is the best motive. Look up the Law of Parsimony. Also known as the Keep It Simple Stupid principle."

"So, you think I'm on the right track with someone seeking revenge on the jury?" I know this is belaboring the point, but I'd expected more resistance and am a little off my footing.

Warren shrugs and sips again. "It's a good start. Who you got?"

I flip open my file, feeling nervous for some reason. He didn't even throw shade at me. Who is this guy? "Three people. A relative, close coworker and the girlfriend, now fiancé."

He rubs his hands together, exaggerating anticipation like an old-time

Vaudevillian actor. "My money is on the girlfriend."

"You haven't heard anything else yet."

"Don't need to. Girlfriend."

I sift through my workup sheets. From trial records I pulled information like address, aliases, date of birth and anything else that seemed pertinent. "Kelly Gorman. She was the other woman when Johannsen murdered his wife and testified on his behalf."

Warren snorts out loud. "She wants to marry a dude who killed his first wife? Talk about walking the high wire. Hope they celebrate with something other than a toast."

"Living dangerously," I murmur as I pull the second sheet up. "Number two. There's a cousin, Jeffrey Highland. He ran interference on the witness stand. Based on that alone it's worth a look."

Warren grunts and motions for Highland's workup. He scans it and grunts again, which I interpret as agreement.

"Last," I look at the third sheet. "Gus Hoover, fellow stockbroker with the defendant. He was suspected of lying under oath. Told the detectives and DA one story then changed it during testimony."

"Anything happen from that?"

"I don't know but I'll find out. If this verdict impacted his life due to perjury that could be motive."

Warren pauses and looks straight at me. He jabs up one finger. "Wait, you just picked up these transcripts yesterday. And you've read everything already? What are you, some kind of speed reader?"

Now it's my turn to shrug. "It's not like I have a lot else going on in my life. Being single does that to you. And yes, I do speed read."

He shakes his head and mutters, "Kids nowadays. What do you need from me?"

"Past arrest records if any, additional contact information or addresses. Essentially anything else you can find that isn't on my workups."

"Vague, but okay." He collects the copies I'd made to leave with him. "What are you doing until then?"

"Not waiting on you. After this I'm

taking a drive past each last known address. If it looks like someone is home, I'm knocking."

This answer gives Warren pause and I can see his gears turning, sorting out thoughts and possibilities. "You know, there's nothing that says you can't ask random people questions, but you could be treading a thin line here, Arch. If this turns into a criminal case, it goes over to the Kenosha police, probably my buddy Paul Richardson. No one is going to be excited picking up after a citizen inquiry. It means taking a risk."

"Well, no one else is looking into this. Without me doing the leg work there is no case to jeopardize. If a killer truly is walking free right now, your friend can get over it and pick up from me."

Warren stacks his sheets, tapping them on the desk to line up edges. "Yeah, sure. He'll be thrilled. Let me see what I can get you by tomorrow morning."

"Sooner would be better, but whatever. Now," I level a look at him. "Ted."

This brings a sharp shake of

Warren's head. "Not your guy, I'm telling you. I've known him most of my life. He wanted nothing more than to be married. No way he has a hand in this. I'll stake my life on it."

Even though I don't really see Ted as a suspect either, I'm a stickler for procedure. Or I was until the Noah Bell case made me go rogue. Maybe I'm just now overcompensating. "Then he should have a solid alibi."

"He called me to look after this in the first place. Why do that if he was guilty?"

"Red herring. Diversion. Plausible deniability. Who knows? We've seen it before, like arsonists who offer statements to police while everything burns. Someone willing to kill can't be judged by what you and I see as rational."

"Jesus, such a pain in my ass." Warren opens a drawer and pulls out a slim folder. "I talked to him yesterday, thanks for the uncomfortable discussion. He gave me a receipt from Steak N Shake, that one in Gurnee at the outlet malls. Time stamp was 8:21. Ordering takes 10 minutes at least; I go there all the time. Place is always busy. Eating, let's say 15 minutes, so now we're at 8:45. It's thirty minutes to Sunnyside so the soonest he could have been there was 9:15. You said the group started leaving by 10. The math is tight."

I motion for the receipt to which Warren states, "Now you're double-checking me?"

The last four digits of a credit card are displayed. It's the only way to tie him to the receipt. "Reconcile Ted's card to this and that will be good enough for me."

"Thanks for your approval," Warren spits out sarcastically.

"Autopsy?"

"Tomorrow end of day at the latest. It's the same lady who did the Johannsen wife, so she knows what to look for. Add another day for lab processing and you're looking at Friday soonest."

"If it comes back positive for ethylene glycol?" That's the million-dollar question I need answered and putting Warren on the spot is the only way I get it.

He shifts and breaks eye contact. I know what he's thinking. He set me on this thinking it would lead nowhere and he gets to keep his friend happy. Now that there's death with a not-small chance of it being homicide, he'll have to act on the results. That means scrutiny of the evidence I'm gathering, scrutiny on his adherence to protocol. He broke that link from the start by calling me, everything else will be framed as dereliction of department policy. The thing he fears the most in this world – accountability – could be coming home to roost and there is nowhere else he can point the finger. It's what happened to me in Chicago and from someone who was all too recently hoisted on such a petard, it's not a great place to be.

It leads to an empty apartment between two worlds and a lot of soul-searching.

"I can buy you a day, maybe two, but you know I'll have to refer this over to Kenosha. I don't know what to tell my captain. He's going to chew me a new asshole."

The response is not what I expected. I thought I'd hear some dissembling, blah-blah-blah about looking into further, whatever would keep him disengaged.

"Look at you, taking responsibility. You just might become a real detective yet."

"Get the fuck outta here," he shoots back, but without any true heat.

I double-rap his desk with my knuckles and get the fuck outta there.

There are generally two options to determine whether someone belongs on a suspect list:

- Surveil until there's enough proof to confront the person then work towards a confession. Or…

- Embark on a fishing expedition and interview someone right off the jump, see if anything emerges that confirms or corrects an initial suspicion.

The clock is ticking. I'm working under the assumption an autopsy will reveal ethylene glycol poisoning as cause of death. Time is too precious to consider otherwise.

So, I go with option two.

Kelly Gorman's last known address

is on Meadowlands Circle, a closed loop drive with a dozen townhome units identical in nature and appearance. There's newness to them, as evidenced by some yards that still have black construction wrap around the perimeter. I recite house numbers under my breath as I idle along the road to the address.

There's a car in the shared driveway. My information is a year old, hopefully she still lives here and is home on a Wednesday morning. I pull over to the curb and take a beat, mentally rehearsing my script. It's hard to cold call someone when you know they could end up being your prime suspect. You don't want to tip them off or give them time to compose a different story. You also don't want to shoot your own case in the foot by not uncovering the truth. It's a fine line and you have to feel your way through it on the fly.

I give two loud raps on the door, followed by one press of the doorbell. Standard knock pattern to convey authority.

Seconds pass before the door opens and I'm facing a petite woman with short brown hair, pursed lips and glasses. I've seen pictures from the trial. It's her. "Help you?" She asks in a tone hinting that such help may not be easy to obtain.

Unbuttoning my jacket, I give my best disarming smile and purposely jump right into it. No sense soft peddling around my presence at her front door. "Hello ma'am, Aramis White. I'm looking into the circumstances surrounding Nicole Wright from last Friday night and hoping you might be able to help. Apologize for the suddenness of this all." My wording and vocal intonation are those of a law enforcement officer. Maybe she won't notice my lack of identification.

There's no reaction to the mention of Nicole, other than brows knitting in confusion. "Who?"

I'd hoped spouting the name right off the bat would trigger a reaction of surprise or recognition, perhaps defensiveness that someone had tracked her down quickly after she poured antifreeze into Nicole's drink. I'm denied.

One more try.

"Nicole Wright," I repeat. "Do you

know her?"

Consideration causes her eyes to lose focus as she thinks then shakes her head. "Sorry, can't help you."

Might as well unload with both barrels and see if I can knock something loose. "She was the jury foreman for Mark's trial."

Now those eyes grow hard behind the lenses and her face stiffens. "Really."

"Yes, really. There was an incident with her last Friday."

"Well, too bad but nothing to do with me. Everything about that can go straight to hell."

I glance down at her left hand. The ring finger is bare and I kick myself for not noticing right away. "You're no longer with him."

"I am not," she states flatly. There's a truckload of emotion pushing out those three words and now I'm off my bead. It was not a scenario I'd considered. Such a rookie mistake.

Dammit, Arch.

"You were not at or near the Sunnyside bar Friday evening?"

"Not that it's anyone's business but I was on a flight that landed in O'Hare at 10:14pm. You come back with a warrant and I'll show you the ticket. Otherwise, get out of here. My day is now ruined remembering the shit-show of last year."

The door slams shut, solid and final.

I shuffle back to my car, cheeks on fire with self-recrimination. As I accelerate away, a glance in the mirror shows she re-emerged from her house, standing with crossed arms in the driveway, watching me depart.

Shake it off.

I'd been caught unprepared for an answer and had no regroup. That can't keep happening, not if I want to walk into the Kenosha police department and hand over a packet of evidence. I can't have them looking at me side-eye, thinking '*Hobby cop. Get him away from here.*'

It's from Chicago, this new habit of over-thinking. Everything that happened there has only eroded my confidence. I dwell on the past, reliving each decision that led to me to this lonely place and flog myself for not taking the smart play. I know I shouldn't do it, that looking backwards prevents you from looking forward, but I can't help it. So many mistakes and my name plastered to each one.

Now I'm on a quest to rebuild my reputation, my skills. My confidence in who I am. Is that why I'm hunting this case like a hound dog? Or is this case unfolding for me because I'm a hound dog?

I don't know the answer. Part of me is afraid to find out.

The last known address for Gus Hoover is off County Road KR and it takes me a few minutes to realize the KR probably stands for Kenosha-Racine. Clever, those civic planners.

His house is a single-story mid-century design, nearly identical to so many others I've seen around here. Red brick graces the front, window frames white and clean. The sidewalk leading to his front door is neatly bordered by colorful plants. If this is still Hoover's house, he takes pride in maintaining it, which is worth noting.

The driveway is empty, window curtains drawn and a general sense of no one home. I pull in, blocking the end with my car and repeat my knock-knock-doorbell sequence, but there's no response after a few minutes. It's not unreasonable to think the occupants are away at work. The trial transcripts for Hoover listed his employer, but not the actual address. There are a half dozen locations for the company within the Southeast Wisconsin area and rather than driving to each one, I decide to jump the queue and move onto my third suspect. This will give Warren time to verify Hoover's addresses for me.

Let's have a talk with Highland.

I pause beside my car door, looking up at the blue June sky, at deep green trees surrounding me, the buzz of insects doing whatever it is insects do. The road is slender, stacked in a symmetrical line with neat houses similar to this one. Lawns are tended, flowers spark color and there's a sense of calm nearly visible to the eye. The scene is beautiful to behold, postcard worthy.

My arrival diminishes the vibrancy and turns the natural sounds discordant, like a harbinger of grim tidings. I've brought on a wave of bad omens, carrying with me questions designed to unveil the darker side of humanity, which cannot coexist with beauty.

Something will have to give.

256

15

TUESDAY, JUNE 1, 1999, 1:05PM –
DAY 14

The Memorial Day weekend provided a three-day respite from the trial but very few jurors looked refreshed. Some had part-time jobs, which gave them no relief. Others simply had duties to attend, normal life tasks that had been disrupted by the grind. Everyone needed more than a long weekend to re-center themselves.

They were in the Dog Days. So much evidence and testimony had been presented that accuracy faded, names and faces blurred, critical information was blunted by the relentless surge of more, more, more.

Millick thanked his jurors at the beginning of each session, truly meaning it, but he could see the slog taking a toll. Charles, Justyna and Margaret no longer bothered to hide their droopy eyes. Danny stared straight ahead with a blank expression, clearly somewhere else in his thoughts. Nicole often stood near an open window behind the second row to stay alert. Shelli and Courtney frequently whispered to each other. A shake-up of some kind was needed.

Enter: Jeffrey Highland.

"We would like to call our next witness," attorney Cruise announced after lunch.

The courtroom doors opened to admit a tall, gaunt man in jeans and wrinkled polo shirt. He pulled off his faded ballcap to reveal a full head of graying hair. There was resemblance to Mark Johannsen in his lanky frame, his bone structure and eyes, but Highland was the roughly used copy, edges ragged and blistered from the sun.

He walked slowly towards the witness stand, eyeing the jury members one by one with a squint on his face. When he raised his hand to take the oath, it was bony and scarred, knuckles enlarged, one finger missing after the first joint. In many ways, this was symbolic of Highland's life.

The creases and pale skin lining his eyes revealed a man who wore sunglasses but still never stopped squinting.

Cruise straightened her jacket. "Mr. Highland, can you state your connection with Mark Johannsen for the court?"

"Yeah, sure. Cousin, close cousin." His voice was a match for his gravelly appearance, vocal cords scraping raw his throat. Highland was someone unafraid to yell.

"And how would you characterize your relationship to Mark?"

"I just said close cousin," he said, tone betraying his temperament and distrust of the judicial proceedings. "I know you heard me."

Justyna leaned over to Travis. "Someone got up on the wrong side of the bed."

"No kidding. Look at his hair. I got hedges don't stick up that straight."

Justyna snorted.

Cruise nodded and gave a plastic smile. "I did hear you, yes. It's to make sure the jury hears you."

He looked from the witness box to the Breakfast Jury, eyes flinty, and appeared on the edge of speaking directly to them. As if sensing the same thing, Cruise quickly moved on. She established a background between him and the defendant, two cousins growing up close together throughout their lives. Johannsen and Highland, getting into the mischief young boys get into, sharing many of the same experiences.

This phase of questioning took them to the afternoon break and in those two hours she repeatedly used Highland's answers to frame Mark as a devoted husband who lived only for his wife but was shattered by her infidelity. Conversely, she painted Julie as a wife suffering remorse over the affair, on a ledge of her own making, until there was no other option but to leap off into suicide.

"She stopped talking to me in the final few months," Highland groused at one point. "After I yelled at her during a family

Easter brunch, she told Mark not to let me come around anymore. Isn't that something? Cutting off your own family because you can't handle being reminded of your shame? Weak."

His lip curled and he looked over to his cousin, giving a minimal shrug. Mark merely stared back without expression.

"This guy is supposed to help the defense?" Terry whispered to both Danny and Kay.

Danny grunted in agreement. "Fail."

"Jambliss has to be licking his lips."

"Gross," Kay added. "Now I've got that in my head."

As if privy to their whispers, Cruise glanced over before closing. "The defense has no more questions, your Honor."

Millick leaned towards his mic. He made the same hand movement every time he spoke, half-flip, half-wave, revealing muscle memory from years of presiding over trials. "Does the State wish to cross?"

"Absolutely," Jambliss replied and fairly jumped up from his seat.

This enthusiasm had a noticeable effect on Highland. He leaned back, face hardening. The DA was an enemy, someone trying to send his cousin away for life. Jaw muscles rolled under leathery skin. The creases edging his eyes and forehead sharpened.

"Good afternoon, Mr. Highland," Jambliss said in a modulated voice.

"Hey," came the reply, just as insincere.

"Did Mark ever discuss with you the harassing pictures supposedly sent to his house and place of work?"

"You mean the dick pics? Yeah, once or twice. They came from that pervert Julie cheated with."

Jambliss latched onto that statement. From his gleeful expression it was apparent even he didn't think this moment would come so soon. "Wait. How do you know that? How do you know Perry Tarrell sent them? Is there any proof?"

"Well, Mark told me." Highland's face betrayed the realization he'd just made a mistake.

"So, under oath, you are making a statement with no factual bearing, placing it on record for the jury to consider in this matter. Am I correct?"

"Whatever," he replied, gruff and annoyed.

Jambliss was not content to accept the win and move on. "If Mark had sent those 'dick pics', as you call them, would he have told you?"

"He didn't."

"That's not an answer to my question." Jambliss clearly didn't care though, not enough to repeat the question. He quickly moved on. "Did he ever tell you about the thousands of penis pictures he had? The tens and hundreds of folders categorizing them by size, shape and state of erection? The hours spent searching and saving those image files for his own pleasure?"

"Bullshit," Highland spat. "That's sick."

Jambliss jabbed one finger in the air, an exaggerated pantomime of someone making a critical point. "Ah, but we have the evidence. A forensic examination of his computer revealed them all. A computer analyst verified them. Did you know that?"

"I don't believe it."

"We're not asking you to believe anything. It's an undeniable fact and the jury has also heard of these pictures."

"But never seen any," Nicole groused under her breath.

"And also," Jambliss continued. "Did you know that the police themselves thought Mark was planting them around the house? That they told Julie this? All for the purpose of harassment and emotional manipulation. Did Mark tell you any of that?"

Highland's jaw rolled and bunched. "No."

"No? That's surprising, considering how close you two were." The DA smiled thinly. "And did Mark also tell you about his affair with Kelly? His plan to take her on a cruise after he removed Julie from the picture because, according to him, she was just a 'minor' detail?"

"Objection," Cruise spouted. "Subjective."

"Sustained."

But Jambliss was on a roll now. He plowed forward without acknowledging Millick's words. "If he wasn't willing to share those things, what else did he keep from you, his closest relative?"

"You don't know what you're talking about."

"Oh, I think I do, Mr. Highland. Your cousin is charged with murder, and you can't accept it. You cannot comprehend the man that you grew up with is capable of killing his wife with poison."

"Objection, argumentative."

"Sustained."

"You see, Mr. Highland, Mark is not who you think he is. He committed the very act you despised in Julie. If you hated her for having an affair, then you must also hate Mark for his own infidelity. The person sending dick pics was not indeed Perry Tarrell but your own cousin. How does that realization strike you? How does it make you feel to know that Mark is the pervert you claimed Tarrell to be?"

"You're lying."

"According to testimony, Mark mentally tortured Julie for years. He used her affair as a weapon against her whenever it suited him. He concocted a sham scenario of harassment simply to increase the pressure on her. And when finally an opportunity came to eliminate her from the picture, he did so without hesitation."

"Fucking lies."

The sound of camera shutters clicking added a buzz to the escalating tension. Millick loudly demanded decorum in his court. Mark looked nervously from his cousin to the jury, to the judge and then his lawyers. Things were boiling up and he was helpless to stop them. The bailiffs and sheriff's deputies were alert in their chairs, attention pinned to the witness.

Jambliss turned up the wick. "In fact, you don't know the kind of man he is. You show up here thinking you can tell the court he didn't do anything wrong, when in fact you have no idea what he did, do you Mr. Highland? Your family relation blinds you to the fact that Mark Johannsen is a cold-blooded killer."

"Shut up." Highland's face radiated fury, nose and lips twisted into a snarl.

"Decorum!" Millick pounded his gavel.

Cameras clicked, capturing the raw displays of emotion.

"I'd argue that your presence here today did more to damage him than help. You, his closest friend," Jambliss made air quotes. "You don't even know him and if you don't, who does? If he could hide his monstrous nature from you, then he could hide it from everyone."

"You shut your mouth!"

"Mark hid it from you because he could. Because he planned how and when to kill Julie, manipulating and driving her mad in the weeks leading up to it, cutting her off from others, all so he could take his collection of penis pictures and start a new life with Kelly Gorman. Why should we believe your words when all that went unnoticed? How does your character assessment carry any weight? Your cousin is a pervert and murderer, and nothing you say changes it."

"Objection!"

"Sustained."

Click, click, click…

Highland finally snapped. "FUCKING KILL YOU!" He leapt over the witness box wall, thudding on the floor with his heavy work boots, startling the recorder.

Larry the bailiff was ready. Though half a foot shorter and decades older, he shouldered Highland, timing it perfectly.

The cousin tumbled forward to one knee, slapping his hands on the floor to brace himself. Jambliss stepped back, keeping the prosecutor's table between them. His face showed no alarm. Rather a smirk tugged up one corner. If he felt imminent danger from an unleashed witness, it didn't show.

Both deputies vaulted from their seats, burly men with stern looks and corded forearms. Before Highland regained his feet, they grabbed his arms and shoved him back.

All three tumbled into the jury box wall, sending Courtney and Shelli backward in their chairs. Notebooks flew. Charles and Bryan jumped to their feet, alarmed. Chuckie yelled something.

Chaos exploded, sounds and motion, Millick pounded his gavel, photographers jockeyed against each other in the gallery, deputies wrestled with the manic Highland, reporters shuffled for a better view. Camera shutters were in constant stream, freezing each moment with clarity. Cruise and her lawyers sat back down, failing to hide their dismay as Highland's credibility evaporated. Mark kept his head lowered, refusing to watch the pandemonium.

"Well, I must say," Charles noted as the jury room door closed. "I didn't have a courtroom fight on my Bingo card today. Anyone else?"

Laughter rose as others released tension.

"Crazy," Justyna said with a barked laugh.

"They almost hit me," Courtney added and examined one of her notepads. Several pages were now torn.

"I know a lot of dudes like that," Danny stated. "We get them on the job site and they last maybe a day or two. Just can't keep it together."

Nicole huffed. "That's more than not keeping it together. Guy was crazy. Hope we never see him again."

A momentary pause was cut short

by Shelli. "Guys," she said. "I have a confession. I know him, I know Highland."

She held off questions by raising both hands. "But not personally. He's done some work on our house. My husband is the one who deals with him. I recognized his face right away but didn't want to say anything after what Travis went through. I didn't want to risk Millick sending me home. After this long, I want to finish out the trial and have a say in the verdict."

Kay cleared her throat. "Same. Highland's done work for us too, tree cutting and patching our roof after a storm. Although he never finished the job and there was an argument over payment. I don't know what happened after that."

Danny grunted. "Of course."

Silence fell as each juror considered the courtroom action, decompressing from the adrenaline surge in their own way.

After a few minutes, Courtney broke it up. "Well, if anyone cares, I think that's the end of the witnesses." She flipped through one of her notepads. "Millick mentioned ninety witnesses and we've done that many."

It had only been three weeks since jury selection, fourteen solid days of testimony after opening arguments. Did the court severely misjudge their initial estimate or was there something else still to be presented? Silence in the room hinted at a similar thought across the group.

Margaret broke the silence. "I don't know what the defense was thinking, bringing this guy in," she blurted.

Grunts of agreement arose in response.

"In fact, both sides had a problem with witnesses," Bryan replied. "That prison dude, Travis' buddy, was shady as hell."

"You heard he testified in return for a reduced sentence, right?" Jean asked. "I mean, if that doesn't taint him I don't know what does."

"Then the Hoover guy," Dennis chimed in. "He lied at some point, either to us or Jambliss."

Travis cleared his throat. "It's going to be hard coming to a verdict. We all have our own ideas, but we'll need to be able to back up our decisions. Hard evidence is the key. Too many of these witnesses have question marks."

The door opened and Larry poked in his head. An angry red scrape above the right ear showed the aftereffects of his tussle. His normal twinkle no longer shown. "Judge is letting all you guys go early. The rest of today is a waste. He's got to get with the attorneys."

"To yell at Cruise?" Terry asked.

That elicited a glimmer of Larry's default cheeriness. He grunted a laugh. "Good guess." With a glance over his shoulder to the hallway, he said, "The court has been cleared, you all can leave whenever."

The early release did little to change anyone's mood. They were facing the end of Mark Johannsen's case, a moment everyone knew would come but hadn't verbally acknowledged. Beyond the hurdle of coming to a verdict, there was the other elephant in the room.

Shelli had the fortitude to say it. "You guys, are we staying in touch after this?" Her voice was soft, as if anticipating a negative answer. "How many people have gone through what we have?"

No one immediately replied. Charles took up the challenge. "I think it's fair to call you friends. We've gotten to know each other in a different way than normal. The usual pattern of friendship was accelerated, being thrown together like this, forced to work together day after day, all day. We're supposedly the longest trial in state history. That counts for something and even if no one else cares, we should."

Margaret looked over at him, her lunchtime walking partner, then beamed a smile at the room. "Everyone, may I introduce Charles the Wise?"

Murmurs rolled through the room, agreement and appreciation, expressed in varying ways.

"Well, shit," Nicole spouted. "Y'all are pretty cool. I could handle more friends."

"Anyone ever in the mood for a round of golf, hit me up," Travis said. He held up his left hand to show the tan lines left by his glove.

Chuckie lifted a roughened finger up to make a point. "I'm going to take Jean out to dinner one of these days. She'll wear down and say yes. Then breakfast." He fake-flinched as Jean punched him in the arm with a laugh.

"Hey," Travis stood and hovered his hand flat over the table center. "We're the Breakfast Jury and don't ever forget it!"

Danny looked at him, at the hand. "What?"

"Go team, on three!"

"Are you copying me? I did that on day one!"

"One, two, three…"

No one joined Travis, much to the delight of Danny. He sat back in his chair, bottom lip pushed out in an exaggerated expression of satisfaction.

Courtney and Shelli looked at each other. Then both wadded up a notepad page and threw it at Travis. "Weirdo," they said in unison.

Laughter still hung in the air when Kay took her leave, the first to break contain, followed closely by Terry and Rick. Conversation bounced off the room's walls as they exited, fellow jurors chatting as they slowly packed up their belongings, delving into topics ranging far from the murder of a wife by her husband.

The timing worked out so most of the jury headed towards their cars as a group. The sun hung in the western sky, still hours away from the horizon but with enough of an angle to cut tight shadows.

The chatter of random subjects continued amongst the jurors as they migrated towards their cars. No one sensed the stare from a lone figure, watching intently from a building behind as they parted ways.

276

16

WEDNESDAY, JUNE 14, 2000, 2:01PM

My money is on Highland. Call it intuition, a hunch, or the result of my investigation. They all lead to the same conclusion.

I'd read his testimony and looked up news articles. Everything painted the picture of a man unable to control his emotions, someone who harbored resentment and distrust of authority. His transcript was a master class in half-formed thoughts, convoluted sentences and harsh declarations. The fact that he tried to attack the DA simply frosts the cake.

I have no idea what the defense was thinking putting that guy on the stand.

They were probably desperate for character witnesses to rebut the evidence and took a chance with him.

Swing and a miss.

Highland lives west of Kenosha in the town of Paris. My path takes me past a restaurant I'd overheard a couple of locals discussing last night in the library, so I stop on a whim. It's a place called Tenuta's; I order something called a Muffo-lotta to eat in my car. Good, but woof. People eat these things on the regular?

By the time I arrive in Paris my innards are roiling from the vinegar and oil dressing.

He'd listed his occupation as 'Handyman' on the witness profile sheet. His response to background questioning on the witness stand, verbatim: "You know, like drywall and plumbing and maybe some roofing. Landscaping, cutting down trees. Stuff like that."

Stuff like that.

One year ago such a vague description would have earned scorn from me, Mr. Career Detective, but at the moment mine was similarly vague: *Private investigations, criminal procedure advice and stuff like that.*

I have no room to talk.

However, I do have a personality profile banging around my brain. I've come across others like him plenty of times. Big talkers, full of plans large and small that never see the light of day somehow, because there's always a reason out of their control. Their lives are in a constant state of leaping from one idea to the next, rarely finishing anything. I once surveilled a guy like that, professional looking, nice house in the suburbs, good life from the outside but just a burning mess on the inside. His car's passenger door once stood open for days because he received a phone call while unloading groceries and started talking about launching an internet business, selling pet supplies online or some such. Under later questioning, it turns out he left a gallon of milk sitting in the seat to spoil. When he couldn't find it in the fridge he grounded his kids thinking they drank it. As a capper, his car battery died from the interior light drawing power.

None of that ever helped him evade

charges of drug dealing to raise money for Pets.com or whatever it was named.

Highland's house is tucked far back from the road, down a long gravel drive that bends to the right, thick oak trees obscuring a clear view. Similar to Hoover's, his house is a mid-century design, nearly identical in layout. However, neglected maintenance gives it a completely different aspect. Decorative brick bracketing the front door is dingy, showing splotches of green where moss has gained footing. A broken shutter hangs over one window and there's a ladder leaning against the roof. I spot a stack of shingles on the peak, with leaves and twigs collecting atop them. He started a shingle patch at some point and then abandoned or forgot it, propping up my assumptions. The guy doesn't finish anything. Dandelions peek through grass that hasn't been cut in weeks despite the presence of a mower sitting outside the garage door.

I'm having trouble being objective and there's a tremor in my system when I consider his potential as a suspect.

Parking my car behind an old Ford pickup truck, I hear barking from somewhere in the backyard. It's deep, a big dog, and frantic, warning me of risk.

Before I've proceeded more than a few steps, a man appears from behind the house, shovel dangling from his left hand. He's tall, close to my height, and built lean like me. But where mine is a result of youth and sensible diet (Muffo-lotta monster sandwich non-withstanding), his is the stringy gauntness of hard choices. He's several decades older, judging by the wrinkles around his eyes and strands of gray escaping a dirty ball cap. A grungy flannel shirt hangs untucked over jean shorts, with white gym socks sticking up from work boots.

He stops and stabs the shovel point into the ground like a stake past which I dare not trespass. Nothing comes from him by way of greeting, just a steely stare.

I read his not-so-subtle body language and stop a dozen feet away. The dog continues to bark, echoing over the roof. It must be chained or confined to a kennel. "Are you Jeffrey Highland?"

"Certainly hope so. Otherwise it's gonna be awkward when he gets home." His sarcastic response carries a gravelly tone, one I recognize from people who've spent decades smoking.

"I'll take that as a yes then." I move a couple steps closer. He doesn't react. "Sorry to bother but I'm hoping you can help shed some light on a case that's currently active. Don't worry. You are not in trouble over anything."

Yet.

"Good, 'cuz I ain't done nothing wrong. Day's young, however."

Now is when I find out how this discussion will go. "It's related to the jury in your cousin's trial."

Instantly his demeanor hardens and he re-grips the shovel handle. "What about them?"

"You're probably aware the one-year anniversary of his verdict just passed. They had a reunion for the occasion and I have reason to believe someone made an attempt on their lives."

I bite back on the cringe even before

the words finish leaving my mouth. *Terrible phrasing, Arch.*

Highland catches it though, lowering his voice to a growl. It's a match for the barking dog. "You mean those folk were partying? After what they did? Fuckers."

"My apologies for characterizing it that way. Not my intention to sound callous. But there's a theory it was revenge." I give a beat for my next words to load. "You testified on behalf of Mark, right?"

It's a redundant question that needs no response. We both know he did. We both also know why I asked.

His eyes hold mine from under the shadowed brim of his hat then break away for a second.

Got you.

It's a tell, interview 101 basic instruction. When the subject avoids eye contact, it's a sign they've been caught out. It doesn't indict him on anything, it just reveals that a path has suddenly opened for me. I press on.

"I've read the transcripts. You were

adamant that Mark was innocent. Your testimony ended with you being removed from the courtroom under duress, right?"

"Damn right," he spits. "Whole thing was rigged from the get. I known Mark better than anyone. He may not have had a perfect marriage but ain't no way he'd kill her. That wasn't him but the judge didn't care. He just wanted to be The Man, longest trial in state history, blah blah. Cameras everywhere, reporters from TV, articles on the Yahoo internet. Fucking disgrace is what it was."

His body language betrays growing irritation, emotions simmering over long-held resentment. He clearly has not gotten over it and if I'm not careful, I'll trigger him past the point of responding. Everything he's shown matches my mental profile, so I've got a good handle on him. I need to throttle back. That way I can edge back around to my line of questioning.

With a non-committal shrug, I convey my neutrality on the matter. It's important he doesn't see me as an adversary. "I didn't live around here when the trial happened. I'd never even heard about it until Monday, so excuse me if I state anything wrong."

"Yeah? Where you come from?"

"Chicago, up until a few months ago."

This time the spit from Highland is real, a wad of phlegm hacked up and shot at the ground before my feet. "So you're a FIB."

"A what?"

"Fuckin' Illinois Bastard. FIB. Bears still suck, go Pack go."

I think my mouth opens and closes three times, seeking the right comeback and failing miserably. I'm not even sure what he means, sports is not my world.

He doesn't wait for me to assemble a response. "Ain't got nothing more for you. You want to ask me about Friday, ask down at the station all formal and shit. That happens and I'll sue you right out of your fancy suit. Now get off my property."

Highland hawks another spit ball, this one closer, and turns away. As he disappears around the corner of his house, incessant dog barking turns to whines, a pet begging favor from an owner.

I'm left standing there like a dunce.

This is turning into a crappy day, nothing is going as intended. I return to my car and let it idle at the end of his driveway while I jot down my thoughts about our encounter, in no hurry to comply with his demand. I admit, it's also a passive-aggressive move, daring him to do something about me still on his property. Yes, it's weak.

Nothing about our interaction puts me off Highland as a suspect. If anything, I'm more triggered now. He gave me the signs I needed to carve deeper with my questions, but I blew it. Who knew there was such a border battle between the two states? I mean, was this a thing?

However, I've now lost the element of surprise, lost the tactic of loading him with a question to gauge his response. Face to face interaction is out the door now, time for subtler techniques. After a few minutes I back out of his driveway and head east, retracing my route. Plans and actions are running through my mind. There are a couple of loose ends I should tie up first before taking further action on Highland.

Clear the plate of other potential suspects so I can fully focus on what I need to pin him down.

I'm a few miles away when it hits me, a thunderclap that nearly causes me to cross the center line. I never said anything about the party being on Friday.

He already knew.

I'm not quite sure what to do with such a revelation. My instinct is to rip back around and confront Highland, but as I rewind the encounter, a different decision emerges. If I'm accurate in my profile, an accusation over his gaffe would only send him to ground, make any further clues that much harder to uncover.

No, I'm going to let him simmer a bit.

Even now I picture him digging at whatever he's digging, mulling over our conversation in his head like a record on repeat, inspecting the moments for anything that could have betrayed him. Natural reaction will have him focus more on my words, any verbal slip that indicated

I knew more than I let on. At some point he'll realize his mistake and will be forced to act on it. That's when my next opportunity arrives. I can't press, not yet.

Let it breathe, Arch. Some cases are like fine wine.

Griff once said that to me, an overwrought analogy that caused him to immediately laugh at his own corny advice. But it fits.

I call Ted. He answers immediately, as if waiting on my ring. It doesn't help settle my nerves. This is a guy that offered me a lot of money to look into his wife's situation. Based on the way the cards have fallen, he could also be a suspect. Accusing your employer of murder is a fine line to walk. I mean, we're talking about a lot of money, to me anyway. Since being ejected from the Chicago PD, I don't exactly have an excess of it floating around.

He cuts short my greeting. "You asked George to sniff on me, yes?" His flat accent gives no hint as to his mental state. This man just lost his wife, but you couldn't tell from his voice. Maybe he's just that stoic, maybe he's good at hiding it. "You think I poisoned her?"

This is a conversation I've tumbled in my mind, knowing it would eventually come. I gather the words I'd assembled for such a question, hoping they will be enough. "There's a different perspective for me, Ted. It's not that I think you did it. I must rule out the possibility you *could have*. If this goes the way I think it will, you'll be subject to less scrutiny because of my request. I asked George to add a layer of official law enforcement inquiry, to help buffer for what will come."

He grunts, once, twice, clearly mulling over my answer. Finally: "Is good. You are thorough. He said you are like that."

I'm assuming the 'he' in this case is Warren so I don't respond.

"Is now three days. How many hours do you spend?"

"All of them," I shoot back in a lighter tone, relieved we're over the accusation hurdle. I'm only half-kidding but it might have been too much. He says nothing and I clear my throat. "I'll get you an accounting by the end of today. It is all I've been doing, however."

Another grunt, impossible to read.

"Have you been able to obtain your wife's cell phone logs?"

"Yes, I have. I leave for Chicago soon, to spend rest of week there. This house has no good memories right now. I place phone documents under doormat. You pick up."

"Thank you. As for the autopsy, George told you I asked him to step in and help it along?"

"Yes."

"Okay good. If the medical examiner finds what we both suspect he will find, this case morphs into something much larger. It moves to law enforcement control. There's little I will be able to do once that happens. Even George will be limited due to jurisdictional boundaries. I'll help the detectives by providing everything I've been able to find but they will take it from the start as a brand-new case. That means re-interviewing witnesses I've already contacted and gathering forensic evidence.

Essentially, they will be repeating everything I've done."

"I pay you to find the person who did this. If you do not, then what payment is for?"

"I did. I'm just preparing you for the eventuality that it may take weeks for an arrest."

"Is too long. You and Georgie, you do arrest. Then you get paid."

With that he abruptly ends the call, off to Chicago. I realize there will be no more answering on the first ring. He's set forth a demand in the manner of his contractual fulfillment and I'm left wondering how to do what he wants.

My next call to Warren doesn't relieve any pressure. I can practically hear him shrug over the line. "Whaddya going to do? That's the way Ted is. You don't get to his level by being patient."

Now there's the Warren I know. He doesn't care. His paycheck doesn't hang in the balance. He can hand the case off to Kenosha, call Ted and give some weasel-like excuse then go about his day. Meanwhile, I'm in this up to my neck, with a direct line to my dangerously thin wallet.

At least my call nets what I need for my three suspects. Warren has their files ready for me. Instead of driving all the way to Grand Haven, I end up back at the Kenosha library where, for $.25 per page, I'm able to receive his fax. It costs almost twenty dollars.

The librarian looks a little unsure when I pull out cash to pay, like she's never handled a money transaction before. I suppose with everyone just emailing each other now there isn't much use for faxes. Maybe one of these days I'll get my own email. I end up throwing the bill down on the counter when she calls someone for assistance, telling her to keep the change. I'm eager to dissect Gorman, Hoover and, especially, Highland.

Grabbing a table in the far corner, I spread out the pages and group them by person, looking at them in ascending order of suspicion like I'm building a plot to the climax of my own novel.

First up, Kelly Gorman. She's had a

slew of home and work addresses, hopping jobs as much as residences. There's nothing of note with any criminal history, just a few traffic violations. It's the profile of someone completely uninteresting from a legal perspective. She's a good citizen.

Second, Gus Hoover. He also doesn't have much, some traffics, a drunk and disorderly from decades ago. Doing the math on his birth date would put him around college age then. Who hasn't had one of those? I mean, besides me? The home I visited was indeed his and now I've got his true work address. He still seems to be employed as a financial guy so that's a likely explanation why he wasn't home. The location is in Racine, twenty minutes to the north.

I set aside his pages. I'll pay him a visit at work, if only to check off the box and clear him.

Lastly, Highland. The majority of fax pages are his and I feel a growing sense of satisfaction that my suspicions are gaining steam. The charges leveled against him across the years are wide and varied.

Disorderly conduct. Trespassing.

Assault. Assault and battery.
Resisting arrest. Brandishing a firearm.
Harassment. DUI.

Holy Christ, this guy is a walking jacket. Four decades of arrests, again and again, often for the same or similar crime. He doesn't learn. None of the charges are for homicide but that doesn't put me off. There's a small gap between assault and murder. It's easy to imagine someone running as hot as Highland could cross that threshold if the stakes are high enough.

Like a family member done wrong by the justice system and a year to mull over it.

I pull out the most recent arrest complaint. It's from March. March 3, 2000, in fact. Midnight at a local bar called One Night Stan's. What a great name.

Highland began arguing with another patron Glenn Scott, which escalated to shouting and eventually physical fighting. No witnesses reported knowing what the argument was about, just that the two guys knew each other, and both were inebriated. Highland ended up being hauled downtown to dry out. There's nothing unusual in the report, happens every night across the country.

It's what follows that grabs my attention.

Two nights later. Cops responded to a possible home invasion call. Highland, banging on the front door of Scott's house, demanding to talk. Scott wasn't home but his wife freaked out – rightfully so – and called 911. He's still there when they show, sitting on the steps like a sulking child, anger spent but belligerent drunk. Highland allows them to search his car and in doing so, they discover duct tape, plastic bags, and a metal pipe in his trunk. He was charged with intent to do bodily harm, the theory being that he'd planned to kidnap and torture his former friend as an extension of their fight. The DA was eventually forced to dismiss charges as Scott proved to be an uncooperative victim, meaning he simply never responded to anything.

The DA may not have been able to link intent and motive, but I've got a much lower burden of proof.

It's staring me right in the face,

easier to see when I spread the flimsy fax papers across the table and order them in chronological sequence. This is one of the hardest things to do when embroiled in the mundane day-to-day routine. Gaining perspective across months and years is invaluable, creating a portrait that isn't obvious standing up close.

With Highland there's a pattern, a direct cause and effect. Some inciting action kicks it off, like heated disagreements or fights, followed by a time of inaction. Then, out of nowhere, an act of retribution, some kind of violence enacted as a result.

It's like he stews over the grievance, letting it build in his mind until he's forced to relieve the pressure. If you apologize immediately, he moves on. But refuse to apologize and at some point he will come for you. Jeffrey Highland is a man who cannot let go of a grudge, nurturing it deep within his soul until action is the only course to absolution.

My blood stirs, vindication bubbling up. Fuck Warren and all his grousing, there's no way he would ever have knit all this together into a story. He'd probably just kick it down to a squad and send them around asking pointless questions.

Gather all your facts, Griff once said, then step back and let the case form on its own. That's what I've done. I developed a set of potential suspects and supported their classification with their own history.

Just like he would have handled it.

Grabbing up my stack of faxes, I head out of the library. It's nearing 4:30. If I time it right, I'll catch Hoover leaving his office for the day. A few questions are required to clear him from my list, to get satisfactory answers and cross off his name. Despite my certainty over Highland, I'm still careful to ensure my diligence has been completed.

17

WEDNESDAY JUNE 2, 1999, 11:58AM – DAY 15

"Folks, trusted jurors, my friends," Jambliss said with a syrupy tone.

Nicole and Justyna simultaneously groaned at the pandering.

"For weeks now I've presented forensic evidence and computer evidence and personal testimony. I've brought before you witnesses who knew the deceased or who had a role in the investigation, and showed that Mark cruelly murdered his wife. The order of this is specific and deliberate, strategically designed."

He looked around with a dramatic flair. "I now have one last witness, the ultimate testimony. A final nail in the coffin if you will. This evidence will prove beyond a reasonable doubt that the defendant did as the State has charged."

A pronounced pause, Jambliss surveying the assembled court, before announcing: "We're going to hear from Julie herself."

A collective gasp rolled through the jury box and gallery alike.

Jambliss glanced at the clock. "After lunch, your Honor?"

"Plot twist," Charles announced as the jury room door closed behind them all.

"What a dick tease," Danny said. "Drop a bomb like that and then send us off to lunch? My PB&J can't measure up to that."

Bryan laughed and held up his ham sandwich. A lettuce chunk dropped out.

Shelli, laying out her Tupperware containers in a precise half circle, also laughed.

"You know right now reporters are rushing to write up something, be the first,"

Terry noted as he cracked open a small cooler at his feet and pulled out soup. "He planned the timing purposely for show."

No one disagreed. They'd come to understand the trial was one half evidence, the other half publicity.

"If he trots out a puppet made to look like Julie and goes into a ventriloquist act, I'm going to lose it," Nicole said with a sarcastic laugh.

Sadly, the following laughs were only partially sincere. Every juror had come to recognize the lengths to which Jambliss would go for a conviction. Chuckie held up his right hand to mimic a puppet and began chirping in a female voice. "Hey everyone! My husband fed me antifreeze and then shoved my head into a pillow. Wish you were here. Write back!"

This time the laughs were mixed with gasps at the morbidity and several in the room shook their head. Jean smacked him on the arm and did not look amused.

When they returned to the courtroom, anticipation hung in the air like storm clouds, a sensation thick and tangible. The door repeatedly banged as people entered to bear witness. Reporters who'd been tipped, photographers in tow. Court watchers who'd heard rumors. Courthouse employees curious about what Jambliss had up his sleeve.

These groups and more crowded the gallery, packing into open seats, raising the level of stuffiness.

As the jury filed into the room, they too felt the weight of expectation. "Jambliss better deliver," Travis declared from his last spot in line.

Millick brought the court to order. "I hope everyone had a good lunch. If not, blame Mr. Jambliss. That was a bit of dirty pool to leave you all hanging like that." Laughter tittered through the crowd, dying quickly.

"I promise, it will be worth the wait." Jambliss got to his feet and faced the jurors. "I've been practicing law for decades, always from the side of prosecution. Sometimes we're given irrefutable evidence, the proverbial 'smoking gun.' Other times, often, the evidence is circumstantial.

Everything you've heard thus far in this case fits into that category. Witnesses telling us what Mark said, experts showing forensic evidence, that sort of thing. Never have I, in my years of law, had something like this. The victim is dead, long gone from this world, but she can still testify."

He nodded at the court clerk and then to the TV monitor on the wall. "Folks, I give you Julie's last words." The screen flared to life, displaying a photo of an unlined piece of paper, standard size found in home and office printers. Handwriting filled the page, level and evenly spaced, female in nature.

"From the grave, Julie has sent us a letter identifying Mark as her killer."

Silence dropped thunderously in the court as every set of eyes stared at the monitor.

'I took this picture & am writing this on Saturday 11-21-98 at 7AM. This "list" was in my husband's business daily planner - not meant for me to see, I don't know what it means, but if anything happens to me, he would be my first suspect. Our relationship has deteriorated to the

polite superficial. I know he's never forgiven me for the brief affair I had with that creep seven years ago. Mark lives for work & the kids; he's an avid surfer of the Internet...'

'Anyway - I do not smoke or drink. My mother was an alcoholic, so I limit my drinking to one or two a week. Mark wants me to drink more - with him in the evenings. I don't. I would never take my life because of my kids - they are everything to me! I regularly take Tylenol & multi-vitamins; occasionally take OTC stuff for colds, Zantac, or Immodium; have one prescription for migraine tablets, which Mark uses more than I. I pray I'm wrong & nothing happens... but I am suspicious of Mark's suspicious behaviors & fear for my early demise.'

The jurors traded glances amongst each other. Kay ignored them, focusing instead on Mark Johannsen. He shifted his beady stare from the monitor to the jury box, scanning along both rows, presumably trying to read their reactions. When he landed on Kay, she shook her head.

The lawyers likewise appraised the

sixteen sets of faces, gauging impact. For Jambliss a sly smile crossed his face, secure in the assumption that this was a gut-punch to the defense's case. Attorney Cruise and her cohort maintained neutral expressions, unwilling to let any sign of concern appear. To do so would only validate Jambliss' tactic.

After several moments pregnant with expectation, the DA stood and adjusted his jacket, taking up position beside the prosecution's table. "Interesting, isn't it?" he asked in a disingenuous tone. "Julie knew what was happening to her. She suspected it. Right there, the last lines. She knew and wanted to point law enforcement in the right direction if what she feared most were to come true."

He cleared his throat and stepped closer. "Mark's intentions toward her were so blatantly obvious that Julie felt compelled to write this 'letter from the grave' and give it to a friend just days before her death. I'll be honest, I don't know what's more damning: The words in the letter or the act of writing it. She knew what was about to happen and wanted to make sure everyone else eventually did too."

"Objection, your Honor," Cruise stated, but her voice lacked the usual stridency, as if revealing a defeated emotion. "Speculation towards the intent of a witness who cannot testify."

"Sustained," Millick agreed. "Mr. Jambliss, move it along. Who are you calling to the stand?"

He smiled. "I will start with the person who received it straight from Julie herself."

Maggie Volk was called. A neighbor and friend, she was the first salvo in Jambliss' legal bombing raid. "On Saturday, November 21, did you receive an envelope from Julie Johannsen?"

Maggie appeared similar in age to Julie, with a nervous demeanor. Her eyes flicked rapidly from Jambliss, to jury, to the gallery, to the sheriff's deputies standing guard in the back. "Yes, she handed it to me."

"Please tell us what instructions she gave you."

"I was to call the police and give this

envelope to Detective Richardson if something happened to Julie." Her voice quivered slightly, betraying her emotions.

"And as we all know, something most unfortunate happened. But did Julie give you any hint what the envelope contained? Did she say why you had to call the police?"

Maggie shook her head. "She was scattered in her thoughts, tripping over words. Not like she was talking too quickly, but like she was in shock and unsure. I asked several times what it was. She just kept saying to make sure the police got it."

"Did this happen often with her? I mean, secret letters or other mysterious requests?"

Maggie blinked several times, clearly confused by the seemingly obvious answer. "No. Never."

Jambliss spent another hour picking at details. Was the envelope sealed? Was there writing on the outside? When did she find out about Julie's death and then when did she call the police? Who received the envelope? Maggie patiently answered each question, clearly and succinctly.

When it came time for cross, Cruise had a little more buoyancy in her step, as if the testimony was less damning than expected.

"Mrs. Volk," she began with a thin smile. "Did you see Julie write the letter?"

"No, I did not."

"So, no verification she penned it? No notary-level of signature?"

"Um, no and no."

Cruise nodded. "Would you agree that the only factual evidence is that Julie handed you an envelope with something inside but would not tell you what it was? You never saw the actual letter."

Maggie looked around with an expression that showed she thought it was a trick question. "I guess?"

"It's a yes or no. Please answer it as such."

"Then, yes."

THURSDAY, JUNE 10, 1999, 4:49PM – DAY 21

"I'm never handwriting anything again," Jean groused. "How many days now have we been talking about that letter?"

Courtney glanced at one of her notepads. "Today is day seven. Nine witnesses, fifty-one objections…"

"Okay, okay. I withdraw the question."

"At this point," Charles said with his usual sense of timing. "I have written my own letter and will provide all of you copies. In the event I expire in the jury box, of course."

Travis and Margaret laughed in unison. Kay smiled and shook her head. She looked around the table to see who else heard the joke.

"I mean," Nicole said. "We can all read it ourselves. The defense is acting like someone else could have written it but that makes no sense."

"No," Kay replied. "Let's play Devil's Advocate. What proof do we have Julie wrote it?"

Nicole threw up her hands. "Why why why would anyone else have? How fucking stupid to think that."

"Not as stupid as thinking absence of proof is the same thing."

The rest of the table quieted over this exchange. Shelli shrugged. "When all other explanations have been ruled out, the most obvious one is usually correct."

A few grunts of agreement rolled around the room. Terry, sitting next to Nicole, also shrugged but with a different intent. "That's the problem. I don't know that all other explanations have been ruled out. I've got some doubts."

Further discussion was abruptly cut off by the door opening. The other bailiff Joe stuck his head in. "All clear, guys. Have a good night, see you tomorrow morning."

The sounds of bags closing, chairs being pushed into the table and the shuffle of muttered goodbyes filled the room. Kay moved slowly, cleaning up the candy wrappers littering her spot.

Nicole continued to mutter under her breath, failing to hide her annoyance at the conversation. When Terry wished her a good night, she simply shook her head.

Several minutes after everyone else departed, Joe walked back in. Surprise showed on his face. "Oh. Thought you guys were all gone."

Kay turned from staring out the window across the courthouse entrance and shook her head. "Sorry, I'm going. Long week."

"Long trial," he countered with a smile. "Can't imagine what it's like for you. At least everyone seems like friends."

Kay slung her purse strap over one shoulder. "We argue like siblings," she replied. "It's an eye-opening experience. I think we'll carry the trial with us for a long time. When you find out about things like this, it changes your worldview. What husbands can do to their wives…"

She trailed off and slipped past him to the door, leaving the thought hanging. "Good night, Joe," she said as she departed.

18

WEDNESDAY, JUNE 16, 1999, 11:38AM – DAY 25

"Members of the jury," Robert Jambliss said in a somber tone, overacting and theatrical. "You've spent all morning listening to the State's closing argument. You are to judge this case on evidence, not opinions or subjective bias and we've spent the last month providing conclusive evidence to be used in your deliberations. You've seen emails between the defendant and Kelly Gorman, his extramarital lover, planning a life together when Julie was no longer in the picture. Mark hated her, he seethed over the brief dalliance she immediately regretted, and he never accepted any attempts to amend their marriage. On the night of her death, Detective Richardson testified to the emotionless response from Mark, as if nothing traumatic had just happened. We heard from a neighbor who witnessed Mark give his father a high-five in the driveway that night, as if he'd achieved some significant victory. What kind of person, with the mother of his children dead inside, has a reason to celebrate anything? We showed via emails that Julie was no more than a footnote in his plans, a minor hurdle he needed to eliminate *by his own words*. We showed how even the police believed he was the source of continual harassment."

He cleared his throat, pausing for effect. "Julie was a smart person, but her husband deceived and manipulated her. For most couples this ends in divorce, an unfortunate event, but something that allows both people to rebuild their lives. Not with Mark, however. He could not stand the thought of her starting over with someone else, possibly finding happiness. Those were his plans. He signed off his emails to Kelly with IDLY, meaning 'I do love you', but he could not allow Julie to ever sign off IDLY with someone else."

"Oooh," Travis murmured. "Burn."

"I'll state it again, with emphasis: We have provided you with irrefutable evidence of Mark's actions. The defense will come up here and tell you that Julie was depressed. That guilt over her affair, despite being years ago, ate away at her until she had no other choice but suicide. Let's think about that. To accept such a proposal means you must believe Julie spent years contemplating it, and then when the day finally came to take her own life, she chose ethylene glycol, undctcctable in the normal autopsy process. She ingested an amount large enough to kill but then also decided to suffocate herself with a pillow. Does any of that make sense? It doesn't to me but here's what is most important for the defense: Where's the evidence? She briefly saw a psychiatrist in the aftermath of her affair but stopped within months. If she remained suicidal all those years in between, where can we hear testimony from a friend who heard Julie say she wanted to end it all? Surely she would have confided in someone. Where can we see an empty glass with residue and her fingerprints all over it? If she truly intended to commit suicide, where's the note?"

Jambliss looked down at his notes and took a breath. "Did you know for every suicide there are on average three previous incidents of self-harm? Eight emergency room visits? These are national statistics gathered over years of research and are viewed as reliable. What signs did Julie display? Where were her warning signs? Nowhere. Zero. Zilch. What she did was document her concerns about Mark in a letter. Somewhere deep in her heart she suspected her husband wanted her dead and made sure she could indict him from the grave. Does any of this portray the picture of someone ready to commit suicide?"

He glanced at the clock. "The defense cannot rebut any of the State's charges nor produce evidence to refute them. Because it simply does not exist. Julie Johannsen did not kill herself. She was manipulated, emotionally tortured and eventually murdered by her husband. Those are the facts and you know he's guilty.

Thank you."

Lunch was unusually solemn. No one left the building to eat elsewhere. Even Margaret and Charles forestalled their noon walk. It was as if each juror weighed the State's argument and now considered how the defense planned to counter.

Attorney Cruise would present her closing statements after lunch, followed by a round or two of rebuttal statements and arguments. But those statements were posturing, lawyers notching points on their imaginary scoreboard. Everything needing to be said will have been said by then.

The jurors knew they soon would be locked away in their room, debating the fate of a man who'd spent the last seven weeks staring at them. The scales of justice would need to be balanced by each person according to their own beliefs and understanding. Despite the seemingly overwhelming evidence against Johannsen, nothing was ever certain.

"Anyone else not hungry?" Shelli said, ending the silence.

"I so want this to be done," Jean answered. "But the hardest part is yet to come. It feels like forever since we first walked into this room. I don't think I can even remember the first witness." She pointed to Courtney. "And I don't need to know."

Courtney paused in the act of opening her first notepad. She looked around the room at every set of eyes focused on her. "Oh okay, sorry."

Laughter relieved some of the tension.

"Does anyone know how it works?" Lian suddenly said. Bryan jumped at the voice coming from behind him. All throughout the trial she'd sat silently, content to remain in the background and observe other interactions. "I mean, do we get instructions on how to pick a foreman or come up with a verdict or anything?"

"I swear I forgot you were there," he blurted.

Another smatter of laughs as looks were exchanged around the table, shrugs and headshakes.

"No one's ever done jury duty

before?" Dennis asked, sounding perplexed that it wasn't ever brought up.

"Never made it past round one," Chuckie replied. He flexed. "They were all in awe of my manliness and thought I'd be a distraction."

"I got picked for a DUI case once," Terry announced. "But the guy quickly plead guilty, so we were dismissed before day two."

Nicole pointed to Courtney. "Question 1: How the hell do we do this? Write that down."

"Question 2," Justyna added. "Where's drinks afterwards?"

The gallery was packed once again. Throughout the previous weeks there were always reporters and photographers, with varying degrees of attendance and interest. Some days only one or two were present. Other days, like there was some underground network of information cluing them in, reporters swarmed the rows. Closing arguments in a trial of this magnitude drew in observers, professional and casual, like moths to a flame.

They all knew history was being written with each word.

Kay felt the closeness of the room, warm bodies jammed up against each other, everyone breathing, the heat of expectation. Millick had ordered the windows closed for arguments as if concerned that someone lurking just outside the first-floor room could eavesdrop. Nicole used her notepad as a fan.

"Members of the jury," Cruise began. "You heard DA Jambliss tout the mountain of evidence he believes is enough to win him this case, and make no mistake, it *is* all about winning for him, not justice. You heard him say it's inconceivable to ignore common sense and consider that Julie Johannsen could have taken her own life. What he did not tell you is that people are complex, more than a collection of documents to explain their thoughts and emotions. They do things that are not always logical or understandable from the outside."

"He did not tell you this case is about humans, flawed humans as we all are, but I will."

"Curve ball," Danny breathed.

Cruise moved to the lectern. She took her time flipping through loose pages, letting anticipation build while camera shutters clicked away. Her face was placid and neutral as she looked up, making eye contact with each juror. "We can acknowledge the mistake of infidelity in both Mark and Julie. That is not what's in dispute here. An affair can arise from and lead to a vast number of circumstances. Julie admitted to cheating on Mark back in 1991. She admitted to regret. She tried to get them both into marriage counseling. Those are actions that can be viewed as apologies for violating the sanctity of their vows. Mark accepted her apology. He did not initiate divorce proceedings and he participated in counseling sessions."

Another pause. "He also paid for Julie to see a mental health professional for depression. They both recognized she was struggling, and he provided support. If he was this scorned husband intent only on tormenting his wife, why do that? He could have simply let her problems persist. Why live with the affair for years and then suddenly decide it's time to start the torture? Perhaps because it was never him in the first place. Much has been made of the penis pictures, an obsession I personally don't understand, but it's not a crime to collect images. You heard Detective Richardson attest to his belief Mark was behind them being sent as a form of harassment. He told Julie the same, yet she never corroborated it. In her own house, which she occupied day after day, she never witnessed her husband planting pictures. Further, she never took any action. She never left, even for a trial separation. If someone knows their loved one is harassing them emotionally, why stay? Are we supposed to accept she somehow was okay with it? Does that fit with the common-sense decision Mr. Jambliss wants you to weigh so heavily? Is it perhaps she never believed Mark did it? That she, herself, never found any of her own evidence to support Richardson's claim?"

Objections were frowned upon during closing arguments and because of this Jambliss looked ready to pop. If Cruise made a blatant misstatement or fabricated testimony he'd be within court rules to object but she didn't, leaving him simmering with counter arguments. His face reddened and he shook his head repeatedly. How much of this was for show and how much was true disagreement was anyone's guess. At least one camera clicked in the gallery with each shake.

"This is a tale of two people unable to see their way through marital issues. In Mark's case, it's a tale of being unable to see the depth of pain Julie endured. Suicide is one of the leading causes of death in our country and less than thirty percent of victims show signs or leave notes. It is not marked by consistent actions, there is no template to follow when assessing someone as a risk. Let's talk about the actual suicide itself. Julie died from ethylene glycol ingestion, a sweet-tasting liquid that does not need to be consumed in large quantities. Why do it that way? Why not hanging or gunshot or jumping off a bridge? Again, I will refer to the theme of suicidal people: They are not predictable. They are not brave. They may be afraid of the terror that comes from jumping or drowning. They may worry what their loved ones will see after the trigger is pulled. Overdoses are common because it's viewed as a gentler descent. Perhaps it's how Julie wanted to go, with a few drinks, some drowsiness, and then an endless sleep. The State pushed the theory that Mark – after supplying her with ethylene glycol – shoved her head into the pillow to speed along the process with suffocation. Their theory was propped up by little more than conjecture. None of the forensic experts, people who've seen numerous deaths, confirmed the theory. There was only circumstantial evidence that it *could* have happened. Here's what also could have happened: Julie drank her last drink. She cleaned out her glass so no one else would have to. Maybe she tidied things up a bit while waiting for the effects to hit. And then when they did, she went to the bedroom because she wanted to be found in a natural pose. And perhaps with that action and unlucky timing she fell face first into her pillow. Does that scenario fit the State's common-sense criteria?"

She paused and observed the jury,

letting the imagery of her words descend upon them.

Several jurors exchanged glances, a move that did not go unnoticed by Jambliss. Even Millick looked over.

Cruise spent another hour countering the State's numerous arguments. True to her initial claim, she focused on the human element of it all, introducing possible reasons why things happened the way they did and backing up each with an example everyone could relate to. She provided food for thought, introduced doubt over Jambliss' certainty and in general weakened her opponent's case.

Though she may not have been likable throughout the trial, there was no doubt she was effective. Attorney Cruise didn't need to sway everyone, just one. If a single juror voted differently, Mark Johannsen would walk as a free man.

"Folks," Millick started when the

jury returned from the afternoon break. "The duties of counsel and court have been performed. The case has been argued and you have been instructed by a court of law on the rules that govern you in your deliberations. The time has now come when a fair and conscientious decision of this case is to be thrown wholly upon you, the jurors. Do not be swayed by sympathy, prejudice or passion. I charge you to keep your duties steadfastly in mind as upright citizens to render a just and true verdict. The following two forms of verdict will be submitted to you for your consideration:

- We, the jury, find the defendant Mark Johannsen guilty of intentional homicide in the first degree, or,
- We, the jury, find the defendant Mark Johannsen not guilty of intentional homicide in the first degree."

The silence in the courtroom was oppressive, a palpable thing pressing down. The enormity of their task came towards the jurors like a ponderous wave, propelled by Millick's officious directive. Gone were the side glances and murmured asides, the inside comments on Cruise's expressions or Jambliss' behavior. No matter their personal opinion, each juror wanted to do it right.

"This is a criminal, not a civil case," he continued. "Therefore, the verdict must be reached unanimously. All twelve jurors must agree in order to arrive at a verdict. When you retire to the jury room, select one of your members to preside over your deliberations. The presiding juror's vote is entitled to no greater weight than any other juror's. When you have agreed upon your verdict, have it signed and dated by the person selected as your presiding juror. At this time, the bailiffs will escort you to the jury room where you may begin your deliberations."

Back in the jury room Courtney looked down at her notepad then back up to everyone. "What the shit, guys." She flicked a finger at question number one. "There's your answer. We don't know anything more about how to do this than we did two hours ago."

The room had shrunk by four. Danny, Bryan, Justyna and Rick were selected as alternate jurors, segregated to another room. Only if one of the remaining twelve was unable to complete his or her duties would an alternate be called. If that didn't occur, their duty in this case was fulfilled.

"Imagine," Travis said. "Sitting here for weeks listening to all the testimony and paying attention but then not being allowed to deliberate on a verdict. That would suck."

Several grunted in agreement but there were no follow-up comments. The room grew heavy with expectation for the first step: Selecting the foreman. It was an awkward moment, burdened by conflicting thoughts between those who wanted nothing to do with the responsibility, and those who did but wanted to avoid nominating themselves.

"Well," Nicole announced. "If no one else wants to, I can be foreman. Forewoman, whatever."

Dennis and Chuckie looked over to

Travis, who raised his hands in surrender. "I can't because of Aaron Daball. There's a conflict of interest."

A few more glances were scattered throughout the room but there were no other volunteers. "I guess congrats are in order," Terry said. "Where do you want to start?"

Jean spoke first. "We should take a vote before anything else, get an idea where we stand as a group."

"Good idea," Margaret said. She started passing around a Post-It pad. "Write your verdict and fold it up."

Shelli emptied out a small wicker basket holding plasticware. "Put them all in here."

Within a minute the votes were cast and Shelli handed the basket to Nicole.

"Moment of truth," Charles noted.

Anticipation rose within the silence as Nicole unfolded each vote and read it before placing the paper upside down on the table. Soft crinkling filled the room, amplified by the weight of their judgment.

When finished, she looked around the table. "Eight guilty, four not."

There was no immediate response, just glances around the table. Perhaps shock that the vote was not unanimous.

It appeared evident that the Breakfast Jury was not of a single mind.

"Well," Chuckie announced. "Here we go."

19

WEDNESDAY, JUNE 14, 2000, 4:54PM

Racine sits directly north of Kenosha, a sister town squatting on Lake Michigan's shoreline. The downtown portion looks much the same, except fifty percent more run down. Some of the neighborhoods I pass through are sketchy as hell, to the point I glance over at my passenger door to verify it's locked. Funny how two nearly identical towns just a few miles apart can be so different.

Near the lakefront things start to brighten. The graffiti disappears, young males no longer loiter on street corners, eyeballing me as I wait for a stoplight; commercial buildings start looking refreshed and clean. Signs of renovation are everywhere, in construction fencing, dump trucks blocking lanes, the warning chimes of industrial machines in reverse.

I find the offices of Stifel-Nicolaus overlooking Racine's primary marina, a three-story structure with massive glass panes that bounce back streaks of afternoon sun. It's blasted hot and sweat tunnels down my spine as I walk from my car across the asphalt. A wash of cool air greets me in the lobby and I linger more than necessary reading the directory, letting my body cool down. The Stifel offices are on the top floor, sharing space with an accounting firm.

A young receptionist makes eye contact with a smile as I enter. "Who are you here to see?" She asks, efficient. An appointment book lies open on the desk before here. There are no entries for this late in the day.

It's a small cluster, four glass-walled offices along the back wall, a half dozen cubicles in front of them like sentries.

I spot Hoover in his office, recognized from trial photos. "Him," I reply to the receptionist and stride around her desk. She huffs in exasperation but makes no move to stop me.

Hoover's brow lifts in confusion as I open his door. He half rises from his chair. "Can I help you?"

I wait until his door swishes fully closed and stop across the desk from him. "Mr. Hoover, I need a moment of your time. My name is Aramis White."

The uncertainty fades a little as he jumps to an incorrect conclusion. "Oh yes, absolutely, but it's the end of my day. I'd ask you to make an appoint…"

"It's about the Johannsen trial."

Color rushes his cheeks, clapping shut his mouth. He slams back down in his chair. "Jesus. What now?" He growls.

"The jury gathered last Friday on the one-year anniversary and it appears there were attempts to harm them as a group."

"Let me guess, antifreeze?" He laughs sarcastically but when I simply meet his eyes the expression drops. "What, really?"

I remain a bit longer, waiting for the

dots to connect.

"Oh. Christ." His face flushes even deeper. "You're serious. Someone went after those people? Oh, no. No. And you think I had something to do with it."

"There seems to be strong indications of someone seeking vengeance, which is motive. It then follows that someone would have a vested interest." I glance casually out the window behind him, seeing the vast blue water of a Great Lake. "You testified on Mark's behalf, correct?"

He licks his lips. "No, I mean yes. But you know what I really did?"

"Tell me."

"I screwed over my life because I was gullible. He begged me for an alibi. We'd been friends for a few years, I couldn't bring myself to see him as a murderer. Seriously, we'd hung out multiple times. No one wants to believe they've been friends with a person capable of killing. So, I believed his story about Julie's depression and how it looked from the outside. Then I went up there and gave a story he helped me develop."

"You were one of the early

witnesses, correct?"

"Yeah, in the second week. And that was the problem. Everyone who came after me contradicted my statements, and it was obvious I lied. I knew then I was in trouble."

"Then you didn't believe Mark was truly innocent?"

"Hell no! Did you see the mountain of evidence? How could any jury find him innocent? Clearly, I messed up." He leans forward and braces crossed arms on the desk, head shaking in slow movements. "I'm never going to be free of this, am I?"

"Perjury will do that to you."

"It wasn't perjury, just an obviously false recollection of events. I got discredited in a very public trial. No charges were brought, and I thought that would be it. But no. Stifel isn't that big of a company. Gossip travels and within a week everyone had heard. You know how it looks now when I attend conferences? The looks when I cross paths with executives who also knew Mark? I'm the guy who used extremely poor judgment to defend a murderer, not enough to be fired but more than enough to be punished. Many of our clients are based in the Midwest. I lost all of mine, the bosses reassigned them to someone else with less baggage. Now I'm stuck with pissy little coastal accounts that pay half what I used to make. So, yeah, I fucked over my life. My fault, I accept that. But I never wanted revenge against the jury. I don't even know who they are."

Bitterness rings clear in his tone. The guy's either telling the truth or an excellent actor. I don't pick at the scab. Like Kelly Gorman, he's been burned by association with Johannsen, regretting past decisions and struggling to deal with the consequences. If anything, his anger is directed at his former friend, not twelve faceless people.

"I believe you, Mr. Hoover. The trial did damage to a lot of people. This visit is just me clearing the decks of potential suspects and witnesses. One last question: Where were you Friday night?"

He spins away to look out the window and grunts. "Client dinner, down at the Hob Knob in Kenosha. See my secretary on your way out, she'll get you a copy of the tab and guest names. I'd ask that you contact none of them, they have nothing to do with this. Now please, go."

THURSDAY, JUNE 15, 2000, 9:18AM

I'm early to Sunnyside, before they officially open. Leonard has a few more questions coming his way.

He looks the same as the other day, groggy, unkempt. If I didn't know he kept an apartment upstairs, I'd assume he sleeps in his car. The look he gives is vacant, absent of any recognition. It's only been three days since we last spoke. "Help you?" He drags a wet towel across the bar top.

I don't bother reintroducing myself and hold up one of Highland's most recent mug shots. Warren had provided a variety spanning the years. There were plenty to choose from. "Last Friday evening, did you see this man in here?"

Leonard tucks long hair behind his ear and leans forward. His reddened eyes flick from the portrait to me and back.

"Yeah, yeah. I seen him Friday. He comes around every now and then. James, Jeff, something J. I'm not sure."

Vibrations rill down my spine, the sensation of rightness filling me. He'd been here, present at the same time as the jurors.

I point to the far corner. "Nicole Wright was there with her friends. Did you ever see him interact with any of them? Passing by on his way to the bathroom, conversing, anything?"

Leonard grunts. "Not that I saw, but I got a job to do. Lots of people. I just remember him sitting over there." He motions to the far end of the bar. It was a direct line of sight to the juror's table. Highland could sit at his spot and easily keep everyone in view.

"How long was he around? He say anything to you?"

The bartender shrugs as he examines liquor bottles by lifting them up against the light, occasionally writing on a scrap of paper, making a supply list. He's avoiding eye contact, unnerved by my questions probably. "Most of the night. Nothing specific I remember, bitching about something probably. One of those guys."

If 'those guys' means someone willing to kill in return for a verdict, then yeah.

"Anything about Nicole and her friends?"

Another shrug. "He did ask what they were doing, as if I'd know." He sets down the last bottle along the rail. "Hey, you need anything? Bloody Mary? Screwdriver?"

As I shake my head he turns away. "Okay, I got stuff to do." He shuffles towards the back room, paper clutched in his fingers.

With the bar empty, I move to Highland's spot and slowly spin, envisioning this place packed with people on a Friday evening. They're milling and laughing and drinking. He's sitting here, stewing in the juice of vengeance. Bathrooms are beyond the jury's table, down a short hallway, and it creates a natural choke point. Put a dozen people trying to pass in both directions and it wouldn't be hard for someone to sneak an arm through the press, pouring antifreeze into drinks. Would the color even be noticed?

A few passes like that, just some random guy making trips to the bathroom, unnoticed or ignored, and suddenly you've got high concentrations of ethylene glycol being consumed. Did he target Nicole specifically? Or just any juror and she happened to drink the most?

The smile refuses to diminish on my face as I mentally walk through the scene again and again, like an invisible time traveler watching events play out to my content. I've established a motive. Now I've got opportunity as well.

Time to transition from talking to doing.

Surveillance is about a few key elements, chiefly patience and a strong bladder. The objective is to build a profile of actions, creating a verifiable narrative to support your evidence, thus resulting in legal charges. Usually, you begin surveilling only after there's enough data points to make it worthwhile. You don't surveil as a filtering mechanism, simply because manpower is precious. No department can afford to send out multiple squads to watch people and determine whether they should be a suspect.

In my case, there's an ideal ratio: One man, one suspect. The data points are quantifiable in my view.

Highland's road is a long dead-end with one entrance and ditches that fall away from crumbling asphalt. There's no yellow stripe, drivers take the middle unless there's another car. This level of isolation is peaceful but also strips me of anonymity. I stand out as a strange car to the residents, easily noticed. In Chicago cars sit along the curb at all hours, indistinguishable amongst each other. There it's easy to tuck your car a block away and slouch down. No one pays attention.

Here I'm forced to be more creative.

I find a gravel driveway one hundred yards beyond Highland's place, tucked between two stout trees. A chain stretches across weed-stricken path, hung with a *No Trespassing* sign several car lengths back from the road's edge.

Backing in, I have enough of an angle to see his driveway. Unless he decides to depart on foot through his rear property, I've got him coming and going. The house itself is set too far back for a direct line of sight from my position but I can hear the frantic barking of the dog out back. It makes me think he's outside. Moments later my guess is confirmed as morning stillness is shredded by a chainsaw ripping to life, followed shortly by the wail of metal teeth chewing wood.

Forty-two minutes into my stakeout Warren calls.

"Tell me you have results," I demand, bypassing greetings.

He pauses. "Where are you? Sounds like a sawmill."

I turn my head and roll up the car window. "Is the autopsy done?"

"Not yet. Richardson called and said it's scheduled for this afternoon. I've burned just about every favor getting it fast tracked so you better be on target."

"Actually, I'm over the target as we speak."

"What the hell does that mean?"

"It was Highland after all. I've got eyes on the guy. He profiles out, I built his timeline from Friday and there are witness statements putting him on the scene."

Warren starts sputtering. "Wait, what? You're surveilling? Motherfu – Christ, I'm getting fired. Listen to me, White. Get your ass away from wherever you are. Now."

I ignore him. "When that examiner report comes back positive for ethylene glycol, because it will, I'll have a nice package for you guys. There will be enough to set a warrant and probably wrap it all up by next week. Trust me."

"Oh God. Godgodgod…" Warren chants. His voice recedes, like he's holding the phone away from his mouth and I imagine him slowly banging his head against the desk surface. This is his every nightmare coming to life across the phone line. "So fucked," he mutters on repeat.

I leverage his natural fear of responsibility to manipulate the moment. "Tell you what, why don't you set a meet for later today and I can walk you through everything I have so far. Maybe that will help stage it up for Richardson." It's dirty on my part because I know Warren will grasp at my offer as a way for him to unload the problem. That's fine. I want to get this officially opened as a case. If preying on his primary weakness does it, I'll provide an escape hatch.

He'll think I'm doing his work. We're using each other.

I want Richardson to see what I've done and nod in affirmation. I want it recognized I still have my detective chops. I'm never getting my badge back, I know that, but chipping away at my reputation as an uncontrollable wild card matters to me and always will. Maybe one day someone will say it aloud: *Aramis White was damned good before he was damned.*

Warren's still mumbling to himself when I close the sale. "See you in a few hours."

Out of sight the chainsaw continues to carve wood and the dog continues to bark for attention.

Sometime after lunch, long after the chainsaw ceased howling, I spot a set of Ford truck taillights flare through the tree branches. The sound of an engine coughing to life lifts up in the quiet air. Within seconds Highland backs out of his driveway and heads away from my position.

I've mentally rehearsed this part of the play. There wasn't much else to do while he worked in the backyard.

I wait until his truck disappears around a slow bend in the road. Then I pull out and let my car idle along, keeping space between us. Because it's a dead-end road with few houses, I assume he'd notice my car if he saw it. He struck me as the paranoid type, driving with one eye on the rearview mirror. Staying out of sight is my best bet.

I come into view in time to see him accelerating away on a busy county road. With the additional traffic there's more ways to hide and I'm able to keep him in sight as we drive.

We head south until Highway 50 appears, onto which he turns west. I get the impression of someone driving hesitantly, uncertain of his route. This is backed up by more than one instance of his turn signal coming on, then off, and a surge of acceleration as he bypasses a crossroad. I don't think he's trying to lose me, I'm not that close and the driving behavior is different. There's an image in my mind of him driving with scribbled directions on a slip of paper gripped to his steering wheel.

After a few minutes we turn south once again, onto Highway O. It feels like we're nearly to the Illinois border by now. He winds through a town called Twin Lakes. I see water off to one side of the road and take a wild guess there's another lake nearby, maybe a twin even.

Eventually we wind up on a narrow lane freshly stripped of mature trees to both sides. Houses are spattered along the road, bare lots providing no cover. I'm now also exposed, easily visible, so I drop back further until his truck is a blur. Thankfully the road is arrow straight and I can see him.

Movement in my rearview mirror shows a car pulling into a driveway but otherwise there's no one else here. I need to be careful.

Brake lights flare as Highland reaches a four-way stop. The Ford idles through the intersection and pulls over at the first house. Two hundred yards back, I match the move and then we're both sitting on the side of this empty lane.

What is he doing?

After a few seconds he accelerates away, tires chirping for traction on the warm asphalt. There's no way I can mimic his departure without it being obvious, I'm forced to move at a more sedate pace. His truck disappears beyond a dip in the road. By the time I hit the four-way stop he's nowhere to be seen as the road curves away past the dip.

He'd paused at the first house past the intersection, a neatly tended Cape Cod design. Hosta plants line the front walk, newly planted trees march along the side yard, lower portions wrapped in netting to keep small animals from nibbling bark. Whoever lives here takes pride in upkeep.

My knock on the door is met with silence. A peek through the front window shows no signs of life inside. It seems the homeowner isn't home. Around back there are old tractors and lawn mowers, in various states of disassembly or repair. Looks like a retired guy hobby yard to me.

I return to my car, mulling over this. Why did Highland drive all the way out here only to speed away? He'd driven like someone following directions, so I discard the idea of visiting friends. He should already know the way and plus, I can't envision him having any.

Clicking my pen in thought, I go to write down the address and as I peer around for the street name, it hits me. The full address flags in my mind. I flip through my folders until I get to the juror information.

Shit, shit, shit.

This is Chuck Fire's house. One of four who'd skipped the reunion.

Thoughts and implications jam up my skull, questions and counters, consequences. Did Highland come all the way out here for unfinished business with a juror? Did Lady Luck dab her wand by the fact of Chuck's absence?

And was Highland at this very moment making his way to the other remaining jurors' houses, intent on completing his revenge? Skimming through the profile sheets I can tell Rick, Dennis and Lian are spread across Kenosha County. There's no way I can cover that much ground to prevent something bad. My mind continues to race, assembling and discarding plans in rapid fire.

The ring of my cell phone disrupts the train. Warren. "Four o'clock," he growls, still unhappy. "The autopsy came through. I got the results."

"And?"

"You know already. Me calling is your answer."

My limbs tingle with validation. I knew there would be ethylene glycol but having it confirmed by a medical examiner vindicates my efforts.

I glance at my watch. It's 3:22, just enough time to get back into Kenosha. "There's more, Warren. I caught Jeffrey Highland in the act. He just scoped out a house for one of the jurors that missed Friday night, but no one was home. I think he wants to tie up loose ends. There are three others. We need to get squads out on welfare checks."

"Stop it. Stop it all, now," he hisses back. "Just get to the station." And hangs up.

I swear under my breath. Somebody needs to warn them. My next call is to Dennis, but it goes straight to voicemail. I better enlist help since I'll soon be tied up with Warren and Richardson.

Kay answers on the third ring. Her voice is uncertain after I give my name. "I already told you everything."

"No, this is different. I need you to call Chuck, Lian, Rick and Dennis, tell them that Jeffery Highland may be coming and should be considered dangerous. Someone needs to confirm they're alright. I won't be able to in a few minutes."

"Wait." Confusion colors her words. "The cousin? What's going on?"

"Let's just say some things have come to light since we spoke. I have good reason to think Highland is a threat. Those four need to be warned. I already tried Dennis, but he didn't answer." My words tumble over each other, syllables mashed up and barely intelligible.

Kay takes a deep breath, loudly exhaling. "Hang on. I can help. I'll call. What are they supposed to do?"

"If Highland approaches them in any way, call 911. I'll be meeting with the detective taking over this case but it's going to take him time to mobilize assistance." I'm embellishing the truth but urgency causes me to cast aside minor concerns.

"Hold on. The police are now involved? Why? What happened?" Panic undercuts her words, and I don't blame her. Every juror is a potential victim if Highland truly intends to exact his vengeance.

I put her off, doing my best to keep a lid on the emotional part. Maybe a little too late if I'm being honest. "Give me time to get my ducks in a row and then I can fill you in." I don't want to tell her Nicole is dead, that's not going to help.

"Will you come by after you've met with the police?" she asks, plaintive in tone. "I'm freaking out. Should we all be worried? Oh, God."

"Yes, I will. For now call the others, tell them what I said."

Before I hang up, I offer one last

piece of advice. "And lock your doors."

20

THURSDAY, JUNE 17, 1999, 7:59AM – DAY 26

"Well, fancy seeing you here," Dennis stated as he walked into the room. Nicole was seated in her usual spot, staring at the large sheets of paper hung on the opposite wall. Scribbles littered each one, points of evidence, counterpoints, notes, questions; some circled and others crossed off. Multiple markers had been used, creating a colorful display that concealed the serious subject matter. "I don't think you've ever been first one in."

"Dude," she scrubbed her eyes. "I couldn't sleep. Spent all night thinking about this."

"Same."

Their deliberations had only lasted an hour before Millick announced the day was over. During that time the group went back and forth on what evidence to consider, what to discard. The judge instructed them to go home, discuss the case with no one, not even each other, and come ready in the morning.

"Terry, Kay, Margaret," Dennis continued, listing the not-guilty votes.

"Me," she added.

"And you." His tone was neutral.

Other jurors filtered in over the next twenty minutes. Travis, Chuckie and Charles arrived together. Shelli and Courtney, followed shortly by Terry, Rick and Lian. Margaret and Kay were last to arrive.

Tired eyes ringed the table, furrowed brows over steaming cups of coffee. "Anyone else sleep like shit?" Courtney asked.

The nods were unanimous. This weighed more heavily than anyone anticipated. They'd spent weeks making snarky comments over lawyers and witnesses, mocking behaviors they'd come to dislike, generally acting like high school students locked in detention.

Now the enormity of their burden had arrived.

Margaret cleared her throat. "It's not that I think Julie committed suicide. I don't believe that. I think Mark killed her but I'm struggling with whether there's enough evidence to convict. The signs are there, where's the actual evidence? I know we've seen all this stuff showing his mindset but it's not the same thing. This is someone's life we're talking about. He has people who love him, too." She spoke quietly, drawing down the room's mood, and shook her head to keep the emotion controlled.

"That's where I'm at," Nicole answered. "I think Mark's an asshole and sociopath but that's not illegal. What do we have to convict him on?"

Chuckie set down his coffee. "Hearing from dozens of witnesses isn't enough? The high-five with dad in the driveway? He told other people he did it."

"Oh, so we're just swallowing the

word of a career criminal who's getting a reduced sentence by tattling? Sure, he's trustworthy." Her words were sharp, irritated.

"You can toss him out and there are still plenty of others." Courtney snapped back, tapping her stack of notepads. "When everyone says the same thing, what else do you need to hear?"

Travis interrupted. "You heard Millick. Go by the evidence."

"But which evidence?" Jean asked. "I mean, do we give the same weight to everyone as the computer guy? Or the psych doctors? One of them did testify that Julie was depressed."

"But he didn't say she was suicidal," Shelli countered. "Those two are not the same thing."

"Plus, that forensic tech was an idiot." Terry shook his head. "Can't trust anything he said. Kiddie scripter, splashing in the deep end of the pool with no idea what he's doing."

The room paused, distant tension like a winged creature hovering over their heads, ready to pounce.

Terry wasn't done. "What if she set this all up?"

To that several in the room turned to him in unison. "*What?*"

"Think about it. She knew the marriage wasn't good. It's what made her depressed. She doesn't want to lose the kids, so she makes it look like Mark tried to poison her. Frames him for attempted murder. He gets locked away and now she's scot-free with her children. But somehow she miscalculates and ends up dying."

Stunned silence greets his theory and more than one juror exchanges glances across the table. It's finally Nicole who says what everyone else is thinking. "Terry, that is some Scooby Doo shit. Where did you come up with that?"

He simply shrugs. "Think about it."

"Nope, won't."

Charles leans forward. Thus far he'd remained silent and withdrawn, observing the room dynamics. "There are a lot of differing opinions here, as there should be. It's not getting us anywhere by picking and choosing information to support each opinion. I'd like to make a suggestion. Let's first decide what can be used in our deliberations. Keep some, discard some. This will reduce side discussions and allow us to focus on the remaining evidence. Does that seem like a reasonable approach?"

Murmured consent traveled the room. Leave it to a wise elder to get them on track.

Kay leaned back in her chair and flipped a hand towards Nicole. "Foreman lady. You going to sit there or do something? Let's move it."

Nicole stood with fresh sheets of paper adorning the wall behind her. Uncertainty colored her expression, but she plunged ahead. "Okay, how about this? We list out good witnesses from those who aren't. Like Daball, Hoover and Highland."

Doubt flared across several jurors and Shelli voiced their thoughts. "That seems subjective. One of us could think someone was good that no one else does."

"I liked one of the office worker witnesses. She seemed trustworthy," Chuckie said and nudged Dennis with his elbow. "And blond."

Dennis responded with a head shake. "There were about ten of those and they said maybe ten words each in testimony. How can you even remember?"

"Mind like a steel trap. Clang, clang, brother."

Travis laughed, drawing an echo from Shelli. Margaret snorted. Terry and Jean tried to talk at the same time, drowning each other out. Courtney flipped furiously through her notepads, looking for who knows what.

As the noise level rose, Kay stood up and rapped her knuckles hard on the table. "This is getting us nowhere. Can I propose a different approach? Let's set aside all witnesses. If their contribution was nothing more than words, discard them from consideration for now. Take subjectivity out of the equation. Instead, we use what we saw, things like emails, forensic reports, pictures. Those are less open to dispute."

Looks were traded around the room, shrugs and nods following. Jean spoke first. "I think that's a great idea. Use the hard data and remove opinion. In a case like this, it will be important to look back and be able to say what we considered and why. Good suggestion."

Kay glanced around, ending up with Nicole. "There. Was that so hard?"

Lian, Margaret and Travis exchanged looks, thoughts echoing the other jurors. Maybe they picked the wrong person to be foreman.

Ignoring Kay's sarcasm, Nicole wrote a large number '1' on the first sheet. "Emails. What do they show?"

"Intent," Charles replied. "We have Mark's words in black and white. Those are irrefutable. There might be differing interpretation of the meaning, but I think the messages are pretty clear."

"Also," Courtney added. "The internet searches. No one ever denied Julie died from ethylene glycol, the only question is how it got into her system. Did she drink it as part of a suicide? Or did he force-slash-trick her? The answer to either question is our verdict."

"Oh!" Margaret blurted. "We should create a timeline between his emails and his internet searches. That will show if there's a connection. It will help me anyway."

Nicole smiled. "Now we're getting somewhere." She looked towards the end of the table. "Courtney, first search. When did it happen?"

And so they were off. Forgotten were the room dynamics and personality tensions, everyone referencing their own notes to supplement Courtney's master compilation. At Shelli's suggestion Nicole drew two parallel lines. Top line showed emails, bottom line showed internet searches. Calendar dates became the header for each connection.

The morning ticked by with this exercise, minutes, an hour, then two. Someone called for a break and while no one disputed it, no one stopped discussing the evidence either. Jurors removed themselves to fetch a snack or use the restroom but quickly rejoined.

By lunch a diagram had emerged in Nicole's handwriting. The first email occupied a top left position.

The subject in blue: '*What are you going to do?*'

Directly below, connected by a

green vertical line…

"Holy shit," Chuckie breathed.

"Holy is right," Margaret.

There it was, in colored marker across the paper.

"Look at the times," Charles said. "Kelly's email came during the day. She's asking questions about Julie; I think we can all agree. Then, 11:04 that night, Mark searches out poison for the first time."

Silence befell the room at the significance of what they'd created. This was not something Jambliss, with all his prosecutorial gamesmanship, had established. It was born of their own hands. Thus, it held more weight.

"Okay, I'm good now," Nicole said. "Guilty."

21

THURSDAY, JUNE 15, 2000, 3:56PM

Detective Paul Richardson stands eye to eye with me but with significantly more bulk. If I stood behind him, I'd disappear. It's clear from our initial greeting that he does not rely on his size for a psychological advantage. He's soft-spoken with watery blue eyes behind glasses. The smile that crosses his face fails to hide distaste for this meeting. To him I'm simply another crackpot and he's already regretting the decision to let Warren trade favors. He's thinking of the quickest way to humor me and get out of the conference room without hassle.

Next to him, Warren is intent on

offloading this case. He may be buddies with Richardson, but self-preservation takes no prisoners. This whole situation guarantees he will never again call me for something he doesn't want to handle. I wonder how many other gray-area investigators he knows.

Richardson comes out swinging. "I'm aware of your issues down in Chicago, Mr. White. It was something I closely followed out of professional interest. Frankly, you earned the dismissal with your antics, a case study in what not to do as an officer. You've got an uphill battle here. Tell me why I need to listen."

If he meant to set me off my bead, it worked. I'm instantly defensive. "If you stayed abreast of things then you would have learned I was fully vindicated by the department. Does your case study include that tidbit?"

"You lost your tin. It's a final rendering of judgment. Nothing else counts." He takes charge of the conversation with his placid tone. "Anyway, moving on. Warren briefed me but let's hear from you."

Much as I want to debate this detective on my history and current merits, it's more critical I get him on board and tracking Highland. I'd mentally rehearsed my words over and over on the drive, anticipating resistance to my request for an official investigation. The sooner I secure that, the sooner those jurors will be safe from harm. Echoes of Kay's voice, and the panic threatening to consume her, roll through my mind.

I tap the thick folder sitting on the table in front of me. "You were lead detective for the Mark Johannsen homicide case. You testified as a key witness for the State. Your name is forever connected to his."

None of these were questions.

He leans back. "It was only a year ago. I *do* remember."

"Johannsen was found guilty and sentenced to life in prison."

"Why are you telling me things I already know?" He looks at Warren. "Is he going to keep on like this?"

Before Warren responds, I cut in. "Because you need to hear the things you don't know. Like the fact this case is not over. We're now in the second phase."

"Which is?"

"Someone exacting revenge on the jury for their verdict. Someone using the same method of poisoning as a point of ultimate irony." I point to Warren. "His friend's wife is dead and if we don't move now, she won't be the last."

Richardson's eyes are flat behind his glasses, narrow and squinting. He blinks a couple of times before pronouncing, "Bullshit."

I point to the autopsy report lying on the table, putting him on the spot. "Are you calling bullshit on the ME's findings too? Doesn't it seem a little too coincidental that almost exactly one year later, during a reunion of their verdict, someone from the jury dies from ethylene glycol? I'd love to hear how you think those events could possibly be unrelated."

He glances down as if reading the words printed across the report, but I know he's simply buying time to run through his own decision tree. No detective likes to think about opening a case based on the words of a civilian. But more so, no detective ever wants to be held up to the light if they received information about potential crimes and ignored them. There really is no win for him either way.

The silence grows and I don't want to give him too much consideration. "Tell you what," I say. "Let me walk you through what I have so far. If, after I'm done, you think it's bullshit, fine. Start over. However, I can save you a lot of time and legwork."

I pivot to Warren. "You handed me this. It didn't go where you thought it would, but you know there's something here. If you don't back me now, you're either admitting you made the wrong call or you're too weak to see it through."

I'm engaging in emotional blackmail, and I don't care. I warned him, more than once. You call me in and I'm in until it's all done.

With a huff he succumbs to my subliminal pressure and turns to Richardson. "Listen to the kid. He's done a good job packaging everything up."

They lock stares, two seasoned cops, opposites in the extreme. Wheels turn in each of their brains, practically audible. Richardson comes to his decision and looks back at me. "As a professional courtesy only, paid by George. You have five minutes. Go."

Odd, I remember saying something similar to Warren when he first called me. Must be a common cop tactic.

I cap off my five minutes by sliding over Highland's most recent mugshot. It joins a pile of other papers, my notes, key trial transcripts with handwritten annotations, juror profiles and anything else supporting my request for an investigation. I've done my part. The decision now rests in the hands of a detective I don't know but who thinks he knows me from media reports. Tenuous is a good description of my confidence level, but I don't let it show.

Richardson picks up the mug shot. "I remember this guy. Another officer did the initial interview, but I was in the gallery the day he testified. You could tell even then there was something off about him."

His voice retains the same soft intensity, and I can't tell if he's talking to us or himself. He spins the picture with two fingers and meets my eyes. "You're positive it was a juror house he visited today?"

"One hundred percent."

"And you confirmed he was at Sunnyside when they all were."

"Bartender corroborated it."

The next question isn't asked, I answer anyway. "I don't have any signed witness statements. I'll leave that to you guys, but the information is solid. I'm telling you, Highland is out there right now scoping targets. If he was willing to poison an entire group in a public setting, what happens when he gets a juror alone?"

"You still vouching for this?" Richardson asks Warren.

"Right or wrong, White is a known name. If the media sniffs him out in connection with this and word comes out that you slow-walked it, you're going to burn." I almost feel bad for Richardson. Warren took the first opportunity to drop a mess onto his friend's lap. The guy has to do something, his arm has been bent.

"Okay, okay," he says. "Understood. Let's move. I'll send around squads to check on those four jurors. We'll start interviewing the rest and get our statements in order. In the meantime, I'll run this up my chain of command. It won't be tonight but tomorrow we should be knocking on Highland's door." He swivels his watery gaze my way. "That make you happy?"

"Absolutely, especially if I get to ride shotgun when we knock on his door. He needs to be off the street."

Of us three, Warren is the most pleased. He's successfully evaded another career-impacting case. His friend, however, looks glum, the expression of someone forced to act out of his control and worried about it.

"It'll be fine," I reassure him. The words don't change his demeanor.

Kay Standin has apparently been waiting eagerly on my arrival. She's in her driveway when I pull up. There's frenetic jerkiness to her movements, like she's uncertain of each step, worried about making the wrong decision. I feel bad. Maybe I shouldn't have weighed her down with the task of warning others. You never know how someone is going to react when under stress.

"What's going on?" She blurts as I open my car door. "I did what you asked and called everyone. What's happened? What should I be doing?"

Interesting. Two days ago she had no time for me. Now she's looking at me like I'm her savior. Funny what the threat of danger will do.

I hold up my hands to stall off any more rapid-fire questions. "Stop. One thing at a time. You called the other jurors?"

At her nod, I continued. "And did any of them report seeing Highland?

"No. Chuckie is up north visiting his kids. Rick and Lian are at work. Dennis is out riding, somewhere far past Lake Geneva."

That eases my internal pressure a bit. Richardson has breathing room to get officers mobilized. Maybe we can keep everyone safe yet.

I look around. The neighboring houses are quiet, no visible movement, but it's nearing the end of a workday and soon cars will be pulling into their respective driveways. No need to stir up curiosity.

"Perhaps we should step inside."

Kay doesn't hear me. She's wrapped her arms tight around her torso, looking inward. Haunted eyes lift to mine, reddened. "I think Highland had something to do with my husband's disappearance." Her tone is fragile, wavering.

What?

"Why didn't you say anything before?" I fire back. "You said he left you. What's changed?"

She shakes her head. Not in the way someone does when they disagree, but rather the repeated shake of disbelief. Back and forth, her dark hair stirring from the movement. "I never made a connection."

Pulling out my notepad, I flip to a blank page. I'm not sure where we're going with this or how it will impact the material I provided to Richardson, but a sinking feeling weighs me down, like I completely overlooked a critical piece of information.

"Tell me everything."

Kay leans against my car, close enough to nearly breach that comfort buffer we all carry. Her arm bumps against my elbow. "Jonathan followed me to Sunnyside on Friday. We'd been having issues because of his cheating. I think he thought I was having an affair of my own and wanted to catch me in the act. One of those deals where two wrongs offset each other."

This is random information and doesn't provide me with any insight, but I write down '*cheating accusation – Jonathan*' anyway, so she can see I'm taking her seriously.

"I didn't know Highland was there, that part of the bar was behind me. I think Shelli noticed him first. I turned in time to see him storm out, angry look on his face. We were all shocked. I mean, what are the odds of that guy being there?"

I stare at my page and the sparse scribbling. "You're losing me. Where's the link to your husband?"

"Well, as he left, I looked where he came from and saw Jonathan standing by himself. I didn't know he'd followed me. His face was really red, just as angry, like they had argued. I don't think he saw me through the crowd."

"I still don't understand."

Kay dips her head then glances around the area much like I did. I'm uncertain whether for the same reason, though. "We know Jeffrey Highland. Jonathan and he graduated high school together. He's done work for us, repairing our deck, cutting down a bunch of trees. After the last job, we weren't happy with the results. Sloppy work. I don't even remember which job; I think he left tree stumps and wasn't supposed to. Jonathan refused to pay the bill until he came back. He never did so we never paid. And that was the end of it."

Except Highland's history shows there's never an end unless it's the end he chooses. I think about all the reports of his retribution for seemingly minor confrontations. The guy clearly holds grudges against those he felt wronged him. Holding back payment for a job certainly could qualify for that. Does making someone disappear fall into the pattern? I think back to the incident with duct tape and plastic tarps in his trunk. Nothing ever came of the charges, but those items were there for a reason.

"What did your husband say? What did he do? Did he go after Highland?"

Guilt washes over Kay, a visible effect. She rubs at her eyes and sends out a distant gaze. "I pretended I didn't see him and simply turned back to the group. I didn't want drama. No one else knows Jonathan. They were just happy to be together again and letting my domestic issues come up wasn't the right thing to do." She dips her head again, fingers pressed into eye sockets like she could blot out the image. "I didn't know that would be the last time I saw him though."

"Kay, it's been almost a week."

"I know." She nods and looks up at me, eyes reddened. "I told you, we're not good. He's disappeared on other occasions, sometimes for days at a time. Then he'll suddenly turn up, act like nothing happened and on we go. Rinse and repeat, it's our damnation."

I recall our first conversation.

"That's why you told me you'd looked in the harbor where your boat is stored. It's his go-to hideout."

A stifled sob shudders through her. "How pathetic that he even has a go-to. We're so broken."

Kay's words strike hard. I'm surrounded by brokenness. Mark Johannsen hated his wife and ended up poisoning her. Victim to poison of his own, he robbed his children of a mother because he saw no other way to course correct his life.

Jonathan and Kay bear some of the same hallmarks: A relationship corrupted by infidelity, leading to distrust and gamesmanship, leading to arguments which result in her agonizing over his whereabouts.

What does this say about parallels between Sheila and me? Our daughter's death fractured the bonds we'd spent years building. There were so many plans yet ahead, a brighter future marked by birthdays and milestones and happy emotions. Then, boom, all of them gone when Anna took her last breath. Sheila handled it better than I did, processing her grief without losing anchor. I did not. Have not. My process stole me away, physically and emotionally, to the point I've become a ghost, evading definition or capture. She'd call. I'd ignore it. If I answered, the distance remained great.

I look down at Kay, huddled and small.

Is Sheila even now clenching herself, wondering if I'm lost to the unknown, never to return? A sudden wave of sadness takes me and I forcibly tamp it down.

It's easier to deal with bad guys and problems that have clear resolution.

"I don't know how you want me to help."

Kay moves away, still hugging herself. "Can you come in?"

As she walks towards the front door, I pause. In every investigation there are moments when the case turns an unexpected corner, when the detective is forced to consider new evidence and determine for himself whether it adds or detracts. Experienced cops recognize the difference and know how to react.

If I follow, it means I think Jonathan's disappearance is directly related to Highland, and I'll need to provide Richardson with this new thread. If I don't follow, I'm leaving Kay to sort out her own domestic situation that, while not new, may have new results.

The decision isn't hard.

I catch up before she opens the door. "I'll do what I can," I promise.

And mean it.

22

FRIDAY, JUNE 18, 1999, 9:18AM – DELIBERATION

The bleary eyes on day two of deliberation are no better. They had spent yesterday establishing links between conversations and actions. The diagram approach did wonders for drawing out causal connections, showing the jury how Mark reacted to Kelly's questions about their future.

"Why didn't Jambliss do something like this for us?" Travis groused at one point. "It's so easy to see when you can draw a line from an email to an internet search."

"Goddamn lawyers," Dennis

muttered in response, eliciting agreement from several others.

As the morning wore on, they worked through every connection point they could. Courtney provided details on dates and times, Nicole listed them on the wall and as a group they would decide whether it was enough to count as evidence.

By the time everyone needed a break, two walls of the jury room lay covered with paper. The email and internet search timelines spanned one side to the other, thick marker denoting the items they would include in consideration.

Chuckie got up to brew another pot of coffee while others queued up for the bathroom. Side conversations broke out in pockets. Shelli and Courtney huddled close, comparing their notes and making an occasional scribble.

Margaret whispered to Charles, receiving slow nods in response. Jean and Travis talked about the neighborhood they shared, a fact unknown to either until this trial.

Kay remained silent, content to watch these people and their interactions.

Her own notepad lay open to the page for ethylene glycol stages of poisoning, embellished with notes she'd added during their discussions. A half-eaten donut rested on a napkin next to it and she idly swished her cold coffee with a stir straw.

As Nicole came back from the bathroom and resumed her position along the wall of evidence, Margaret motioned her close. "I think you should call for another vote," she said.

Nicole nodded. "Thank God, I don't know what else to write."

When everyone had reassembled, a second round of votes went up.

Ten guilty, two non-guilty.

Terry shook his head again and again. "It's that letter from the grave. I can't get past it. If she wanted to set up Mark and get him thrown in jail, something like that is perfect. The fact that she screwed up and drank too much antifreeze doesn't change anything."

Exasperation colored Nicole's face. She was not the only one. "But there literally – *literally* – was no testimony for any kind of conspiracy on her part. We can't just make up things to explain evidence."

He leaned back and folded his arms. Stubbornness set his jaw.

Nicole turned her attention to Kay. "And what about you?"

"I think she really was depressed. She should have been. If I cheated on my husband, I would be. None of those internet searches for poisoning are conclusive proof Mark did it. She could have been the one doing them."

"And doing them during times when he was home so a pattern was established," Terry added with a nod.

"So, nothing about how those searches coincided with Kelly's emails?" Travis asked, swiveling his head back and forth between the two holdout jurors.

This produced a shrug from Kay. "Look at the chart. It's not like there's a ton of direct connections."

Every head turned to look at the diagram on the wall. It was true that only a handful of searches came on the same day when an email contained some reference to the future. In most of the juror's eyes, those were enough.

Apparently not for Kay.

"The letter from the grave?" Jean asked. "I mean, how else do you explain it?"

Again, Kay shrugged. "There's no proof Julie actually wrote it. No handwriting comparison, no signature. It could have come from anyone. It was obvious none of the neighbors liked Mark. What if one of them did it to pin everything on him because they sympathized with Julie?"

Terry nodded to her. "Excellent point. Others were in on it."

This caused Shelli to throw up her hands and look to the ceiling. However, hints of doubt appeared in some of the jurors' eyes. Courtney shook her head and began flipping through a notepad. Margaret and Charles exchanged a look, both with compressed lips. Dennis lowered his head into his hand, shading eyes as he wrote something down.

"Smells like a stalemate in here," Travis remarked, and they knew what it meant. "Takes all twelve of us."

Silence settled over the room as

everyone considered the ramifications. For those steadfast in their guilty vote, the potential of Mark walking free upset them. It would be the same as saying he was innocent when no one thought that.

After a few minutes, Shelli raised her hand. Chuckie looked at her, at her hand. "Really?"

She blushed. "Sorry, don't know why I did that. Anyway, here's a thought. Why don't we also consider as evidence things Mark didn't do?"

Looks crisscrossed the room. "What do you mean?" Nicole asked.

Shelli got up and moved to a blank sheet of paper hanging on the wall. Nicole tossed her a marker and she drew out a grid for the first week of December. "Julie died on Thursday December 3rd, right? Around 4 or 5pm." Heads nodded, the time and date had been drilled into their minds throughout the course of the trial. Shelli traced around the square for Thursday in thick red lines.

"What happened in the days prior to Thursday?"

Courtney flipped a notepad page and

scanned down it. "Monday. Mark stopped at her doctor and asked for a prescription of Ambien because Julie was not sleeping."

"Yep," Jean added. "He was trying to help her sleep."

"And Wednesday?" *Tap, tap.*

"She didn't do her weekly volunteer session at school," Margaret said. "Didn't call in, didn't show, which was unlike her."

"When the principal called, Mark answered and said she would be sleeping for a long time," Travis said. "He laughed when he said it."

Tap, Thursday.

"The kids said mommy was really sick in bed," Jean again. "They told the teacher."

Comprehension rolled across the faces staring back at Shelli. She nodded. "If you're so worried about your wife being sick, if the kids are worried, why wouldn't you call 911? Or bring her to the walk-in clinic?"

Chuckie grunted. "On the day she was dying the dude did nothing to help her."

"Not only that," Charles added.

"Remember one of his coworkers testified he went to pick up a client check. He left her home alone despite how sick she was."

"And maybe pushed her face into the pillow when he came back," Dennis said with a shake of his head.

"Because she was still alive. He couldn't have that when the kids came home," Travis said. "They would insist he bring her to the doctor."

"Thereby," Charles lifted one finger in a professorial manner. "Undoing all his plans."

"Now we're just speculating," Kay countered. "We don't know why he acted the way he did."

"Well, can we agree Mark didn't act in a way that a caring husband should?" Shelli raised her hand again.

This time every hand raised in agreement, including Terry and Kay.

Terry was last, unwilling to let go of the conspiracy angle. "But what about the letter?"

Nicole picked up the thread of Shelli's logic. "What about it? If it didn't exist, does that change anything?" She circled Shelli's diagram, drew arrows to the emails and internet searches. These were indisputable pieces of evidence, the foundation of the case.

Pausing with an open mouth, Terry considered it then shook his head. "No, it doesn't." He paused again, staring at the diagrams, letting the room settle as others watched thoughts cross his face. Finally, he nodded. "Guilty."

All eyes turned to Kay now. She met each stare with a set jaw, as if straining against weighted opinions. Nicole opened her mouth to speak and Kay stabbed a finger towards her. "Shut up. Let me think."

The room fell silent, everyone sensing enormity in the moment. Kay was not someone to be swayed by eloquence or bullied into agreement. Over the course of the trial she'd emerged as a wild card, friendly one minute, antagonistic the next. She now held the balance of their verdict in her hand.

Kay says not guilty and Mark Johannsen walks free.

Kay votes with everyone else and Mark becomes a convicted murderer.

"At the end of all this, we're dealing with a domestic affair," she said, as much to herself as the others. "Husband and wife, letting the rot of infidelity into their marriage. She tried to make amends and when it didn't work, grew depressed. He let it fester until the poison spilled over onto her." She held a breath. "Pun intended."

No one interrupted this stream of consciousness, knowing Kay, like Terry, needed to work it through on her own. She pointed to the emails. "There's no proof Mark conducted all those searches, but there's also no evidence he didn't." She looked at Shelli. "To use your angle."

"We don't have solid evidence he fed Julie the antifreeze. There's no photo, no video clip of him forcing her to drink, no witness who saw it. There's not even a glass with fingerprints. All we have is circumstantial evidence painting an image of how it could have happened. We get left with the job of filling in the colors, using logic and common sense to complete the picture. In the end we either indict Julie for sparking it all with her affair, or we penalize Mark for escalating things beyond a normal reaction."

Kay sipped another breath. Her eyes traveled the room, once again locking upon each of her fellow jurors. The moment drew long and suspenseful. She exhaled, loud and punctured, arriving at a decision.

"He's guilty."

23

FRIDAY, JUNE 23, 2000, 9:01AM

There's a Groundhog effect at play this week. Wake up, shower, eat, review my notes, wait impatiently until I think people are available to call.

Call.

"Yes," Richardson replies to my abrupt greeting. "I received your voicemails when I arrived this morning. All of them." There's dry sarcasm in his voice. My habit of shooting out a phone call when something occurs to me doesn't always sit well with others. I don't care.

"Okay, good. As noted, there may be an additional victim, Jonathan Roberts. His wife is certain Highland had something to do with his disappearance."

"And this is the wife who admits to having a bad marriage where her husband has vanished in prior instances? Who has not filed a missing person report? Who is speculating without any evidence whatsoever?"

"Well, yeah, but…"

He sighs. "Listen, White, I get that you're vested in this for whatever reason. Your passion is admirable and gives a glimpse into why things in Chicago went down the way they did. That's not how I work, though."

I hear subtle condemnation in his modulated voice.

"You've compiled evidence to target Highland in the death of Nicole Wright. It's thorough, maybe not enough to get a warrant but at the very least worth bringing him in for an interview. That's all I'm willing to do right now. If his interview turns up more smoke, I'll follow my process. This idea you can lop on more angles to the case, disabuse yourself of it."

"You're not…"

"Let me finish. I am expending this

effort as a courtesy, to George first and yourself second. That's not the same as buying into your theories. If something about the husband surfaces, it will be handled as with any other investigation. I'm not one to ignore my procedural requirements. Is that clear?"

My cheeks are flushed, heated by the lecture. I'm forced to remember that the goal is justice. Redemption is a secondary effect. "Sure. Of course," I manage to squeeze out.

It means I'm on my own to handle Kay's issue.

Richardson is not done though. As if regretting the condescending tone in his words, he throws me a bone. "George asked that you be included during the interview. I'll allow it, but we'll place you in the adjoining observation room. No talking directly with Highland. If I need reference, perhaps to clarify something in your packet, I will come to you. Those are the only terms I can accept for your presence. Understood?"

"I appreciate that, detective." It's passive-aggressive on my part, dropping his name, and makes me feel petty, but my blood is simmering. Anything else and I might have said what I really thought. "I'm just happy to be of assistance."

"Keep your phone handy. We're moving today." And with that the line cuts.

There's the sole positive I can take away from our conversation. If he's moving this quickly it means my evidence was solid and actionable. Someone as hidebound as Richardson needs the T's crossed and the I's dotted.

I did both.

I'm in a bit of limbo, waiting for the next move, so I call Kay and give her an update.

"They're never going to find him, are they?" She blurts. "Where would they even begin looking?"

She's jumping to the conclusion that police are already looking for her husband. The question is laden with such worry I don't have the heart to correct her assumption. "During Highland's interview, if it becomes apparent he has information on Jonathan, I'll personally handle it."

Only because no one else will.

"No, I get that," she replies. "I'm asking where they would look if Highland doesn't talk. What would they do?"

"You must initiate things, Kay. A missing person's report. Then interviews with you to get an idea of his movements on Friday. A list of places he might choose to stay, people who might visit harm on him. That sort of thing. There's no magic wand that sends them on the hunt."

"Okay, I understand." A hint of relief tinges her words, like she feels better knowing what the path forward is. "It's on me to provide the information best as I can."

"Pretty much, yeah. I can get a head start with some of the details you gave me yesterday, start building a profile if it becomes necessary."

She's quiet for a moment. "We didn't have the best marriage but it wasn't all bad."

"You're speaking as if it's over. Think positive. You have my word I will stay with this to the end."

We cut the call after she extracts a promise to keep her updated, regardless of how insignificant the information. I close my phone, not certain how I'm going to keep my side of the bargain. They seemed like such throwaway words, but they bind me to a distinct quest that may not end up having any connection to Ted's original charge. How did this happen?

To kill time, I decide to check out the marina where Kay and Jonathan keep their boat. If he'd escaped there during past arguments, it's a good starting spot. I should have mentioned it to her in case there are gate codes or other such access permissions I'd need, but I don't want to be pressed for more answers I can't provide, so I don't call back. I'll figure it out when I get there.

The Prairie Harbor Yacht Club sits right on the border between Wisconsin and Illinois, secluded and expensive. A man-made channel leads out onto Lake Michigan.

I'm no stranger to boats, my parents

owned several in my youth. My dad loved boats, trains and the Rule of Law. Only one of those loves passed onto me.

I recognize the standard club setup, almost like there's a common blueprint for these places. Tennis courts, swimming pool, a restaurant and other amenities entice boaters to hang around, to spend on food and drink, or branded apparel. A variety of slips fill the actual marina, from 40' to 80' in length. On this sunny Friday morning many are already empty as members get a jump on the coming weekend.

I can feel the buzz as other owners make ready their vessels and chat with slip neighbors. It brings back memories from my own youth. The noise of children splashing in the pool drifts over the clubhouse.

A family walks with their little red wagon full of food and drink, pulled by a young boy in a sailing cap. I speed up my pace and hold open the locked gate for him after mom punches in the code. She tugs her daughter's hand to move her along and gives me a smile of thanks, to which I mutter, "Sure," and close the gate after us, just in case anyone is worried about strangers wandering the docks.

Jonathan and Kay's boat is a 30' Chapparel *Signature* cuddy, white with green striping along the flanks, tucked in the row of slips farthest from the gate and clubhouse. Pricey rig, capable of navigating big lake waters. The name stenciled on the back is *Money Robber*. She mentioned he worked in finance and with a last name like Roberts, I assume it's a play on words and not a direct statement.

Precisely-tied hitch knots secure dock lines to pier cleats, bumpers hanging out to protect the hull. At the bow I note an anchor line angled downward into the water. You don't usually need one in a protected berth. Jonathan must be a careful guy. Then again, the hitch is tied differently from the dock lines so maybe it wasn't him.

There's little foot traffic in this part of the marina. With a furtive glance to make sure no one's paying attention, I step on the rear swim platform and begin unsnapping the cabin cover, keeping my movements natural, like I belong. The young boy stands by his wagon, watching me from across the marina, scratching his scalp under the cap. I lift away enough of the cover to slide underneath.

It's steamy hot, dark green canvas trapping the summer heat. Sweat instantly beads across my forehead as I crab forward to the cuddy, a shallow area in the bow ringed with seating. Cushions can be laid across the center to make a bed for overnight stays.

I don't really know what I'm looking for, just something that seems out of place.

Jonathan keeps his boat tidy, there's no trash left on the floor, the cushions are placed evenly around the cuddy space, and everything appears properly tucked. The scent of Simple Green cleaner is strong, confirming his attention to detail. My dad would nod favorably at the upkeep of *Money Robber*.

There's no sign anyone has been staying here, seething over marital issues, biding time until it felt right to return home. If anything, this boat has been sitting for some time.

With nothing else to see, I back my

way out and stand up from under the cover, breathing in cool air.

The young boy stands on the dock, still staring. A man who I assume is dad stands behind him. "What are you doing?" His tone is tilted towards confrontation. My answer will determine what happens next.

I swipe at the sweat, making a show of it to buy a beat. "Jon asked me to check on his battery charge. He's traveling home today and wanted to take it out this weekend. I think he had one of those '*did I plug it in*' moments."

"Jonathan Roberts?"

I nod. "Jon, to some of us."

"Oh, okay." He looks at the boat and I use that moment to begin re-snapping the cover, like I'm humoring his questions while I attend to other matters. "I thought I saw his wife here just the other day."

"It's possible, but she's no boater. He wanted someone a little more familiar with them."

"Got it, makes sense. Everything good?"

"Well," I fasten the last snap. "She's

fully charged but lonely. Needs more hours."

This produces a laugh, the knowing kind among those with shared knowledge. "Don't they all."

We start re-tracing our path to the entrance. "You're friends with them?" The boy is on the other side of dad, eyes fixed on me. I give him a smile and he shies away.

"Just enough to say hi. More him than her. He's often on his own." He glances over his shoulder at the Chappy. "Boy's toys, you know."

I throw out some bait. "Yeah, he was last here over the weekend."

The dad shrugs. "Could be. We didn't come up."

I motion to the general area of his boat. "Weekends are precious around here. You're neglecting the captain's most important duty to his craft: Usage."

This pulls another laugh so I put out my hand. I might need to talk to him again at some point. It's a good ploy to make introductions. "Samuel Whitman." But there's no way I'm giving my real name.

He shakes it. "Steve McConnell. Nice to meet you, Sam."

We walk the marina perimeter in comfortable silence until reaching his slip. "Well, have a good day," Steve says and herds his son aboard their boat, a Sea Ray 40' *Sundancer*.

I pause by the gate, scanning. When I worked the Noah Bell case in Chicago, a breakthrough happened due to security cameras from a neighboring business, giving me a grainy glimpse of the crime. It doesn't seem like I'll have the same luck here. There are no cameras mounted on the pier poles or clubhouse walls, silently watching over the marina. You'd think there would, with millions in boat value secured only by dock lines, sailor's hitches and a gate anyone could easily vault.

Giving one last glance over the marina, I let the gate clank closed and head towards the clubhouse. A stroll around the exterior also reveals no surveillance cameras. People are milling around in the unique way of those for whom money isn't an issue. I don't know exactly how to describe it, but there's an aura of self-absorbed relaxation about them. They control their own clock and thus are perfectly fine lounging under the summer sun on a patio with Mimosa, Bloody Mary, or Irish coffee in hand. If they stay and drink or move onto other activities, it doesn't really matter. Things happen at their leisure, not the reverse.

No one pays attention as I wander past the pool and enter the clubhouse through a rear door reserved for members.

After an hour of speaking with employees and wandering the grounds, there's not much left to explore. Everyone knew Jonathan and Kay as long-time members, but none had seen him recently. It doesn't appear that he retreated here after their latest argument. While it fails add weight to her theory about Highland, it also doesn't detract.

As I'm leaving the club, my phone goes off. I don't recognize the number and flip it open hoping to hear Richardson's voice.

"This is Margaret, with the

Johannsen jury," the voice on the other end says softly. I'd not spoken with her in person when checking on the jurors, we'd simply traded voicemails, but I recognize the tone.

"How can I help you?"

"Can you meet this morning? I need to talk."

She doesn't address my return question as to why, keeping her responses vague, so I agree to a place called the Red School Cafe. I'll take her meeting in case there's any further details she provides, things not captured on the trial transcript that can fill between the lines.

The request gives me just enough time to head west, driving parallel to the state line, and come north on highway 45.

My hesitation at the café entrance flags me. A blond woman gets up from her booth and approaches. "Are you Aramis?" She asks.

I nod. "Margaret?"

She gestures for me to follow and re-takes her seat. Two other people are in the booth. A grizzled older man grips my hand firmly and introduces himself as

Chuckie. He's got sun wrinkles and buzz-cut hair. Calloused fingers pick at the tabletop.

Courtney is the third person, short and dark-haired, with inquisitive eyes that dart everywhere.

"Call me Arch." I meet their look. "I can guess you have a lot questions."

"What's going on?" Courtney asks as if she could no longer contain the question.

"First you call us asking about Sunnyside," Margaret says.

"Then a cop calls me to watch out for that Highland guy," Chuckie finishes.

Placing my hands flat on the table, I reply. "There's limited information I can provide as it's an active investigation, but it appears there was an attempt to poison all of you. Nicole was affected the most but everyone else reported similar effects."

"Dude." Courtney cuts me off. "We know this. You don't think we talk? We heard Nicole died. Then the news about Highland comes out. We can put together the puzzle pieces. Is he hunting us? What's being done?"

"It's not a great night's sleep knowing a killer drove by my house when I was out," Chuckie adds. "I'm thinking about leaving town for a while."

"I understand and don't blame you. At this point Jeffrey Highland is a person of interest. We're looking to interview him soon and get answers about his movement on Friday. I've read his trial transcripts and there's strong motive."

"If you need more than what's in the transcripts, let me know. I have notes," Courtney says.

Margaret shoots her an astonished look. "Courtney!"

"I couldn't help it," she responds. "They were my babies."

At my look of confusion, Courtney sheepishly clarifies. "We weren't supposed to take our notes from the jury room on the last day, but I snuck them out in my backpack." She glances up to see Chuckie's raised eyebrows. "What? They were going to just shred them!"

He grunts. "There goes an entire tree."

Getting us back on track, I look at

the two ladies. "Do either of you remember seeing Highland at Sunnyside?"

This startles both. "He was there? In the bar with us?" Alarm fills their expressions as they trade glances. Margaret breaks the stare to answer. "I never saw him. My back was to the main bar though. I'd have left right away if I did."

"Same," Courtney adds. "He freaked me out on the stand. I don't ever want to meet him in person."

"Yes, he was there. Both the bartender and Kay confirmed it. That gives us the opportunity to pair with motive."

Chuckie snorts. "I wouldn't trust Kay's recollection. She was as drunk as Nicole. Those two were going shot for shot."

"There's also a side-angle to this." I hold up Jonathan's business card with his picture in one corner. "Kay's husband was also there. I have reason to believe he and Highland had words. Now he's missing."

This brings yet another snort of derision from Chuckie. "Probably wanted to talk Highland into offing his wife."

"Chuck!" Margaret says. Looking

over at me, she adds, "Kay is a little…severe."

Courtney nods. "More like a moody bitch." Margaret winces.

A waitress stops at our booth with an order pad in hand. Just as she's opening her mouth, my phone buzzes. I snap it to my ear with one finger held up to stall her off.

"We're cleared for an interview and only an interview," Richardson says. "Forty minutes, Highland's house." He hangs up without any further words.

I abruptly stand, banging into the waitress, and mutter an apology. "I have to go. Now."

"You just got here!" Margaret's expression is unfettered dismay. "What are we supposed to do?"

"You can't leave us hanging," Courtney says.

"I'm sorry. I just got word that we're bringing Highland in for questioning. Who knows where it will lead but do what the police advised. Keep your eyes open and aware of your surroundings. Lock your doors. If you see him after we've completed the interview, call 911 immediately.”

Chuckie points at me with a rough-hewn finger. “Buddy, we’re out in the county. When seconds matter, the cops are only minutes away.”

I simply nod and offer no response to his sarcasm as I rush out.

410

24

FRIDAY, JUNE 18, 1999, 1:08PM - VERDICT

The jury filed back into the courtroom, one last procession before they no longer would be needed to render judgment on another human. This time they were in a new order, entering in the sequence of number cards they'd received from Larry. Travis looked over his shoulder as if jealous that someone else now occupied his spot at the end.

Nicole carried the verdict, a simple sheet of paper with two lines of print, Mark Johannsen's fate summarized in twelve-point Times New Roman font. She kept the paper pinned close to her thigh as they entered the jury box, trying to minimize her foreman role.

The courtroom was packed tighter than ever, brimming with media. Camera shutters continuously snapped; low murmurs hummed throughout the room as the jurors shuffled into their new seats.

Terry, spoiled by seven weeks in an office chair, let out a hiss as he sat in the fixed chair. "These things suck." His knee banged against the jury box wall when he tried to lean back.

Kay nodded in agreement. Her chair canted to one side, forcing her to angle her torso the other way for counterbalance. She glanced over her shoulder at Chuckie, the former occupant. "You sat this way the whole time?"

"Welcome to the clown show," he whispered back with a wink.

Lawyers peered at them, eyes intent, trying to interpret the verdict from body language and facial expression. They would soon find out together, but it seemed as if neither side could bear waiting that long.

Judge Millick shuffled papers around his desk before speaking, in no apparent hurry to end the trial. "We're back on the record. Let's have the appearances one last time."

Jambliss announced his name and role as prosecutor on behalf of the state.

Then it was the defense's turn. "Good afternoon, your Honor. Attorney Bridget Cruise, appearing on behalf of Mr. Mark Johannsen, who appears in person."

"The jury is in the courtroom, all twelve jurors who deliberated and the four alternate jurors who did not. Does the jury have a verdict?" Millick asked.

"They do, Your Honor," Larry answered on their behalf.

"Please bring the verdict sheet."

As the bailiff retrieved the verdict and walked it to the bench, Kay snuck a look at Nicole. Over the last month plus she'd come to recognize those small tells everyone gives off and knew Nicole felt nervous. Her head twitched in minute movements, like someone shaking away a mosquito buzzing their ear. Kay didn't blame her.

Several of the other jurors were equally nervous. Courtney darted her eyes everywhere, as if danger would erupt at any second. Travis sniffed repeatedly and shrugged his shoulders. Shelli clasped and unclasped her hands.

Millick studied the verdict sheet, longer than necessary for two short sentences. This intensified the tension in the room as everyone tried to read his expression.

Finally, he cleared his throat. "State of Wisconsin versus Mark Johannsen 1998CF314 verdict," he stated, announcing the case for the record. He then moved onto the verdict sheet. "We the jury find the defendant Mark Johannsen guilty of intentional homicide in the first degree as charged in the information. Dated this eighteenth day of June 1999 and signed by the foreperson."

He paused to let the reaction flow. Cameras clicked rapid fire. Somewhere in the back of the gallery an audible sob lifted loudly but it wasn't clear whether from relief at the verdict or a man's fate.

The jurors glanced at each other. Though their expressions were neutral, behind each set of eyes was a sense of duty fulfilled. They'd listened to a seemingly endless array of witnesses, endured the antics of lawyers and developed interpersonal connections that would outlive this day.

"Does the defense wish to have the jury polled?" Millick asked.

Cruise nodded. "Yes, your Honor."

Millick stood and directed his attention to the jury box. "The twelve voting jurors have been given numbers. I'm just going to ask in the order of those numbers to make it easier. Juror number one, is this your verdict?"

Terry, gripping his plastic number card, replied, "Yes, it is."

"Juror number two, is this your verdict?"

Dennis nodded and said, "Yes sir."

Millick continued down the line, asking each member of the jury the same question, receiving the same response. When finished, he sat back down. "The record should reflect I've polled each individual juror and each indicated this is their verdict."

The court remained silent. Mark

Johannsen looked at the jury from under his lowered brow, expression seething. Not one of them met his stare. He had been assessed by a jury of his peers.

Together they'd been party to his life, watched as evidence and testimony stripped him to his dark core. They heard his words, read his emailed thoughts, bore witness to his twisted obsession with penises. At the end of it all, they pronounced judgment on his actions, in consequence determined the remaining path of his life.

And to a person, no one wanted anything more to do with him.

"I'm going to excuse the jury one last time while we tend to housekeeping," Millick continued and directed his attention to them. "Folks, I don't know what to say. I might come in here Monday and look over expecting to see you. You've been wonderful, you showed up on time, short lunches, a lot of witnesses, exhibits, videos. You were patient with us when we had to do our legal arguments. I want to thank you on behalf of all the judges in the county for your service and hopefully it's been an impactful experience."

It was a statement not intended to invoke a reply and none was forthcoming. A few jurors merely nodded, ready to go.

Judge Millick didn't know how prophetic his statement would become.

"I need a drink," Nicole announced as they re-entered the jury room for the last time.

"You always need one," Shelli answered.

"Where we going?" Chuckie asked.

A few local spots were thrown out. Sunnyside, Cooler Near the Lake, Spanky's, Boat House. Eventually they settled on the Brat Stop out by Interstate 94, an iconic Kenosha haunt that had been around for decades.

Larry stepped into the room just as the decision was made. "You guys are free to go now. Leave all the notepads, please. These get destroyed once the trial is done."

Every eye swiveled to Courtney.

"Ripping a baby right from her mother's arms," Travis observed. "Savage."

As backpacks and bags were packed, the buzz of conversation arose. It was light, punctuated by short laughs and exclamations, traveling from person to person, infectious. They shared a sensation of relief, of coming through to the other end of Wisconsin's longest trial with a verdict derived correctly and justly. They could all lay their head down at night with no second thoughts.

Kay, Bryan, and Rick were first to leave. The two men chatted loudly, creating echoes in the courthouse hallway. She stayed silent out front but laughed at one of Bryan's comments.

When she opened a door to the lobby, a wave of sound rolled in. People talking and arguing, reporters staked out in corners with cameras on bright, delivering the latest news. At first glimpse of the Breakfast Jury, noise exploded and they swarmed towards the first three jurors, shouting to be heard, rifling questions, pressing close.

Kay felt Bryan put his arm around her shoulders and propel her forward, repeating '*No Comment*' as he did, parting the crush. Directly beside her Rick used his arm to stave off reporters from the other side while muttering with annoyance.

It was overwhelming, the amount of questions lobbed their way. Other jurors negotiated the same gauntlet in their wake, acting the same way. As a group they'd all agreed to forego any public comment, for fear of saying something wrong. The defense could demand a re-trial if just one of them made the verdict appear biased. None of the jurors had any idea what potentially could vacate the verdict, so better to remain tight-lipped. No one else should be made to endure this trial again. Once was enough.

Nicole endured the heaviest onslaught. Reporters had been present when she handed over the verdict, revealing her role as foreperson. By default, that put her in position to speak on behalf of the jury, but she simply shook her head over and over, pushing towards the exit.

"Somebody fire Larry," Danny said. "Isn't there some secret tunnel we could have used?"

"This isn't the Batcave," Terry

scoffed. "This is good ole Kenosha."

They finally emerged into the afternoon sun. The throng of reporters and photographers did not lessen out in the open air. If anything, it made the crowd seem larger as they were spread across the curved entrance steps and along the sidewalk below.

Plus, the jury was now unprotected by trial privacy. No pictures were allowed of jurors while in service but once it was over, they were simply citizens in a public setting with no expectation of anonymity. Television cameras swung in their direction, catching B-roll for later edits, focusing on reporters as they spoke with jurors framed in the background. Photographers scurried between bodies, snapping pics like infantry charging an enemy stronghold.

This madness followed as everyone made their way around the building exterior to the parking lot. They moved together as a unit, men instinctively taking an outer position, keeping the women inside their ad-hoc perimeter. There was little said amongst them, apart from Justyna swearing that a reporter stepped on her foot.

Finally, the group made it to the lot and quickly entered their cars. Kay, sliding into the driver's seat of her husband's Mercedes that Travis liked so much, looked in her rear mirror to see a reporter scribbling down the license plate. Good God, she thought. They're going to stalk our houses.

At that moment, the enormity of what they did fully hit her. She'd spent the last seven weeks immersed in trial detail, getting to know her fellow jurors, developing likes and dislikes. It had been an insular world inhabited only by fifteen other people during that time. Now, seeing how the outer world reacted, she wondered about what she would do going forward. There would be scrutiny on all of them for some time. She had plans, things she wanted to do, actions to take. Would random reporters seeking a scoop ruin those plans?

She shook her head and backed out, flooring the accelerator as she tore away from the parking lot.

"That. Was. Nuts." Courtney declared as she entered the Brat Stop and approached the others. Everyone else had already arrived and were gripping drinks.

"The fame and fortune of a juror," Charles said, winking.

At 3pm on a Friday, the bar buzzed. Not yet to capacity, but enough that there was a wait to be served. Dennis and Chuckie, first to arrive, had pulled together a couple of tables along one wall.

When Courtney returned with her drink, the Breakfast Jury stood assembled one last time. Travis lifted his glass. "Here's to a good verdict, my friends."

"And to the end of all this shit," Nicole added.

"This should give us a pass from ever serving again," Jean said. "I mean, we've done the equivalent of three or four trials at least, don't you think?"

Shelli laughed. "Don't forget the Jambliss factor. That adds another week or two just from the mental torture."

"Between him and Cruise's eye rolls," Bryan said. "We've done a year's worth of service. If I never hear her voice again that will still be too soon."

Small pockets of conversation broke out as they ordered more drinks and continued to decompress. Terry bought a round of shots. Then Danny. They cheered each other.

At one point two older women crossed the room. "Sorry to interrupt, but are you the people that sentenced Johanssen to prison?"

"We found him guilty," Margaret corrected. "Sentencing comes later."

"Oh God, that's so great. Way to go! Get that creep off the streets."

The conversation attracted attention and soon the jurors found themselves surrounded by people asking about the trial. Some, like Justyna and Jean, willingly engaged. Kay, Travis, and Danny were the opposite, sidling away and avoiding interaction.

"So," Travis turned to Kay. "Back to the normal world, huh?"

She didn't answer right away, a distant look in her eyes. "What's normal? Do you feel the same as before this?"

"Well, I guess, yeah. Nothing's really changed. Still tee times to make this weekend, still work on Monday. It's more like I had a seven week break from my routine. Seemingly you got more out of it."

Kay nodded, avoiding his gaze as she looked at the other jurors. "You could say that. We saw people stripped bare of the face they show the world, peeked behind a curtain of secrets, and I can't ignore what I now know. It can't be a lesson unlearned."

A nod in agreement from Danny. "Yeah, I hear that. Who knew there were so many penis pictures floating around?"

That extracted a smile from Kay and a barked laugh from Travis. "I'm glad I don't have anything like that to hide."

"Everyone has things to hide," she countered. "Just not as embarrassing."

"Probably right. My goofy sock collection pales in comparison."

The server brought over another round of drinks as the crowd dissipated back to their tables. This prompted Kay to approach Nicole.

"I owe you an apology," she started, looking up at the taller woman.

"Really?" Nicole appeared equal parts skeptical and startled. "You're fucking with me."

"No, I'm serious. I was rough on you at times. It was more about me than anything else. Just stuff churning inside and I shouldn't have let it out. You did a good job in the end."

"Aw, apology accepted." Nicole spread her arms and leaned in.

Kay forestalled with a stiff palm. "Let's not get carried away. I'm not much for hugs." She backed away. Courtney, watching the exchange, laughed and choked on her drink.

Undeterred, Nicole turned to the group. "You guys," she announced, slurring a bit. "I have an idea."

"Is that the grinding sound I hear?" Chuckie said with a smile. He glanced over at Jean and nudged her with his elbow. She returned the look and mock-shoved him. It had become a common sight between those two.

"Let's get back together one year from today."

"An anniversary celebration?"

Margaret asked.

"Hey," Shelli added. "Why not?"

"I think that's a great idea," Margaret said and raised her glass to clink with Lian. "We spent all this time together. It's worth reuniting."

"Yeah," Travis blurted. "Like a sequel to the movie called *The Breakfast Club: Monday Morning*. I love it!"

Some groaned in response, others laughed but they all agreed right there, right then. Next year on the closest Friday, they would come together once more.

"Cheers to that," Kay said and smiled as she clinked.

25

FRIDAY, JUNE 23, 2000, 12:18PM

By the time I reach Highland's home, Richardson has arrived with backup. Two slickbacks are parked on the road, blocking the driveway. There's no sign of Warren and I'm not the least bit surprised. It's undoubtedly out of his mind already.

Standing with Richardson are two other detectives. One short and lean, the other heavyset, both with stern expressions towards my presence. Shortly and Portly, I dub thee.

I'm feeling the mood, all my legwork paying off in action.

"Stay behind us," Richardson commands me, skipping introductions.

"This is a simple knock request, nothing more. If there's escalation, we will handle it. You won't."

"Copy," I reply. "Appreciate all of this."

Shortly snorts and shakes his head. I don't know the underlying message and he deflects a stare to prevent any interpretation.

We walk up the driveway until Highland's house curves into view, then we split apart. Richardson takes the front door, Portly drifts towards the garage until his line of sight includes the backyard, and Shortly remains planted in the drive. I move across the front yard, wide of Richardson so I have a good sight angle inside when the door opens.

Richardson's initial knuckle rap is met with silence, so he presses the doorbell twice. It might just be my imagination, but I detect authority and impatience in the electronic ring, like he's able to convey his mood.

As the sound fades, I hear a crack from alongside the house, from the side not covered. No one else reacts, perhaps not hearing it, so I drift wider across the yard, keeping my movements casual.

I'm just in time to see Highland wriggle out of a window and tumble to the ground. He doesn't see me as he scrambles up and scurries into the surrounding woods.

"Hey!" I launch into a sprint. My yell is echoed by Richardson but with a completely different intent. I pretend not to hear him as I round the house corner in pursuit. None of the other three look fast enough to catch up so it's on me.

Color flashes through the trees, Highland darting here and there. He's fleeing on blind instinct, seeking escape like a panicked animal. It's an idiotic reaction, leading to charges of evasion and allowing us better leverage in the interview. It's also consistent with his profile. In every arrest report I'd read, he either resisted or attempted to flee. I expected it.

A split rail fence at the back of his property trips him up, literally. Highland tries to vault over, only to catch his toe on the top rail, which sends him tumbling. This is the break I need, allowing me to close the distance.

Before he can regain his feet, I Superman dive over the rail, landing squarely on him with all my weight. Granted, I'm a lean guy with not a lot of mass, but the velocity helps. He grunts loudly in pain as I drive him into a thorny bush, scratching the hell out of us both.

"Got you now," I hiss into his ear. "You're going to tell us everything."

He groans and tries to squirm free. "What the fuck!" Probably not used to being chased down by a young black dude who ran track in high school.

Any further discourse is cut short by Richardson and Shortly clambering over the fence. Portly stays on the other side, implicitly confirming he can't make it over.

"God dammit, White!" Richardson yanks me upward with a surprising show of strength. "I told you to stand back."

"Good thing I didn't. You guys would still be huffing and puffing in pursuit," I shoot back, adrenaline heating my system, leveling a stare at Portly. "I don't think he'd survive."

Highland continues to protest but

does not offer resistance to handcuffs and complies with Shortly prodding him to walk. I'm content to let them handle the mechanics of getting him to the car. I played my role and met my objective.

"You made things worse," Richardson states flatly. "We could have asked a few questions and been on our way. Now we have reports. You come with us."

I nod. So far, so good. Things are going to plan.

My plan.

The Kenosha station house isn't as fancy as Grand Haven's, although I imagine most aren't. It's across the street from the courthouse, adjacent to the birthplace of all this insanity, a squat tan structure, unassuming and unpretentious.

True to Richardson's word, I'm alone in an adjoining room with a view through one-way glass, isolated from the interview. The door does not lock from the outside, but if it did, I'd expect he would have done so.

Highland is cuffed to a small table in

the interrogation room, sitting alone, quietly seething. He's no rookie to this process and understands what is to come but that doesn't hinder his anger. From under the stained brim of his ballcap he shoots repeated looks at the glass. It seems like he can see me but I know I'm hidden, evident when his eyes never quite meet mine. The hostility is palpable, though, hatred for his current predicament. To that I have no sympathy.

We are simply the consequence of his decisions.

Richardson enters the room and takes a seat across the table, studiously ignoring Highland. Behind him trails Shortly, who posts in the corner, also silent.

After a weighted set of moments he uses to slowly flip through a thick folder, Richardson finally looks up. "You seem unable to keep yourself free of trouble," he observes in his placid voice, as if commenting on the weather.

"I ain't did nothing."

"When I look over the entirety of your jacket, Mr. Highland, it presents the portrait of a man unable to control himself, nursing grudges and harms. And when the pressure of those imagined slights becomes too much to bear, you act. There's vengeance and retribution, actions to redress the victimization of yourself. It's a cycle you seem helpless to escape. Does that sound accurate?"

"I don't know what the fuck half those words mean. You a cop or an English teacher? I'm telling you, I didn't do nothing."

Ignoring the reply, Richardson continues. "It's always been petty revenge. Slashing someone's tires, a fight the next time you encounter them, that incident with the duct tape and tarp in your trunk."

"Nothing ever came from that. Those things were for a job. I was just pissed and drunk." He keeps trying to press his point, providing explanations for what happened, repeating the same words over and over.

Richardson simply overtalks him. "All these incidents are telling but limited. You've never taken it farther, never crossed a line that includes premeditated homicide. Why change now?"

That stops Highland's aggressive rebuttals. His eyes peel open in surprise and he glances again at the one-way mirror. "What? You mean murder?"

In the observation room, I give a small fist pump. Richardson had set him up with a good line of questioning. Once a suspect is mentally unsettled, it's easier to extract the truth. A loud pulse beats in my temple. We're on the way to confession.

"Last Friday night. Sunnyside Bar. The jury for your cousin's trial gathered to celebrate the anniversary of their verdict. You were there, we have witness confirmation. That night the jury foreman was poisoned and later passed away. Our medical examiner observed ethylene glycol present in her system, in sufficient quantities to kill. Antifreeze, Mr. Highland. Someone fed her antifreeze, and it killed her. Other jurors reported similar effects but fortunately all have recovered."

His statement comes directly from my report and I feel a sense of pride. My case is solid enough for him to ride it.

Highland claps his mouth open and closed, a fish gasping for one last breath.

He's caught and knows it. Out of reflex, I lean towards the glass as if by one tiny movement I can be in that room, partaking of the confession.

"This is stupid," he snaps at last. "I was there meeting someone is all."

Richardson takes it in stride, concealing whether he believes the statement or not. "Do you have a name for this person? We'd like to corroborate by speaking with them."

Highland slams back in his chair, frustration flooding his face. "No. I ain't got one. She went by a nickname. We did everything by email."

"And the nickname would be?"

He shifts, uncomfortable. I think he's lying, making up an alibi and scrabbling for details. His body language shows it. "She called herself Turtle."

A barked laugh erupts from Shortly, spontaneous. "Like a shell?"

Richardson doesn't react the same as his partner. He stays on track. "And did this Turtle person ever show?"

"No, I got stood up." More redness flushes Highland's face. "That's what happened. I swear. Nothing more."

Now comes a sigh. "You understand this is non-actionable, right? You were in the same bar, same time, as the jury that convicted your cousin. Your expulsion as a witness from the trial is documented and speaks to motive. Being in Sunnyside then speaks to opportunity if you sought revenge against them." He stalls off a reply with one raised hand. "The alibi is that you were supposedly there to meet someone named Turtle. But we have no way to verify that alibi because you don't know who Turtle is. Am I on target so far?"

"Well, what do you want me to fucking say? I got there early, like thirty-minutes-before-the-date early, and waited. I didn't see those jury folk right away, it took me a while to recognize one guy and when I did, another while to put them all together. Soon as I figured it out, I left. Fuck them. Ain't no way I want to be in the same place. Not when Mark is locked up for life because his wife killed herself. I don't know anything about the foreman or who she was."

"Okay, set that aside a moment. At

this point it's a story with no corroboration. Let's talk about the juror whose house you visited."

"What? No. I never went to any of them."

Richardson looks again at my notes. "Yesterday, you drove to a house in the Twin Lakes area."

"Shit, that? It was a job estimate. Some lady called in the morning and asked me to drop some dead trees on her property. She was going to pay extra if I came out right away."

"According to my notes you never spoke to the homeowner. You stopped in front of the house then sped away. That doesn't match. Do you have the lady's name?"

"Yeah. She said her name was Mrs. Fire." Highland shook his head, gritting his teeth. "It was a bare lot, no trees except some seedlings. I tried to call back but no answer. Tree jobs pay well and I need the money. Figured I wrote the address wrong, it pissed me off that I wasted time and gas. So yeah, I left angry."

I happen to know there is no Mrs.

Fire. Chuckie is single.

"Once again, you have a story we can't verify. Understand, Mr. Highland, I am skeptical. Give me something concrete so we can get this resolved. Anything we can check."

Highland rocks in his chair, bottled emotions twisting his expression, darting his eyes around the room as if an alibi were left forgotten in one corner. I can see the gears turning in his head. Because I'm intently studying his face, I see the transformation when revelation comes, instantly changing his expression. "Oh, oh shit yeah! I forgot. In my back pocket."

"What?" Richardson's face is confused.

"Check it. Check my billfold." He leans to one side. "Left side." At a nod from Richardson, Shortly extracts a beaten brown wallet and opens it.

"Behind the fives, there's a gas receipt," Highland says, urgency in his voice. Notes of triumph can be heard, and coldness begins to form in my gut.

Richardson accepts the receipt, studying it. I see numbers written across the top but can't make them out.

"I track my fuel. Every time I fill up, I record the odometer on the receipt and calculate mileage at home. Look at the date and time and location."

There's a packed silence as Richardson studies the slip of paper then writes in his notebook. "You gassed up at 4:41pm, Citgo station along the interstate near county highway 142."

"Yeah. I was supposed to meet Turtle at 4. When it hit 4:15 and she didn't show, I knew I'd been stood up. Then I recognized those people. That's when I left. You know the station, right? It's at least 20 minutes from Sunnyside."

Richardson looks at Shortly and the thoughts are obvious. He then looks over to the glass behind which I'm standing. Even though he can't see through it, I feel his eyes land on me. The look is most distinctly unfriendly. He turns his attention back to Highland. "Do you mind if we make a copy?"

"Make ten for all I fucking care then take these things off me." Highland jangles the handcuff chain against the welded ring.

Bluster fills his words. "You can also take your case and shove it up your ass. I ain't did nothing, told you that. Whoever pointed you at me was dead wrong…wait, was it that black guy? Young skinny fuck dressing like he's going to church? He sold you guys down the river and now I'm gonna sue you right out of that badge."

"Sit tight for a moment." Richardson gets up and hands the receipt to Shortly. They exit and my room door opens a second later.

"He's lying," I shoot out. "He was seen there later than that. You need to corroborate with the bartender. I don't believe the story about cutting trees, he just made it up. Ask him about Kay's husband. His alibi is flimsy. A gas receipt?"

The detective doesn't address any of my protestations. He levels a gaze with his watery eyes. "Get out of my station. Don't ever come back."

26

FRIDAY, JUNE 23, 2000, 4:38PM

I don't give Leonard a chance to close the door in my face. Soon as I hear the knob turn, I smack it open with both palms. He stumbles back with a look of fear and confusion. A mash of alarmed words emerges but I'm beyond listening. He's only got one answer I want to hear.

"Why did you lie?"

The apartment smells like weed, deep-soaked into the walls and carpet. It's tiny, with one corner featuring a kitchen. Dishes litter the short counter and sink. The bedroom door to one side is open, revealing a futon mattress on the floor, no sheets, just a thin blanket.

"What the fuck, dude! You can't just barge in. How did you get up here?"

I can see from the glazing in his eyes he's high as a kite. Papers and dime bags are visible behind him on the shabby dinette table.

"Your coworker Morgan. Now: Answer." My demand is emphasized with a threatening step forward. I swung the door closed behind me, letting him know there's no escape.

He squints, hesitating. The indignation has given way to apprehension. "What did you ask again?"

Jesus, he can't even focus.

"I asked you about Jeffrey Highland being here last Friday. You said he was around most of the night. That was a lie. Why?"

Leonard pauses, this time for a different reason. I can see it in his slack expression, some semblance of considered thought. He's likely weighing his options for telling the truth versus whatever answer he can concoct. I've seen the same look many times, people looking for the quickest way out and with the least amount of trouble. You have to show them the path.

I look over his shoulder at the marijuana on his table, a long stare, then return my gaze. It's up to him to interpret my meaning.

"Okay, okay. If I tell you, that's it? Nothing more?"

Good boy. "Yes. The truth and you'll never see me again."

He shuffles over to the kitchen counter and plucks an envelope from under a half full glass of beer. Without saying anything, he hands it over.

My phone buzzes in the hip holster, an incoming call. I ignore it as I peel open the envelope. Whatever the call is about is less important than what I'm holding.

Inside is a piece of paper and a single picture. Jeffrey Highland. Side profile, sitting at the end of the Sunnyside bar, clearly unaware of a camera aimed in his direction. He's lifting a beer mug to drink, staring ahead with a wrinkled glare. Leonard is partially visible just beyond him, speaking with another patron, crooked smile on his face. The wall clock overhead shows 4:10.

"Friday?" I ask, knowing the answer already.

He nods. "When I woke up Sunday this envelope was under my door." He points to the threshold, as if to make sure I knew where. "Inside was a hundred bucks and that letter."

I unfold the paper. '*If someone ever comes asking, this guy was at the bar last night until 10. His name is Jeffrey Highland. Anything else, I know where you live. Money for your trouble.*'

It's a typed font, not handwritten. I could have it dusted, but it's been contaminated with Leonard's and now my fingerprints. Plus, no one that could have it processed is going to take my call, those bridges are burned.

Someone wanted me sniffing around Highland. Why? There are two possible reasons that come to my mind.

One, he was guilty and the mystery person wanted to make sure I landed on his trail. But none of the verifiable evidence points to that scenario. He was not in the presence of the jury long enough. He left before the full group even showed up. That leads to…

Two, it's a red herring. A diversion. Something to keep me off the scent. Which means I'm chasing the author of this letter, whoever it is.

And I have no clues as to a suspect. Might as well be tracking a vapor trail. I'm back at square one.

Leonard clears his throat. He jerks his head back towards the dinette table. "We good?"

I don't respond and slam his door on my way out.

Five days ago I parked my car in front of Ted Wright's house, nerves rattling, and accepted an assignment I felt capable of handling. Now I'm sitting here again, more nerves, wondering how I could have been so wrong.

The call in Leonard's apartment was Ted, returned from making funeral plans in Chicago. His voicemail directed me to come see him.

I have no idea what to expect but I do anticipate it will not be something I want to hear.

As before, he answers the door and gives no greeting, no hint towards his mood. A simple nod and he retreats inside, knowing I'll follow. Which I awkwardly do. "Did you get everything arranged for Nicole?" I ask, making conversation to help shape the atmosphere in this silent house.

"Funeral will be Sunday," he replies in his flat tone. "Her family wished it." Pausing beside the kitchen counter, he stares at me.

"Okay, well that's great," I respond and mentally kick myself. *What a stupid reply.* "Listen, about the investigation…"

Ted waves me off. "The man you had arrested was not the killer." There's fatherly disappointment in his voice, making me feel small. "Where are you now?"

A negative shake is all I can muster. That, and dipping my head to break eye contact. "Nowhere." I recap Leonard's letter, fessing up to the fact that I have no idea who wrote it.

He remains quiet. "You did more than the police. They know now it was murder and must investigate. Georgie says nothing more you can do. Is he right?"

"In the strictly legal investigation sense, yes. I run the risk of official obstruction if I keep chasing suspects."

"And more trouble for the name of Aramis White," he adds with a glint in his eye. This is a man who understands the gray areas of legality. I don't know how to interpret the look, whether he wants me to continue.

Instead, he palms an envelope from the counter and holds it out. "I pay half. You did not find the killer but I honor the work. The Kenosha detective has already called and will take over. It is not my wish, I will abide however."

The envelope is heavy, but not as much as it should be, weighed with partial recompense for the sprint I'd run over the last five days. A reward for the dog with a bone in his teeth. I mumble thanks, disappointed in myself, the sensation of defeat coloring my words and posture. Turning to leave, I make it halfway to the door when Ted stops me.

"The phone number list. Nicole's

calls. You never picked up. It was under my mat. You want still?"

In my frenzy I'd forgotten completely about them. This realization only adds to my beaten mood. *Sloppy, Arch, sloppy.*

I'm of the mind to say toss them, but something keeps me. "Sure." They no longer have value, other than a symbol of closure. Everything I'd listed in my notepad can now at least be checked off, an empty gesture appeasing no one.

He hands me a folded stack of papers. By reflex I open them as I move towards the door. The top sheet is home phone calls, less than a dozen entries for a six-month period. Clearly, she preferred using her cell. The remaining sheets are those phone calls, one page per month. I skim the list. It's nothing more than incoming and outgoing calls, the associated phone number and time length for each. As expected, many rows are repeated numbers, friends or family she spoke with on a regular basis. My original intent was to see who she called on Friday, to corroborate Ted's recollection and see what else shook out. In looking at the list, I only see three calls and two were Ted. The third was received late in the morning.

My feet snag, halting me in mid-step. The phone number...

I take a beat to scan through the other pages, isolating down to that number.

"Is all okay?" Ted asks from behind me.

"No. Maybe. I don't know." I spin back to him. "Do you still have Nicole's phone? Did you listen to any of her voicemails?"

"Yes, mostly calls for her business, the new hair cutting place. I did not understand much."

"Tell me you never erased any."

"I did not. Is her memory."

"Play them again." I hand him back the envelope. "If I'm correct, this is light."

Thirty minutes later I emerged from Ted's house, consumed with new energy, nerves vibrating for a completely different reason. Sometimes cases are broken open with a tiny detail overlooked in the heat of investigation. The movies love to stage these deus ex machina moments as a common occurrence. The reality is it's extremely rare. Cases are solved with diligence and attention to detail, not intuition or wild hunches.

Please let this be an exception to the rule. Let's have a Hollywood ending.

My thumb trembles as it scrolls through the contact list in my phone. I initiate a call and don't wait for a greeting when it's answered.

"I know who killed Nicole, but I need your help to prove it out."

27

SUNDAY, JUNE 25, 2000, 1:51PM

The Breakfast Jury stood somber and subdued at a distance from the mourners attending Nicole Wright's funeral. They knew no one, no one knew them, two groups brought together for a singular reason. The Sunset Ridge cemetery sprawled wide at the corner of Green Bay Road and Highway S. Clouds bumped along the sky, diffusing bright rays of sunlight as if recognizing the moment.

Everyone showed up to pay respects to their foreman, even Chuck, Dennis, Lian and Rick, the four who bypassed Friday's reunion. The funeral service was brief, marked by acknowledgements of her life.

Nicole's picture sat on an easel over the grave. A gilded coffin stood ready to be lowered. The jurors shifted in a loose circle, feeling awkward, wondering how long to stay. Margaret and Shelli had emotion in their eyes. Courtney glanced around with curious intensity while Lian stared wide-eyed at the large group of mourners clustered to either side of the burial plot.

For once Chuckie held his tongue and didn't pick at Jean. Kay stood between Terry and Charles, dwarfed by their height, head down in a respectful pose.

Danny broke the mood. "Travis, I appreciate you letting us all know about this."

Travis nodded and looked around the cemetery yard. "Sure. I thought it was important we come together one last time. It could have been any one of us." He fidgeted, impatient and uncomfortable, the body language of someone waiting on something.

"Doesn't that freak everyone out?" Jean spouted. "I mean, we did our civic duty and now someone wants revenge. I heard they set Highland free. Are we even safe here?"

Several jurors echoed her sentiment, speculating and trading rumors they'd heard. Travis interrupted the chatter. "I spoke with someone on the case and we're not in danger. They've narrowed down to a suspect."

This snapped up the heads of Kay, Courtney, Dennis and Rick first, followed immediately by the rest. "Who?" They all asked in unison.

Travis raised both hands in surrender. Motion beyond Terry and Charles caught his attention. He spotted Aramis White walking across the lawn towards the group, ever-present sport coat flapping unbuttoned in the breeze. Margaret also saw the private investigator. She opened her mouth to speak but Travis' reply cut her off. "Guys, I'm only telling you what I heard. When I know, you'll know."

This quieted the group, a momentary pause which White disrupted with one word as he neared:

"*Turtle.*"

TWO HOURS EARLIER

I stand on the dock, watching beat officers hold off curious onlookers, keeping them outside the yellow crime scene tape strung across the marina entrance. There's no sign of my new friend Steve McConnell, just a couple dozen over-privileged club members craning for a better look. Apparently, money doesn't cure you of morbid curiosity. If anything, they feel entitled to know more than necessary, judging by the indignant words echoing over the water.

The day is cloudy, warm and subdued, as if Mother Nature herself acknowledges an ending to things.

Jonathan's Chapparal bobs in the slip as two forensic techs pull back the cover and climb aboard. I can tell which one is familiar with boats simply by their movement, comfortable with uncertain footing. The other one stumbles against the port side seat with a grunt.

Detective Niman of the Pleasant Prairie police department stands next to me, silent and watchful. "Tell me again why you called this in?" He asks. "How did you know?"

I shrug. "Instinct and a hunch." I'm not in the mood to offer much more. He will have plenty of questions later in a more formal setting and I'll answer then. Saves me the hassle of repeating myself.

Water next to the Chapparal's bow ripples as the surface is broken by the mask of a rescue diver. We stare down in expectation.

The diver looks up at us and nods.

"Goddamn," Niman mutters. He grunts and gives a go-ahead signal by waving one hand.

Across the docks I spot Detective Paul Richardson part the crowd and dip under the barrier tape. He's in khakis and a striped polo shirt, Sunday casual yet professional. I take note there's no sign of a crime scene logbook to document visitors and shake my head in disapproval. Sloppy.

He makes his way around the perimeter, eyes fixed on me, sneakers thumping the aluminum pier as he approaches. "I can't seem to shake you." He hands me a piece of paper.

I scan down the page, nodding in satisfaction, reading the contents. It confirms a critical assumption, turning it into evidence.

"I don't know how many times it has to be said," I state back, picking up his question. "When I get ahold of something, I'm not letting go." Handing back the paper, I say: "This locks down my theory."

With a sigh, he looks over to Niman. There's no indication he wants to hear me out. "What do we have?"

"Dive team just confirmed. Male, middle-aged, fully clothed, looks like he got tangled up with the anchor. Maybe an accident. Could have been tying up his boat, rope got wrapped around his ankle and dragged him down. He probably couldn't get untangled before his oxygen ran out."

From the hereafter, Griff's voice rolls back over me, summoned from the night we walked up to Noah Bell's beaten body. *Don't speculate. Observe the scene and note only the facts. Form a theory based on what exists, don't make what exists fit into a theory you've created.'*

I hope I never stop hearing his

advice. These guys could use some of it.

I'm tempted to repeat Griff's instruction but don't feel like they deserve it. The memory is not something I'm willing to share.

Instead: "No. That's not it."

The water ripples again, his time parting to reveal the body of Jonathan Roberts. He's in a t-shirt and shorts, missing one docksider shoe. Both hands and the visible foot are wrinkled from immersion, a condition traditionally called "washerwoman's hands." Same thing that happens when you sit in the bathtub too long. In this case, multiplied by one week.

There's significant bruising and puffiness on one ankle, the binding marks of a rope wound several times around. His eyes stare blackly past us to the clouds as rescue personnel lift him onto the pier, slack-limbed dead weight. Literally. Across the way comes increased chatter as onlookers catch glimpses. A mix of shock, sadness and wonderment fills the marina, followed by questions on identity. I hear Jonathan's name as some connect the boat ownership. Today will provide plenty of

Mimosa chatter for the rest of summer.

"How do you know?" Richardson asks.

Turning to the beefy detective, I raise one eyebrow. "Now you need something from me? Say please."

He sighs with exaggerated patience. "You know we can't simply run around chasing every suspected crime if there's no reliable evidence. When Highland failed out as a suspect, why would I trust your other information?" He flaps a hand at Jonathan's body. "You'd missed a basic detail and I couldn't count on anything else."

"If I recall, your words were: *'Get out of my station. Don't ever come back.'*"

Choosing to forego a debate on his treatment of me, Richardson looks again at the body. "Convince me. I see nothing here that immediately shouts homicide. A flukey death sure, but not necessarily intentional. What makes you think otherwise?"

I look at the swollen ankle. Bodies decompose more slowly in water, especially as cold as Lake Michigan. After a week submerged there are initial signs of bloat but not enough to distort his features. I can also see red spots on exposed arms and legs, probably fish nibbling at his flesh.

The marks around his ankle are deep, showing the twining of rope. It's possible Jonathan did accidentally get wrapped up and pulled fifteen feet down to slowly drown. Wouldn't be the first time in boating history. My dad shared plenty of those horror stories as he taught me the finer aspects of being a captain. I look again at the anchor line climbing from water to bow cleat, at the knot. But there's a fine line between possible and probable, and the pieces are falling into place. I'm certain of it. This will not be another Highland scenario.

"When you autopsy, you're going to find ethylene glycol and liquor in his stomach. By then I'll have you a suspect. And you can thank me."

Without another word I spin and make my way across the marina, ignoring the stares leveled at me by Prairie Harbor Yacht Club members.

As I approach the crime scene tape, I hear one officer whisper to the other. Neither meets my eyes. "That's the guy from Chicago?"

NOW

"Turtle."

Everyone flinches or jumps in alarm, except Kay.

Travis, who'd been the recipient of Arch's call, sees it. He'd been prepped to watch her reaction, bear witness in case the others needed someone to verify. The cold dread of realization cascades down his spine, locking his jaw tight.

She hunches and keeps her stare fixed on the ground. It's the body language of someone who finally hears the thing they fear most.

Arch walks into the center of the circle, slowly spinning to face her. Confusion runs through the expressions of others, no one understanding why he's here. Some had never met him in person so their confusion is even greater. Who is this guy and what's he doing? Only Travis knew what was coming.

"Kay," Arch states flatly. "Look at

me."

Because he's so much taller than her, she's forced to crane her head upward. The look on her face is villainous.

Courtney is the first to piece it together. "Oh, oh fuck. Really?"

Arch remains silent, staring down at Kay. She likewise returns his stare, a contest of wills, stubbornness meeting determination, winner take all. There's no one else, just them, careening towards resolution.

"You don't know what you're talking about," she finally states, voice hard and challenging.

The group shifts, an unconscious reaction. They rearrange to either side of the two, seeing both, siding with neither. They are neutral parties waiting to hear arguments before rendering judgment.

Like a jury.

"The clues were there; it just took me a minute to assemble them. Sometimes you need to see things from a different angle," Arch says. He ticks off his points one finger at a time. "You had a shopping list on your table during my first visit.

Among other things, a large handle of rum and an anchor. For someone who doesn't drink or know anything about boats, it seemed like a strange list. After a few stops I ended up at Jalensky's sporting goods. Their security cameras have you buying the anchor Friday morning before the party."

Terry, ever the skeptic, interrupts. "C'mon, that's weak. Her husband could have asked her to pick them up."

Arch ignores Terry's comment. "The other item took me a while to figure out. Something called Zerex. Turns out that's a brand of antifreeze used for European cars. Like a Benz."

"Still," Terry states and crosses his arms. Looks of doubt cross the faces of Dennis, Chuck, Justyna. Danny's face is stone, along with Rick and Bryan. Jean is silent, lips clamped tight, cheeks pale.

Now Arch lets his eyes move to the other jurors. "The ER nurse confirmed your description as the person who brought Nicole into ER Friday night. You were the last person to ever speak with her and never mentioned it. Why bother bringing her in at all? Or is that when you administered one last fatal dose, maybe one for the road?"

The only one who doesn't react with dismay or shock is Kay. She firmly sets her jaw. "My husband left. Abandoned me. You said you'd find him."

"And I did. Just so everyone knows, Kay's husband was fished out of their marina a couple hours ago."

This crashes the floodgates. Gasps and exclamations erupt; the group closes tight as they shout questions to each other, to Kay. There is a noticeable lack of compassion.

Arch lets them purge their shock and takes back the reins when a momentary pause occurs. "He drowned with an anchor line wrapped around his ankle. A line that had been tied by someone who's never knotted a cleat in her life. The autopsy will include a check for ethylene glycol in his system. That and large quantities of rum, Captain Morgan if we want to be specific. Expect there to be both present. How much did you feed your husband before he puked? The smell of disinfectant didn't quite cover the smell of vomit in your boat. I didn't catch it right away and thought he was just a neat freak. You loaded him up with rum and Zerex, walked him up to the dock, wrapped the anchor line around his ankle and pushed. How am I doing so far?"

At this point, no one has anything else to say. They want closure and a full telling of the tale. Arch is happy to indulge them. "Maybe you can recap what you said to everyone when I asked you to warn them about Highland. Chuck, how was the visit this week with your kids up north?"

Chuckie jumps, surprised at the call out. "What do you mean? I haven't been up to see them in a month." He looks around like someone needs to confirm.

"You never called anyone," Arch states. "The police did but you wouldn't have known that. You only knew no one was ever in danger from Highland."

Margaret, face flushed red with emotion, begs. "Kay? *Kay?!*" She needs no other words. They know what she's asking.

"When the police conduct a warrant on your house," Arch adds. "What will they find on your computer? Emails using the nickname Turtle, setting up a date with Jeffrey Highland at Sunnyside? Did you get that name from all the porcelain turtles displayed around your house?"

"You're full of shit," Kay retorts, face contorted with a mix of anger and fear. Shelli, staggered by the weight of revelation, clamps one hand over her mouth as if trying to contain a scream.

"Wait," Terry interrupts. "Kay, is that why you called me the other day about deleting temp files? I thought it was strange since we hadn't talked in so long. Were you covering your tracks?"

Arch doesn't give her a chance to respond. "Highland seemed so obvious. I fell hard for Occam's Razor. He was antagonistic, with a history of criminality; his actions on the witness stand only added to the picture. He was a perfect suspect to hide behind. Your story about knowing him is likely the only true statement you've made. I can figure no other way he ended up as your diversion. That was a nice touch."

"So, he has nothing to do with this at all?" Justyna asks but Arch simply continues his dissertation.

"A detective let me look at

Highland's cell phone log. Kay called him less than ten minutes after finding out the police were planning to investigate Nicole's death as a homicide. My guess, she'd anticipated it could come to this and planned in advance. She set up the date, took a picture of him at the bar, paid Leonard to give a fake story. My call put those plans into action." He looks at Kay, eyebrows lifted in contemplative measure. "It's an incredible amount of foresight. I almost feel bad for the guy. He had no idea."

Dennis huffs and shakes his head. "This sounds crazy, like a book plot someone created. That's a lot of things to plan out. I'm not sure I believe it."

"I don't know," Danny says but doesn't explain further.

Near the open grave, mourners begin to take notice of the confrontation. They look over, muttering to each other. A few of the men appear like they want to approach. Ted pats his hands down in a calming gesture, stalling them off.

Arch picks up his argument, clearly trying to draw out Kay. "You're not wrong, Dennis. Completely crazy. The What of all this has been answered. Now she needs to explain the Why."

"I don't need to explain anything," she spits.

"Did you specifically target Nicole? Or was everyone in scope and she just happened to be the fatal victim? I couldn't find anything in your history to indicate you're capable of homicide. So, what caused you to snap? What drove you over the edge?"

"I didn't snap!"

Bryan scoffs. "You bought two pitchers of beer for everyone. You turned me down when I said I'd get next. Now I know why. You dosed us with the beer."

A chorus of questions and exclamations follow his statement. The realization of truth is on them, irrefutable, and as a group they shift towards Arch. An arc forms to either side of him, jurors facing Kay. No longer is there any nod towards impartiality when victims are hearing testimony.

The remaining funeral mourners start to sidle in their direction despite Ted's attempts to keep them at bay.

Kay withstands the onslaught of questions and accusations. No one's yelling – yet – but the primacy in their voices shows that moment is coming. Her eyes dart from one to another. Terry, arms still folded, staring down, Charles peering from the same elevation. Courtney's eyes shooting daggers. Margaret, red with emotion and suspended horror. Justyna and Shelli unable to keep the shock from their expressions, Lian reacting with quivering lips. By now most of the men have crossed their arms, declaring an opinion without saying such.

Feeling the tension reach a breaking point, Kay finally snaps. "Fine! *FINE!* You want to know why? She was cheating with my husband. The day we all traded phone numbers I recognized hers. I'd seen it on his phone but he played it off every time I asked, pretending like it was a work call. I knew he wasn't telling me the truth but didn't know what to think, not until I saw her number. It's like she threw it right in my face. That's when I knew. My husband, the man I was supposed to grow old with, was fucking someone else. You all know how I feel about infidelity. *I could not let them get away with it!"*

Her words drip with betrayal, stunning everyone to shattered silence.

Their time as a jury comes rushing back, each person recalling the times Kay blamed Julie Johannsen for starting it all with her affair, as if she deserved death for her mistake. Her statement that if she ever caught her husband in an affair, she'd kill him.

"I didn't think you were serious," Jean whispers. "It's just something people say. You *are* a sociopath."

Arch nods, the motion of someone who is fitting his own pieces together. "That's what I feared. Here's the problem, Kay. There was no affair. He wasn't cheating."

A phone appears in his hand. "This will be hard for you to hear." He presses the voicemail key. Nicole's voice comes from the speaker.

'Jonathan, hey. What's up?'

'Anything yet? Got an opening date?'

An audible sigh. *'Same as last time, nothing new.'*

'*How long can it take? We've been talking over a year now. I thought you said everything was in order?*'

'*Well, now it is. Took a while. There was a bunch of legal shit that had to get sorted. Soon.*'

Jonathan makes a noise of frustration. '*She needs to get back to work. Crazy suspicions are taking her over. If she thinks I'm cheating she'll bury my body so deep no one will ever find me.*' He snorts. '*It has to be a surprise. There's been so much bad going on, something good needs to happen.*'

'*From what I've heard, a lot of that bad came from her. The thing in Twin Lakes poisoned her name. You can't go psycho on someone just because you disagree with them. No salon owners want someone with a reputation like hers.*' Nicole's coarse laugh rolls out of the speaker. '*Good thing for you I like psychos.*'

The group falls silent as Arch ends the call. "I listened to every single voicemail. He was trying to get you a spot in Nicole's new salon."

"Oh, good lord," Margaret breathes. "That was you at Joan's Designs? The stylist that went crazy and attacked a customer?"

Kay ignores the question, eyes locked on Arch. Her skin grows pale and for the first time her steely façade cracks. "That can't be right. The comments she made, the way she acted. It was all for show. She knew exactly who I was." A pleading look ricochets to her fellow jurors. "You guys saw it, right?"

There's no response.

"How would she make the connection? You never used your husband's last name." Arch offers, as if that changes the circumstance of her actions. "Your revenge was based on the simplest of misunderstandings. You made it something it never needed to be."

Kay presses fists against eye sockets and drops to her knees. She rocks back and forth, "No, no, nonononono…" A scream emerges and she slams her forehead into the ground, crumbling into heaves of despair.

No one comes to her aid. In fact, as one, the group takes a step back, unwilling to extend a hand towards her distress. She'd made her bed.

Travis looks at the others, trading stares. Common thoughts cross their faces, shared sentiment. They were strangers brought together and cast into the boiler room of a murder trial, emerging as different people. Bonds were formed, beliefs challenged, a hard verdict rendered. At the end of it all, new friends existed. Maybe the relationships were lean, maybe they wouldn't last forever, but not a single person considered – not in their wildest imaginations – that one of them would be driven to kill.

I step back, slipping between Danny and Jean, exiting the group. There are no goodbyes for me, I'm not a part of their circle. These people, strangers bound by civic duty, are about to find themselves bound again. They'll go from jury box to witness box, testifying against their own.

Vengeance has a wicked sense of irony.

Pulling out my own phone from one jacket pocket, I lift it to my ear and speak. "You catch all that?"

Richardson's voice comes across the line. "Somewhat muffled but good enough. Two cars on the way."

Snapping the phone shut, I catch Ted's attention as he nears, trailed by a group of funeral goers. I point at Kay and nod. His return look is grim. He accepts Nicole's phone from my hand. His own trembles.

"She was not perfect. A rough woman," he whispers. "But such big heart, wanted everyone only to be happy around her. I tell her often that not all strays can be saved but never she listened to me. Now there is no more saving." His voice cracks, at last revealing emotion, and he turns back to his people. They surround him. This close to Kay, the destroyer of his dreams, I hope Ted doesn't allow emotion to take over and pull him towards an act he'll also regret. It's time for the process of justice to unfold.

As I retreat, one final glance shows Kay encircled by her peers, locked in a horror of her own doing. She'd upended her life, irrevocably altered it because she would not brook any challenge. With intention and premeditation, she committed the ultimate crime in the name of pride. Maybe if she'd eased her severity of judgment there would have been a chance for the truth to emerge naturally, for her misunderstanding to resolve itself into an anecdote she and Jonathan could someday laugh about on *Money Robber*.

'Hey, remember when I thought you were having an affair? When you were sneaking around to get me a new job? You have no idea what I wanted to do if it were true.' Haha, clink, toast to marriage.

Now the anecdote will be told by others.

The tragic nature of her fate is humbling, a lesson in unchecked certainty at the precipice of sanity. One step forward, nothing but endless void. She never sensed the edge and plunged blindly towards doom.

Maybe I too stand alarmingly close to such an abyss. Things have veered so far off track I could be in danger of losing my way back. If I keep it up, will I be sentenced to a prison of my own making like Kay, unable to see I might have been wrong?

More importantly, am I strong enough to pull back? If I recognize what lies ahead and where it leads, do I have the will to course correct?

And what's the cost if I don't?

I continue across the Sunset Ridge grounds, weaving between headstones. Clouds, thick and gray all morning, lose density, allowing the sky to lighten. The dark thoughts that have haunted me also lighten, lessened by the closure of this case.

My phone is still in hand. Perhaps subconsciously I knew it would be needed. Flipping open the cover I scroll down the contact list looking for a specific entry. When I find it there's no hesitation.

I thumb the *Enter* key, hoping Sheila will once more answer.

**** END ****